2

Back to Charing Cross, then down into the little back alleys between the Strand and the river, and I'm home. Villiers Street, then on round the corner and into Whitchurch Street. And here it is, down behind the wine warehouse, past all the black garbage bags – our own staircase. Bring me here blindfold, I'd still know it – it's got its own private smell. Cardboard. I don't know why. It's not the kids that kip down under boxes in the doorway at night – it was cardboard long before they arrived. Always been cardboard.

This is our little world. Parchak & Partners Solicitors on the ground floor. InterGalactic Travel on the first. Jaypro on the second. Then us on top. Not all that different from Whitehall, when you come to think about it. More closed doors, more secrets, only in this case who cares? I don't know what goes on in Parchak & Partners, and I don't much want to know. All I know is if I was looking for a solicitor I wouldn't be looking for one stuck away down here behind a wine warehouse . . . I know one thing about InterGalactic, too – they got trouble in there. Couple of fellows come one day last week and repo'ed the copier . . . Door of Jaypro's open. Fellow standing there in the doorway in a double-breasted brown suit and a pigtail, don't know whether to go out or come in. 'Afternoon,' I say to him. He stares at me. Something funny about the look of me, he's thinking – no pigtail, that's what it is. Woman inside the office is talking to him. 'And no more fingers,' she's saying. 'We've got two gross of fingers in boxes, we've got three gross of fingers in tins, I've got fingers coming out of my ears ...' *They* know why they got five gross of fingers instead of ten like the rest of us – *I* don't.

Third floor, and here's us. Know I got there because I'm puffing. Door ajar – matter of policy – tells the world they can all come in. Shove it open, and the old brass handle jingles snugly against my elbow. Nice sound. And our own private smell. Lovely. What is it? I don't know – I never thought about it before – I think it's women.

Here's Shireen, sliding the glass partition back, smiling up at me from the switch.

'Oh, Terry. Can you ring Peter? Also Mr Mudie and Mr Cherry and someone, I couldn't catch what they said, it's about the White Paper.'

Always smiling, Shireen. Smiles at everyone. Smiles when she answers the phone, they can hear it down the other end of the line. I don't know what she's got to smile about.

Jacqui's clicking away on the Amstrad, doing the newsletter. 'You know you've got some television people coming at four-thirty?' she says. Something a bit funny about her tone of voice, but let that pass. If there's anything she wants to say she can say it. I'm not going to start up another campaign to find out what's going on inside the people in this one. She knows I don't play that sort of game. She ought to, at any rate – she's had five years to learn.

I put my head round the door of the library. Another little world in there. Liz is standing up, looking through a stack of files. I don't know why she don't sit down, like anybody else. Never sits down, Liz. Stands there all day, looking down at her work, and she's got this great fuzzy-wuzz of hair hanging in front of her eyes. I don't know how she can see out. I don't know what it must be like, sitting there in the dark underneath all that lot. Number of things I don't know about Liz.

'I've got something together on the DNI for JS,' she says, holding out a folder. Because, yes, she does the work all right under there, she does marvels. She holds out the folder with one hand, and she scoops up a hundredweight or two of the hair with the other, and pushes it back so she can see me. But the funny thing is, she still don't look at you, even without the hair. Her eyes go running all round the room in a panic, soon as they see the light, like black-beetles when you pick up some old doormat. Funny girl, Liz. Another smiler. Funny lot, smilers.

Don't think I do much smiling. Not so far as I can tell from round the back. You seen me smiling?

Take the folder back into the main office and pick up the phone. 'Get me Mr Cherry, then, love,' I tell Shireen. 'I'll get him out of the way first.'

Behind the glass, inside the copying-room, Kevin's trying to pick up a stack of old newspapers. Every time he gets his arms round the bottom, the ones on top start to slip off. Poor old Kevin. Can't ever get his poor old arms and legs working together. Kent's supposed to do all the jobs like that – nothing wrong with *his* arms and legs. Trouble is, Kent's busy – he's got his nose to pick. He's always gazing into space, picking that nose. With Kevin it's his balls that need scratching.

Having a bit of a go at them now, old Kevin, while he works out what to do with the papers. I think those boys forget we can see them through that window.

Get it all out in the open – yes, that's our philosophy. But not what's up Kent's nose. Not Kevin's testicles.

What's Kent thinking about? Nothing. State of his nostril. Or Shireen. I seen you hanging round the switch, old son, turning on the charm. I seen her smiling away. But you're wasting your time there, lad. She goes out with a black boy and they'll murder her. You'll have her dad and her four brothers and her three uncles down on you. They got some nice cousin back in Pakistan lined up for her.

So here we are – we're home. My ministry, my department. Parchak & Pals don't know who Peter and Mr Mudie and Mr Cherry are. I do. The people in InterGalactic couldn't tell you what DNI or JS stand for. I don't even need to remember they stand for anything. Great experts on fingers they are in Jaypro, but ask them what it smells like in our copying-room and they wouldn't have a clue.

I'm thinking about the smell in the copying-room now. It's not women in there. What is it? A mixture of Kevin and Kent. I suppose they're used to it. Anyone else had to breathe it and we'd be contravening the Factory Act.

Now Kevin's got the top half of the stack of newspapers under control. And he's dropped the bottom half. God help us. What's it like being Kevin? Don't answer that – I don't want to know.

My little world – and it's got five little worlds inside it. No, six – I'm forgetting myself. And all six of us a bit of a mystery to each other. Nothing wrong with that. Moderation in all things.

'Oh, yes, Terry,' says Shireen. 'Linda phoned. I put her on to Jacqui. Was that right?'

She put Linda on to Jacqui. How can anyone be that stupid and still know how to breathe? Beautiful smile Shireen's got. Only trouble is it goes all the way through her head, like Blackpool through the rock, so there's no room for any brains.

'Lovely,' I tell her. 'Wonderful. You're a treasure, Shireen.'

Jacqui's gazing at her Amstrad with her eyes half-closed, so that shiny blue stuff she puts on her eyelids, I never known why, is making her whole face look blue. Her skin's shrunk. It's gone tight over her cheekbones. Only got to Monday, and already she's looking more like sixty than forty. I've discovered what's going on in *that* little world, anyway – it's Linda.

Thank you, Shireen.

I'm out and about again. Never stay in the office long. Going down the House this time, have a chat with one or two people, see what the word on the Hassam business is.

Two women coming along Embankment Gardens, one of them stares at me, then nudges her friend. Don't ask *her* if it's me, love – ask *me*. I'm the expert. I'll tell you. Tell you anything you want to know. Tell anyone.

Is it me? – Yes, it is.

How old am I? – Sixty-one.

I don't look it? – I know I don't.

Height? – Six foot two. Weight? – Fifteen stone, and most of it still above the waterline.

What's my greatest satisfaction in life? – The Campaign. Being Director of the Campaign.

How much do they pay me? – Fourpence ha'penny a week, I'll show you my bank statement.

What's my greatest regret? – No kids.

That it? Curiosity satisfied? Don't want to know about my sex-life? Oh, you do. All right, fire away.

Are me and Jacqui still . . . you know? – You mean, are we still doing it? Yes, we are.

How often? – Oftener than you might think, you nosy bugger.

Who else have I done it with in the last year or two? – Oh, come on, be reasonable.

What does that mean? – That means almost no one.

Who's almost no one? – No one you know. And that's enough of that. Don't push your luck.

So what about Linda? – Oh, you know about Linda, do you? That don't worry me, my darling. There's no secret about Linda. Everyone knows all there is to know about Linda. You won't catch me that way.

An open book, that's me. Put it another way – I got my story ready. Got it all worked out. That's from when I was a kid. You'd be walking down the street, not doing nothing, feeling the handle on the odd car, just in case, and up zooms the law – 'What do you think you're up to, son?' 'Nothing,' say the other kids. 'Right, then, loitering with intent – you're nicked.' They ask me, I tell them: 'Going down the Council offices, my dad works there.'

Going in that unlocked Dolomite there if you hadn't showed up, you big blue bastard. Don't tell them that, though. Straightforward's one thing, daft's another.

Dad working for the Council – might be true – might be trouble. Sometimes off they zoom again. Sometimes not. Worth trying, though.

Had the Special Branch round the office the time we done the Warrington Report. 'I believe you have a spot of form, sir,' says this prat with a great smirk under his moustache. 'I certainly have, colonel,' I tell him. 'Theft, false pretences, and occasioning actual bodily harm. If you want the details, they're all here in this press release we put out.'

And I look straight into their eyes. Always do that. Trained myself when I was in the nick. See into their souls.

9

I'll tell you a funny thing: nobody wants his soul seeing into.

Take this old bugger now, in the short haircut and the highly polished shoes, the one that's staring at me while we're waiting to cross the street. I'll tell you what he is – he's a senior staff officer out of the War Office in mufti. Tell them a mile off. He knows who I am, too, and he don't like it, and he's letting me know it. All right, old lad, you look into my soul, I'll look into yours ... Take your time, make a thorough inspection, ask me to open any bits you can't see ... Oh, and he's thought of something else he wants to look at instead. One or two little items to hide, have you, my old sweetheart, down there in the murky depths? Never mind – I won't tell on you.

Right, what else does anybody want to know? What qualifications I got for doing this job? Experience. What of? Everything. The Thames lighterage, for a start – that's where I began my career. You knew that. Everyone knows that. I'll tell you something you didn't know, then – I've worked in TV, I was an actor. This was when the lighterage went phut. I didn't just sit down on the wharf and give up – I went out and got myself discovered. You can still see me on the box late at night sometimes, third villain from the left, second copper from the right. If someone comes on, you don't know who he is, no one introduced him, and he says 'We gotta get outa here!' or 'You OK, Sarge?' – take a good look, it might be me.

Worked in radio, for that matter. Yes! DJ. Spent three delightful weeks out on some abandoned fort in the Thames Estuary, green mould all over the walls, damp sleeping-bag, ended up with bronchitis and no voice, resigned on the first boat off. Moderation again, you see, always moderation.

I was a journalist once and all. – A journalist? – Certainly.

Features agency in Gravesend. – But you can't spell, Terry! – I can spell all the words I needed to spell for the sort of stories we was doing down there in Gravesend. I can spell 'sex'. I can spell 'vicars' and 'knickers'.

Can't spell? I can spell all right, when I'm the one doing the talking. Listen, old lad, I taught English! I did, you know. At one of the finest schools south of the river. Not half bad at the job, neither – I lasted nearly a whole term. And it wasn't the spelling that done for me – it was the income tax.

Try everything, that's me. Try it – then try something else. I was a Trot once. Of course I was, you tell me. One look at me and you know I been a Trot. Tell us something we don't know. All right, my friend, I will: I also been a fully paid-up member of the Liberal Party. The Liberal Party? you cry, turning pale. I must be joking! I'm not, my old son, I'm not. *They* was – *I* wasn't.

So, anyway, when they ring up – TV, radio, papers – I know what they want, I'm ready for them. 'Put 'em on, then, Shireen.' And I got a quote for them. The lobby system? 'That's where Moses went wrong – he should have put the Ten Commandments out non-attributable.' The Policy Statement on Access to Health Records? 'Got more holes in it than the ozone.'

Ask me a question, I'll give you an answer.

11

3

Always makes me laugh, the House of Commons. Every time I go there I end up with someone murmuring something in my ear. What they're murmuring is usually what everyone there knows already. The Members know it, the lobby correspondents know it, probably the schoolkids up in the public gallery know it. They're all talking about it, only they're not talking about it out loud, all together, on their green sofas, so it's not a debate, it's a secret. This time it's Ted Protheroe – good friend of ours, ex-steelworker, great open face like a plateful of porridge. He's got some tale about a massage-parlour just across Parliament Square which certain Members are finding very handy during all-night sessions because they've installed a Division bell. No use to me – we don't go in for stories like that – but I can trade it later for something I do want. No one's got anything new on Hassam, though, so off I go.

I'm just walking past the Tube station on the other side of the road afterwards, and there's Roy coming out of it. Got his old blue cloth bag on a string over his shoulder, like a kid coming home from school with his gym shoes. What's he doing up Westminster way?

'Roy!' No response – lost in thought. 'Roy!' And he looks

12

round very quick – you'd think he'd got the proceeds from a bank job in that little bag instead of a barrister's wig. Comic, really. But then he's a bit of a comic turn altogether, old Roy, when you look at him, which is what he's always telling you to do. 'Look ...' he's always saying, trying to sound reasonable.

'Oh, hello,' he says now, not all that surprised to see me, and not all that pleased, neither. Perhaps he *has* got someone's payroll in that bag.

No, mustn't speak ill of him. Good bloke – pillar of the Campaign – our tame brief – what should we do without him? Only brains we got between us, apart from Liz. But sometimes you can't help laughing. Something about that face of his. He thinks he done it. I don't know what – I don't suppose he knows what – but if he said to the witness Can you see the man who done it present in this court? – they'd pick him every time.

I walk back towards the crossing with him. 'I couldn't make much headway,' I tell him, 'but you might see if your contacts know anything about Hassam.'

Because I know what he's doing at Westminster soon as I think about it. Going to the House, same as me. Seeing his chums in the Party, putting himself about. I know he's got his sights on a nice Labour seat somewhere, sooner or later.

'Oh, right,' he says. Hassam? Ask questions? Stir things up? It'd never even crossed his mind. Just another item on his CV for the selection committees, that's all the Campaign is to him. Still, let's screw all the use we can out of him while it lasts.

'What do you reckon yourself, Roy?' I ask him.

'How do you mean?' he says.

How do I mean? 'I mean, did they beat him to death in the nick, or was he DOA? Mr Hassam?'

No answer. We've stopped at the lights on the corner, and he's running his hand through his hair distractedly while he waits to cross, thinking about something else altogether. I know what he's going to say. 'Look,' he's going to say, because that's what he always says when he runs his hand through his hair, I don't know why, there's nothing much worth looking at up there.

'Look,' he says. Told you. 'The Government Agencies report. I'll bring the final draft in tomorrow evening. No, hold on, I've got Policy and Finance tomorrow night . . .'

What? Oh, yes, he's on the local Council. He's got committees like a dog's got fleas.

'Wednesday, right?'

Right. Lovely. Now, can we get back to Mr Hassam? No we can't, because he's turned and he's crossing the street. Only not towards the Houses of Parliament – across Whitehall.

'Where are you off to?' I say. 'I thought you was going to the House?'

'No,' he says, 'I'm . . .'

What? He's waving his wig-bag in the other direction, across Parliament Square. Where's that? I don't know, but that's where he's going.

Something a bit funny about all this, I'm not quite sure what. Got a little tiny secret of his own, I think, our Roy.

Not off for a spot of massage, is he, by any chance? Only asking. If you don't know you start to imagine things.

Not much more than half six, and there's the usual pair tucked up for the night already under their cardboard eiderdowns in our doorway.

'Hello, Tina.'

'Oh, hello, Terry!'

'Mind your face, Donna. Got to put my foot down some-where.'

Only got 15p in my pocket. Have to be a fiver, then. Bit of a shock. Bit of a shock for Tina and Donna, too.

'It's all right, Terry. Don't worry. We're OK.'

'Go on. Don't be daft.'

Still someone working in Parchak & Pals. No sign of life at InterGalactic. Got the great padlock on the door of Jay-pro . . . I'm puffed, as usual. The old brass handle jingles. Nice sound. Nice smell. Can't be women this time, must be woman, because there's no one on the switch, no one in the library, no one anywhere except Jacqui, still sitting at her desk.

'Getting late, love,' I tell her, very soft and gentle.

'Why? Are *you* going to do them?' – Not so soft, not so gentle. What's them, then – the books? The Amstrad's switched off, the desk's all covered in bills and messy sums on bits of paper. The books. Right. No, I'm not going to do the books. Why don't she do them on the machine, anyway? We got a disk for it. Why don't she learn to use it?

Do I say this, though? Course not. 'Saw Roy,' I tell her. 'Coming out of the Tube at Westminster. Looking very shifty. Lot of hurried hairdressing. Going somewhere, wouldn't say where. Then off he went across Whitehall. What's all that about?'

Shrugs her shoulders, goes on working. OK, if you don't want to talk . . . I got things to do, too. I take my jacket off, chuck my shirt into the corner of my office, go up the corridor and have a wash. Nothing like a good wash. Arm-pits, neck, great handfuls of cold water over my face. Blow like a whale. Lovely. Towel's as rough as a doormat. Better still. And there I am, in the mirror, where I always am. Still there. Still me. Great long red face like one of them long tomatoes, only with grey curls all round. Look myself in the eye, give myself a grin. Oh, so I do smile sometimes. I was wondering. Looks nice. Try it again. All right, my old friend? All right, we're still in business.

Go back to my office and get a clean shirt out of the cupboard. The pale blue, that's my baby. A clean shirt, in a nice colour – what more can life offer?

Jacqui's still crossing out and scribbling. 'Meeting some girl, I expect,' she says, as I stand in the doorway doing the buttons up.

'Whitehall? Comic place to meet girls.' I'll put a tie on, too. Dark blue on light blue – very restrained. 'Anyway, he's got a girl. What's-her-name, another barrister, on the Council with him.'

Silence. Oh. Exactly, she means. Just what you'd expect.

I'll leave the collar open, though. Tie hanging loose, like that . . . Restrained, but bursting out of it. That's me.

'So,' I ask her, 'what did Linda say?'

Because I think this is a Linda one.

'Nothing much.'

I wait.

'She's got water running down the bedroom wall again. She's been on to the Council several times, but they still haven't done anything.'

Yet another excuse for ringing up, she's thinking. Yet another pathetic attempt to get a bit of attention. But then Jacqui don't know what it's like to have water running down your wall. Jacqui don't understand what it's like to be dependent on people you don't know – people with no names, no faces, and no good reason for caring who you are. Any spare water running loose in Jacqui's house and it's 'Oh, Mr Shirley, could you be an absolute angel as usual . . .?' – 'I'll be over there at once, Mrs Cunningham, we can't have you bothered, can we?' And it's a whacking bill, a whacking cheque back, and a bottle of Scotch at Christmas.

Linda's got her little world way out on one side of London, Jacqui's got hers way out on the other, and never the twain shall meet. And I got *my* little world, right here in the middle.

Fellow got up at the Tory Party Conference couple of years ago and described me as a dangerous extremist. How wrong can you be? The middle – that's where I live.

Married – that'd be extreme. That'd be living way out east with Linda, or way out west with Jacqui. Ted Protheroe's always on about when am I going to get married. He wants to come miles out of town to see me? He wants to bring his wife down from Durham? Charming woman, nothing against her, two nice kids. He wants to bring them all, sit in armchairs, talk about the garden? That's extremism. I tried it, so I know. Went through all that with Linda.

Jacqui's putting on her coat. *She's* got to get all the way out to the middle of Berks, and I feel sorry for her. But she's got her life out there, hasn't she. She's got her house, she's got her daughter coming home soon for the holidays. Got her dogs. Got her cat, and her daughter's pony. Got Mr Shirley.

Got me, come to that. Saturdays and Sundays, any rate, plus Bank Holidays and two weeks in the summer.

My last word as she goes out the door: 'Them two in the doorway – I given them a fiver already.'

And off she goes down the stairs. Told her about Roy – didn't tell her about the knocking-shop with the Division bell in it, though, did I. Not after the way the one about Roy went down. So what's this, then, Terry? Bit of news management going on here inside my own office?

17

To this I say: principles, yes – but applied with discretion, observed with common sense and moderation.

And off I go to my club, to watch the seven o'clock and take a glass of the house champagne. Your club? you say, meaning what sort of rubbish are they letting in at the Garrick these days? Yes, old son, my club. The Swiz. The what? Swizzles. Where all the TV people go, and a lot of people in books and such. Want to know who's for the chop in the Beeb? Which company's got the contract for what on Channel Four? Certainly I do, and I'll find Patrick Wales at the Swiz, I'll find Gina Strozzi and Mark Seuss, they'll tell me, they'll swap it for the one about the brothel with the Division bell. I tell them things – they tell me things. We're trading, we're working. That's how it's done. I work all day, then I go out and work all evening. Lovely.

Halfway up Bedford Street – 'Hello, Terry.' I look round. It's a cab cruising past, driver winding the window down. 'Keep after 'em, boy,' he says.

'I will, don't you worry.'

'Cheers, Terry.'

By this time his window's going up and he's fifty yards along the street.

I haven't got many qualifications for running a political campaign. I'm an ignorant bastard. But I got one: I'm me, and everyone knows it.

Here I am. No messing. Out on the street, six foot two inches from top to bottom, two foot six inches from shoulder to shoulder, with a big red face on top of the shoulders, and curly grey hair on top of that.

Anyone wants me they can usually find me.

4

'Hilary, what do *you* think?' says Stephen Hollis gravely, as if my assessment were the one that really counted, even though I'm the most junior Civil Servant present. '*Have* we got the situation contained?'

Everyone turns to look at me – Tony Fail smiling a little, Michael Orton and Penelope Wass as courteously grave as Stephen himself. We're holding a little post-mortem after the seven o'clock news in Stephen's office.

I can feel the red coming in my cheeks as usual, but I think carefully and speak clearly.

'Well, they're still leading on Hassam,' I say. 'But they'd nothing really new, or at any rate nothing that we hadn't been anticipating. It looks as though we'll have more stone-throwing around the police station this evening, but probably, if the reports I've been getting are right, no serious violence. I'm very cautiously optimistic.'

Stephen nods. 'Good. We're all more or less agreed, then. I'll stay on for a bit myself just in case there are developments, and Penelope – you'll go over to the House, will you, and liaise with Michael and Craig Carr? All right, then – I think the rest of you can safely go home.'

I take the lift back up to my empty office on the tenth

19

floor – Jane Syce-Hill went ages ago – and yawn and stretch and groan aloud with luxurious weariness. I've scarcely had time to draw breath since half past nine this morning. But now at last the day is over. I close up my files and lock them away. Half past seven, though! I'm hopelessly late by this time. I must rush.

But I don't. I can't. I just sink down into my chair instead. I suddenly feel as if all the life had gone out of me.

I make a great effort, and turn my head to look out of the window. From up here on the tenth floor the world outside looks very dark and damp and uninviting. All the humble commercial offices clustering round our knees in Petty France and Queen Anne's Gate have been deserted for an hour or more. Only up here in the department are the lights still burning. Only behind these sealed windows is life continuing. *Contained.* Yes. The situation – everything. Shut away up here inside these walls. What's the point of going out?

They're all out there somewhere – the police who took part in the attack. At least five of them, so far as Michael Orton can establish. Three of them with young children, one who teaches rock-climbing at the local youth club, one with a decoration for bravery. They seem to have been possessed. It's all out there in the darkness somewhere, the whole mess – all the hatred, all the lies that were told, all the grief and anger. But now, thanks to a lot of hard work by a lot of people, *contained.* We think.

I get to my feet eventually and put on my coat. I feel rather disturbed by my sudden inertia – at this rate I'm going to be completely institutionalized by the time I'm thirty. If I'm not already. I see why it's called the Home Office. Michael Orton, Tony Fail, Penelope Wass – these are the family I never had. Ideal uncles and aunts and cousins, who treat you with affection and respect but keep their distance. We have disagreements; we never have rows. Jane Syce-Hill is a kind of older sister – a perfect one, always too absorbed in her work to gossip, but always ready to lift her head for a moment and offer sympathetic and practical advice. All rather silly perhaps, but who else have I got? Apart from Mum. And when I go to see her – I went yesterday, I go almost without fail every other Sunday – do I ever linger like this? Do I ever arrive at half past nine in the morning, stay till half past seven in the evening, and then hesitate on the threshold the way I am now, finding it difficult finally to close the front door?

And when at last I get my office door shut the phone rings, and I rush back inside again, instantly anxious and alive, reprieved from liberty. It's Stephen. 'Oh, Hilary,' he says, 'I hoped I might catch you. Just to say thank you. It's been a rather difficult day for all of us, and your contribution was much appreciated.' The blood comes to my face again and the muscles close in my throat. I can scarcely reply. How many heads of section would take this kind of trouble? How many heads of family, for that matter. As soon as I put the phone down I realize I ought to have thanked *him* for involving me so closely in the management of the Hassam crisis in the first place; I was only brought in initially to brief him on the community relations aspect. He likes me, though. I'm his favourite. He's bringing me on.

Tony Fail gets into the lift on the eighth floor. He's in one of his quietly sardonic moods.

'*Contained*,' he murmurs. 'I wonder.'

I don't respond. I never do to any of Tony's little heretical murmurings. I imagine they are simply his way of dealing with much the same feelings as mine. He was just as caught up as I was in the labours of the day.

He looks at his watch. 'Twenty to eight,' he sighs. 'Do you have such a thing as a private life, Hilary?'

I make a wry face, but say nothing. I'm not sure what the answer is, and in any case I assume the question is rhetorical. He would be as reluctant to hear about any personal arrangements of mine as he would be to tell me about his own. Penelope Wass says he lives with a man, but no one has ever heard Tony so much as mention his name.

The air outside is dank and chill. '*Contained*,' says Tony again, as we walk across the zebra towards the Tube. 'Do you feel like a container, Hilary? Or do you feel more like the contents? I sometimes feel like a half-squeezed tube of toothpaste.' His confidence is cut short, though, because by this time it's clear that our paths are diverging, and that I'm not going into the Underground with him. He stops in surprise. 'Isn't it Kentish Town?' he says. 'Aren't you tubing today, aren't you toothpasting?'

'I think I'll walk on to Charing Cross,' I say. 'Get a breath of air. Save changing.'

For a moment he hesitates, wondering whether he should offer to accompany me. But already I'm beginning to edge away, and he takes the point. He gives a very slight smile, and turns on his heel, pleased with himself. He thinks he has detected a faint trace of deviousness in me, a hint of mystery. I don't know why. I often walk to Charing Cross and get the Northern Line direct. I cross the street, and set off at a brisk pace.

Then as soon as he's disappeared I stop and cross back again. I often walk to Charing Cross, it's true. But not tonight.

I go up the side of the Tube station, towards New Scotland Yard. So what am I doing tonight? Nothing. Don't ask. I don't want to think about it.

What – meeting someone? No. Possibly. I don't know. Almost certainly not.

Meeting who? Just someone. Where? Nowhere. Nowhere? In the street. In this little street just beyond the station. Oh, it's all too silly to think about, especially since he won't be there, he can't *still* be there, I told him not to wait . . .

Only he is. He's walking slowly along the pavement, swinging his leg wide at each step and scuffing the sole of his shoe against the ground, as if to give some purpose and substance to a meaningless exercise. I feel a flash of unfair irritation. I don't know how many times he's been up the street and down it while he waited, but it's somehow characteristic of him that at the moment when I finally appear he happens to be walking away from me instead of towards me.

I follow him along the pavement, the sound of my footsteps evidently drowned by the slow, idle dragging of his own. He passes under a street lamp, and the light falls on the blue wig-bag over his shoulder, then on a rueful hand running through his hair.

I can't think how to let him know I'm behind him. I remember the golden rule for relationships that Chrissie and I once thought we would adopt – Stop now! So I stop walking, at any rate.

He turns round at once, unsurprised, as if he knew I'd been there all the time.

'I told you not to wait,' I say. My voice is cross – the first cross words I have spoken all day.

'I'm sorry,' he says.

Why's he saying he's sorry? What's he sorry about? I suppose he means I should be sorry.

He leans forward, smiling apprehensively. I turn my cheek to the kiss so that I can continue to speak.

'I couldn't get away. I *told* you.'

'Look, I'm sorry about phoning you.'

'We can't go on like this.'

'It's all right. I went and sat in a pub. I worked on my papers for tomorrow.'

He takes my arm. We start walking, in the same direction as usual. Where are we going? We can't walk all the way home tonight – we haven't time.

'What do you want to do?' he asks.

'I don't mind,' I say. I mean I don't want to be asked. There's not much choice, in any case. Indian or Chinese, and then we'll have to find a cab if he's going to be home by ten, which he always has to be on Mondays.

'I just drank mineral water,' he says. Why does he feel he has to tell me that?

'Sorry about this thing,' he says. What thing? What's he apologizing for now? Oh, the wig-bag. 'I'm in court first thing in the morning.'

Inquiries – papers – court in the morning . . . Why doesn't he ask me what *I've* been doing? Because he knows I couldn't tell him. But I could tell him *something*. Actually, he must know perfectly well what I've been working on today. He won't refer to it, though. He has to demonstrate how delicate he always is about this aspect of our relationship.

'What?' he demands.

What does he mean, what?

'What are you thinking about?' he says. 'You've got a funny look on your face.'

What I was thinking about at that moment, as it happens, was what it must be like to appeal for protection, as Mr Hassam did, and to end up under the boots and fists of your protectors, knowing that against *this* there is no one and nothing left to appeal to. How curious. I hadn't thought about it from Mr Hassam's point of view before. I hadn't felt those blows. A shiver passes through me.

'Nothing,' I say. It's true. I'm not thinking about it any more.

He looks at me and pushes his under lip up sympathetically. 'Terrible day, I imagine,' he says.

Oh, he *is* letting me know that he knows. For some reason it merely irritates me further.

'Not at all,' I say. 'It was a good day. I enjoyed it.'

We walk on in silence for a bit. That's stopped him. He doesn't know what to say now I've settled into this mood. Nor do I. I'm being so unjust. He's the one who's had to wait, not me. He's the one who's had to tell lies to be here.

We are crossing St James's Park. The raw November air over the lake is insupportably dismal.

'I'd just like to know what we're going to do,' I say. 'Because I don't think we can go on like this.'

There. I've said it. Stop now. I've done it.

We walk in silence for some way. 'How do you mean?' he asks slowly.

'How do I mean?' What's he talking about? 'How do you mean, how do I mean?'

'*Like this.* How do you mean, *like this?*'

I should have thought the answer was obvious. I don't mean *like this* at all. *Like this* has nothing to do with it. What I mean is that we can't go on!

'You know what I mean,' I say. But my heart fails me. 'I mean what are we going to do?'

We walk on. A few drops of rain begin to fall.

I remember Tony Fail's question. Do I have such a thing as a private life? I suppose I do. I suppose this is it.

*

Like this.

Yes, I know what she means. I know perfectly well what she means. Meeting on Mondays like this, when Fenella's out at her Women Lawyers Group, that's what she means. Meeting when I've got an hour or two I don't have to account for between leaving Chambers and arriving at some committee meeting. Walking through the streets like this. Talking like this.

She means having hurried meals in little Indian and Chinese restaurants off the Euston Road where I think we won't be seen – or rather where she thinks I think we won't be seen – because really it's nothing to do with being seen – it's just that I prefer them – we *both* prefer them – to the kind of supposedly smart places that some people I know frequent.

I know what she means all right. But the absurd thing is that this arrangement almost certainly suits her. She doesn't want to be more committed than this. I *know* she doesn't. And it so happens that we both *like* walking. We often walk all the way back from the Home Office to her flat in Kentish Town. Fenella suddenly picked my shoes up off the floor one morning last week as she was getting out of bed. 'But this is the pair I took to be heeled only the other week!' she cried. 'Darling, what do you *do* with your shoes?'

And we both like talking. Because we do actually talk. Usually. We sometimes talk all the way. I don't know what about. Our lives. Our feelings. We tell each other everything – all the secret, awkward little things you can't normally talk about. We're like two gangling teenagers together. We sometimes have to shout over the noise of the traffic. It doesn't matter.

Then every now and then we get into one of these downward spirals where we can't say anything to each other at all. It's probably nothing to do with me. She must have been under considerable pressure at work today, whatever she says. But that is the one thing we can't talk about.

It's such a waste, such a heartbreaking waste, when we have so little time together.

Yes, what *are* we going to do? Where *are* we going? I can never think when we get into this kind of situation. We haven't got time to walk now. We'll have to find somewhere to eat round here. But where, where? Pall Mall – Haymarket – I don't know anywhere in this part of London.

Anyway, when she says What are we going to do? she doesn't really mean How far are we going to walk, and where are we going to eat? She's saying What are we going to do about our relationship? Are we just going to go on marking time, or are we going to go forwards? She's saying We can't go on like this.

She's saying Stop and put your arms round me.

All right, I will. Now. Here. Halfway up Haymarket.

Or I would. I obviously can't when we're in the kind of situation we're in at the moment.

She's saying Don't just give me a kiss at the end of my street tonight. Don't just squeeze my arm, and watch me go. All right, I'll keep hold of your arm, and take the key out of your hand, and let us both in without a word being said.

Only not tonight, because tonight there won't be time.

How have we got into this situation? It's like being sixteen again! I'm not entirely inexperienced with women, after all! Good God, Fenella and I were in bed together within two days of setting eyes on each other! And that girl I met at the party after Bar Finals . . .

'What?' asks Hilary.

'What?' I didn't speak!

'What's that look supposed to mean?'

27

'What look?'

'*That* look!'

'Which look?'

'"What look – which look . . ."! Why are you being like this?'

Why am I being like what? No, I know perfectly well how I'm being – I know how we're both being. Things are getting worse from one moment to the next. Quick, quick, what *are* we going to do? And *I* don't mean just Indian or Chinese, cab or Tube, though I *do* mean that as well, because I actually have to decide. I mean, am I going to tell Fenella? I mean, how can I tell Fenella, when she's in the middle of her first big case? I mean, *what* can I tell her? There's nothing to tell! Nothing's happened!

I can't tell anyone. That's the terrible thing. I have a sudden picture of Terry's face, for some reason. 'You what, Roy? You walk her home? Then you give her a kiss? Lovely. What next . . .? Oh, you give her arm a little squeeze. Go on . . .' Yes, when I think of Terry and *his* relations with women . . . Wasn't there a story about him and the woman in a checkout somewhere? 'Access,' said Terry, whereupon, without another word being said . . .

'What?' Because I think Hilary has just said something.

'I said it's raining.'

'Is it?'

'*Is it?*' she cries. 'What do you mean, *is it*? I don't understand half the things you say!'

All right, it's raining. I know that. *I'm* getting wet, too, as it happens. So all right, we'll find somewhere to eat. That'll be one thing fixed, at least. There's no shortage of places round here – we're just crossing Shaftesbury Avenue, we're coming into Soho . . . Only we're in the one street in Soho without a single restaurant in it . . . Except this one, which looks somehow unwelcoming, and this one, which looks far too welcoming . . . I know what she's thinking – she's thinking I'm worried about meeting someone I know. That's the last thing I'm thinking about, however. I know the place we finally pick is going to turn out to have the head of Chambers or Fenella's father eating at the next table, but I'm long past caring.

Here we are, then. This one. This'll do. Fairly horrible-looking, but never mind.

I hold the door open for her. She just stands there in surprise, as if she's never seen a restaurant or an open door before. Isn't this what she wants? Well, almost certainly not, any more than I do. There's a noise of success and smartness inside. The waiters and waitresses are specially young and stylish. They don't expect to be called upon to serve people like us.

Nevertheless, this is where we are going.

'The Picarel,' I read off the menu displayed inside, as the receptionist comes towards us, smiling as if we were long-lost friends. 'Oh, yes. I think someone was telling me about this place. I think it's where everyone goes these days.'

5

So Jacqui's right – he *was* meeting a girl, the crafty bugger, and it's not what's-her-name, the regular one, the barrister. How do I know? Because this one's never a barrister – I'll give you ten to one on that. I don't know what she is. Local Sunday School teacher, I should think. She's wearing one of them quilted overcoats – got it as a special offer out of a newspaper – and I think she's cut her own hair. She keeps brushing the raindrops off of it, keeps looking at the door, just wants to get out of the restaurant. Thinks we're all laughing at her, because of course they can't get a table, you never can at the Pic, you can't just walk in out of the rain here, trust Roy not to know that. Lily's showing him – look, every table full! He don't believe her. He's peering round the room suspiciously, looking for holes in the defence. His hair's all wet, too, and he's still got his little picnic-bag over his shoulder, what a clown he is.

Poor girl. Don't worry, love, no one's even noticed. Only me.

Because I'm sitting on my own – I'm here to work. I got my foot on the rail of the chair opposite, ready to slide it out for any passing acquaintance who wants to join me for a bit, have a bit of a chat, tell me what's going on in the world.

Never mind. Do a good turn instead. I call my friend Jean-Luc over.

'One more chair, Jean-Luc, and another couple of glasses of champagne. Tell them two poor orphans we found a home for them.'

I wouldn't say they was overcome with gratitude.

'Oh, it's you,' says Roy, the way you might to a spider you'd washed down the plughole once, and now it's come crawling out again.

'What it usually means when two people keep running into each other like this,' I say, as Jean-Luc sets the extra place, 'is they're falling in love.'

But all Roy does is run his hand through his hair. Always does that when he's feeling a bit got at. I think it's from being in court – he's just checking he's got his little toupee on, only he hasn't, so that makes him even more anxious. Naked human hair! What's the old judge going to say? He looks round to see if there's any escape.

'I'm only slightly infectious,' I reassure him.

'What? Oh. No. It's just . . .' Just what? He can't think without his little tea-cosy on. His brains are all wet and cold.

'Don't worry, I'm halfway through my braised sweetbreads already. I'll keep my eyes shut.'

He looks at his lady-friend, see what she thinks. What she thinks, to judge by the way she's pressing her lips a little closer together and raising her eyebrows a little higher, is that it's either this or a bag of chips in the rain, and it don't make too much difference to her which.

So, Roy puts his hairpiece under the chair, and down they sit.

'I'm Terry,' I tell his lady-friend.

'Oh, sorry,' says Roy. He was just going to say the same

thing himself, funnily enough. He agrees with me. So that's a start – he don't always agree with me.

'Yes,' says his lady-friend. Oh, she knew already. She recognized me. Always longed to meet me, no doubt, but if so keeping her delight very much to herself.

Should be a bit of info coming back about who *she* is, in my experience of the way these things are done, but a good three seconds go by and not a word on the subject. I think Roy's just checking to make sure it isn't covered by the Official Secrets Act, or the Thirty-Year Rule. When he gets to be a Minister he's going to be worse than all the others, he's going to be taking the name off the front of the Ministry.

No, here we go. We're in the clear.

'This is Hilary,' he says.

Hilary. Right, we're away.

'Haven't seen you in here before, have I, Hilary?'

'No.'

No. OK. It's a start. 'Get some funny people in here, Hilary, I'll tell you that.' Because if we're all going to be sitting here having a lovely time together we got to get a bit of conversation going. 'See the fellow over there in the corner? Grey pinstripe, hair dangling in his soup? That's Chris Marsh. Know who he's with? David Constantine. What does that tell us, Hilary? It tells us there's trouble in Park Street.'

Only I can see she's never heard of either of them. Probably don't even know what goes on in Park Street.

'Laurie Lancaster?' I try. 'Just behind you. Heard of him? He's leaving *Newsnight*, so that's our best contact in the business gone. All right, you don't give a monkey's. How about Dan Peel? Even you know who Dan Peel is, Hilary. Got his back to us, don't know we're watching him, but we know what's going on round the other side of his head because we can see the way it's bobbing about – and we can see No written all over the face of that nice friendly merchant banker he's so graciously wining and dining. You got any money invested in Dan's little empire, Hilary? I'd take it out fast if I was you.'

She don't even look round to see. Too busy peering at the glass of champagne that Jean-Luc's putting in front of her.

'What's this?' she says. 'We didn't order this.'

'My compliments,' I say.

She pushes it an inch or two further away, in case it's giving off poisonous fumes. 'Thank you,' she says, after some reflection on the matter.

Well, if you can't break the ice with your right boot try your left.

'So how about you, then, Hilary? What's your racket? You're not a barrister, I know that.'

She glances at Roy, very short and sharp. OK, OK. But if people keep things in the dark they can't be surprised if other people fall over them.

'No, don't tell me,' I say. Not that she was going to. 'Let me guess.'

I don't even need to guess, though, now I've put my mind to it, because it's written all over her. Written in nice tidy handwriting, in nice neat paragraphs and sub-paragraphs. Don't know why I didn't see it at once. Whitehall is where I left him, after all, the devious devil.

'You're a Civil Servant, Hilary, aren't you,' I tell her.

'Can we order?' says Hilary to Roy.

So, she's a Civil Servant. Hang on, this isn't *business*, is it? This isn't Roy doing a bit of the old undercover on behalf of the Campaign?

'Look, would you like to go somewhere else?' says Roy to

Hilary. He's having another go at his hair. He'll be bald before he's forty if he goes on like this.

'I'd just like to order,' says Hilary to Roy. 'I'd just like to get something to eat and get out of here.'

No, this is personal. This is two young people having a lovely evening out together.

'You just talk among yourselves,' I tell them. 'Don't worry about me. All I'm thinking about's my plate of sweetbreads.'

So there we sit, me eating sweetbreads and looking at the back of Dan Peel's head, Roy peering round for the waiter, Hilary staring firmly in the direction of the Exit sign. Well, who'd have thought Roy was doing a bit of the old double-entry? You got to laugh. Comes round to OPEN with his latest report exposing secrecy in Whitehall, then creeps off for a bit of secrecy in Whitehall himself. Wait till I tell Jacqui.

Clever-looking girl, not that I'm looking. No, I'm taking a good look, tell you the truth, because they've stopped not speaking to each other for a moment and they're speaking to Jean-Luc. She's quite a bit younger than Roy – what, twenty-eight, twenty-nine? If I had to describe her I'd say she looked like a helping of rather brainy mashed potatoes. I mean, all there on the plate in front of you. No surprises. Always the same with these mysteries, isn't it. When you finally get to meet them there's no mystery there.

'Anyway, Hilary,' I say, when Jean-Luc's taken their order, 'I've nothing against Civil Servants.' Because I don't want her to sit there suffering just because she's got the wrong idea about me. 'Contrary to what you might have heard. All in favour of them. Great admirer, me. In fact what I want is just to see more of you all. You're a bashful lot, aren't you. Just so long as you're not in the Home Office. They're the only ones I really hate.'

Silence. Hilary glances at Roy, then looks down at the tablecloth and goes a funny kind of red colour.

Oh, no!

Funny thing is, I don't know why I said it. Why do I say half the things I say? Because they jump into my head, that's why, and then they jump out again before I've had time to shut the lid on them. And a good thing, too.

'Sorry about that, Hilary. Can't go back, though, now I've said it, can I. Can't just put it back in the box and stick the label down again. I'll just have to go on and say my piece, then. OK? I'll tell you why I don't like you.'

'Look, Terry . . .' says Roy.

'I'll look, Roy – you listen, you might learn something.'

So might Laurie Lancaster, for that matter, so might Dan Peel, because they've both turned round to see what's going on. I'm not one to keep my voice down. I'm not one to start muttering and whispering to people just because I'm in a restaurant.

'You sitting comfortably, Hilary? Then I'll begin . . .'

I see how he gets away with it. All his hangers-on are like Roy here – nice, well-meaning, well-behaved people who don't know how to cope with such open aggression, who cringe with embarrassment every time he raises his voice in public. He's got this big open face, and this innocent mop of grey curls, and he looks straight at you with his wide-open blue eyes like a child. But he's not innocent and he's not a child. He's shrewd and calculating and he's a bully.

I see it, but I can't do anything about it. I'm looking at the tablecloth, just like Roy. I know I've a bright red patch in each cheek.

'I don't like you, Hilary,' he's saying, 'because you done an awful lot of messing around in my life, and you don't know what you done, and there's no way I can tell you, and *I* don't know why you done it, and there's no way I can find out. For a start you nicked me for something I never done. Not you personally, Hilary, I know that. You wasn't even born. The people you work with. Your mates. The filth. When my mum died you shipped me and my brothers off to homes. One of us this way, one of us that – I ended up in Staffordshire. Why can't I be with my brothers? Because. Never you mind. You just do as you're told. Two years I was up there, Hilary, and you never told us why.'

I just keep my eyes on the tablecloth. Why can't I *say* anything?

Roy tries.

'Terry's got this notorious criminal past,' he says, but it's no good trying to make a joke of it – it's even worse than saying nothing. Terry brushes him aside, in any case, without so much as looking round.

'She don't need you defending her, Roy. She can look after herself. She's just as clever as what you are, I know that, or she wouldn't have passed the exam. Four times as clever as what *I* am, aren't you, Hilary? Only exam I ever passed was my HGV. Just not opening your mouth, are you, Hilary. Just looking wise. Knows things I don't know, she's telling me. Lot she could say if only she chose, etcetera. Not her policy to comment on allegations of this nature, and so on.'

He's right about one thing, anyway. There *is* a lot I could say. I could say how nauseating I find his combination of self-righteousness and charming rascality and self-satisfied humour.

I could tell him I've met him before. That might take him aback for just a moment, because he's plainly unaware of it. But I remember it very clearly. It was at some kind of horrible charity show last winter that I'd got dragged to by a friend of mine. The audience was full of people you thought you knew, only you didn't, you'd just seen them on television, and the worst of them was him. Someone introduced me to him in the foyer during the interval, but he was obviously too busy to notice because he was fully occupied in doing precisely what he's doing now – making humorously insulting remarks to some unfortunate woman he'd just met. She was a doctor, and he was telling her why he hated the medical profession. The woman was laughing and setting her head at various interesting angles and generally making a fool of herself. I imagine that's how I'm supposed to behave. But it wasn't her I was watching – it was him. I watched him quite carefully.

So, yes, there *is* a lot I could say, even if I can't say it.

Roy makes another attempt. 'Look, Terry,' he says, 'it's stupid bringing up things that happened forty years ago . . .'

'Yes, all you done in the last four or five years, Hilary, is listen in to my phone calls and steam open my letters.'

'Let's not be personal about it,' says Roy.

'That's right. Nothing personal, is it, Hilary? Never anything personal. Not your section, the nosepokers, I know that. Never anyone's section. You're in the bit that helps old ladies across the road.'

'All right, you've made your point . . .'

But Terry won't be deflected. I can feel his gaze fixed on me like a light.

'Bet your mum and dad are proud of you, Hilary,' he says. He's dropped his voice. He's talking to me on my own now instead of to the entire restaurant. He sounds almost as if he's forgotten about Roy and the rest of his audience. 'Nice people, are they? Nice little house, nice little garden? Not one of the nobs, are you, like Roy here. Didn't come all that easy for you, any more than what it did for me.'

I lift my eyes and look at him for a moment. He thinks he knows everything, and he doesn't.

'Went down the road to school every day, did you, Hilary? Never messed around with boys? Did all your homework? Passed all your exams? Went off to college? Phoned home every Sunday? Mum and Dad come up to see you get your degree?'

He sounds almost gentle. And he's so right and so wrong, all at the same time. I suddenly feel slightly sorry for him.

'Anyway,' says Roy. 'To change the subject . . .'

'Anyway,' says Terry. 'To change it back again. I don't mind about the phone calls and letters, Hilary. I got nothing to hide. You can listen in all night, as far as I'm concerned. You can steam away like the *Queen Mary* – you don't even need to stick the flaps down again. Just tell me one thing, and I won't say another word. That poor Mr Hassam you been looking after. How did he manage to beat himself to death inside the nick with everyone watching? Or did he beat himself to death somewhere else, and then park himself in the nick just to make trouble?'

I look at him again. He's still looking straight at me. It's another of his little tricks. This time I stare straight back.

Roy has at last been roused to make some coherent protest. The fact that they're running a campaign for open government and public accountability, he's telling Terry, doesn't mean they have to be rude and aggressive to public servants in private. There's a lot more in the same vein – it sounds as though he's in the High Court.

Terry's not listening, though. 'A cat may look at a king,' he says, continuing to stare at me. I continue to stare back. Which of us is the cat and which the king?

I look away. He likes me, that's why. I've only just realized. He's as soft-hearted as Stephen – he's just got a different way of showing it.

I can feel his eyes still on me. 'And a king may find himself looking somewhere else as a result,' he says.

'I never had a father,' I tell him. 'I was brought up by my mother, and we didn't have a house, and we didn't have a garden.'

He goes on looking at me for a bit, and then he turns away and gestures to the waiter.

'OK, Hilary,' he says. 'Fair enough. A very frank answer, in my opinion, even if it's not one to the question I asked. Lot franker and more informative than what you usually get from a Government department.'

He rises to his feet.

'Right, I'll leave you two to get on with it. What tact, what self-sacrifice – I haven't even had my pudding.'

He comes round to my side of the table and puts his hand on my shoulder.

'Nice talking to you, Hilary. I never had much of a father, me neither. He buggered off and left us when I was two.'

I imagine that hand on my shoulder is supposed to be fatherly. He's found the bond between us. He's making up for everything. What a ridiculous man he is.

When he takes it away, though, I feel a fleeting sense of regret. I miss the weight of it.

He puts it on Roy's head instead and runs it through his hair, winking at me. 'Just saving him a job,' he says. He makes his way to the door, bestowing blessings on more heads and shoulders on the way.

'What?' I ask suddenly, because I've just realized that Roy is saying something.

'I said I'll tell her as soon as she's finished her case.'

I look at him. He's smoothing down the hair that Terry ruffled. It's getting quite thin in front. I've no idea what he's talking about.

6

'Cats!'

This is me, coming into the office like a madman just when they're all thinking about lunch. Door handle jingling, no breath, just –

'Cats!'

'Oh, Terry,' smiles Shireen. 'Can you call Peter and Mr Philips and Janet Parker, and someone, I couldn't quite get it, but it's his pension, he was in the army, it's all to do with the Ministry of Defence . . .'

But all I tell her is –

'Cats!'

It just come to me on my way back from Bush House. Always get ideas walking up the Strand!

'Cats!' I shout at Jacqui.

'What?' says Jacqui, frowning.

'Cats!' I whisper to the great fuzzy-wuzz hanging over the files in the library. Two hands come up and raise the curtain.

'What did you think of Hilary?' says Liz, smiling, her eyes here, there, and everywhere.

'Never mind about Hilary. Think about cats.'

Who's Hilary? Oh – Roy's pal? How does she know I met

Hilary? But I'm out of the library by this time, banging on the glass of the copying-room. Kevin and Kent look up from their stack of envelopes.

'Cats!' I mouth to them. They gaze at me – they don't know what I'm talking about. I lick my paw and wash my face. I go miaouw. Kevin's mouth falls open. Though it don't take much to make that happen.

Lot of bad days in this business, but every now and then you get a winner. This one's coming home a furlong ahead at a hundred to one.

'You for a start,' I say to Jacqui. 'You got a cat. You got a cat the size of a pig.'

'Terry . . .' says Jacqui, in her tired voice. Always does the tired voice when I come up with one of my ideas. Loves it really. They all love it. Old Terry raging round the office shouting at everyone – it's as good as telly.

'Put it in a basket,' I tell her. 'We'll take it with us.'

'Take it with us?'

'On Saturday.'

Here's Liz at the door of the library, obviously intrigued, because she's holding her hair out of her eyes with both hands. How does she wash her face? Stand on one leg and use her foot?

'What do you mean, cats?' she says.

'Liz, you got cats. You got four cats. All four of them, Liz. On parade. On Saturday.'

'On Saturday?'

'Of course! So we make the Sundays!'

'I don't . . .' says Kevin – him and Kent have emerged from the copying-room by this time.

'You don't have a cat. All right, Kevin. We'll think of something.'

'I don't . . .' says Kevin, because once he gets started he

has to keep going back to the beginning and starting all over again.

'Never mind, Kevin. Shireen – has Shireen got a cat?'

'I got a call for you, Terry,' says Shireen.

'Forget the call. We're not taking calls, we're collecting cats.'

'I don't . . .' says Kevin.

'Give Roy a tinkle, Shireen, see if he's got a cat.'

'It's *World at One*!' says Shireen. 'You're on it!'

Christ in concrete, so I am! Gone right out of my head.

'Put them on, then, Shireen.'

'I don't . . .' says Kevin.

I pick up the phone. 'Stand by, will you, Terry,' says the girl at the other end. 'You hadn't forgotten, had you?'

'Forget you, my sweetheart, how could I?'

'I don't . . .' says Kevin.

'All right, Kevin,' I tell him, because it's one of those days where you can do three things at once, 'you don't have a cat – you can *be* a cat. Yellow Pages, Jacqui – theatrical costumes – pantomime cat – rent an outfit. And don't tell me it's the newsletter today, because I'm telling you it's the newsletter tomorrow. It's cats today. What are *you* doing, Kent?'

'Me?' says Kent. Instant look of being somewhere else, with witnesses to prove it. 'I'm not doing nothing.'

Lovely. Just what I knew he was going to say, that being what he always says if you ask him what he's doing.

'Nothing. Right. You're another cat, then.'

Gotcha. Beautiful. One of those days when it all drops into your hand like liquid soap. It don't work every time, that trick. People don't always say what they always say, in my experience.

'So two cat outfits, Jacqui, one for Kevin, one for Kent.

One black cat, one white. Black cat takes his head off and he's white. White cat takes his head off and he's black. That's for the quality Sundays.'

'Are you there, Terry?' says the voice in my ear. 'Here we go.'

Moment of panic. Jam my hand over the phone.

'Quick – what am I talking about?'

'You mean . . . cats?' says Liz.

World of her own, Liz.

'The Hassam case,' says Jacqui.

'Thank you, my love.'

James's already on. '. . . Now I know you want to see more whistle-blowers, Terry, but would even the most as-siduous of whistle-blowers have been able to do much to save Mr Hassam?'

Whistle-blowers? Lovely. Right. I'm away. 'We don't just want to see whistle-blowers, James. What we want to see are some trumpet-blowers. Like the fellow in the Bible. We want to see people lifting up their trumpets and blowing till the walls come tumbling down . . .'

And off I go. *World at One?* It's World-at-Onederful. And so am I.

'Great,' says Liz, as soon as I put the phone down.

'Rather on form today,' says Jacqui.

'The mad lady in Dorset,' says Shireen. 'She's on the line already.'

'I don't . . .' says Kevin.

And what do *I* say? 'Chorleywood,' I say. 'West Selvedge Lane. Eleven o'clock. Saturday. All the London support groups, all our tame celebs. With cats. Cats in baskets. Cats on strings. Beautiful girls in catsuits. Hundreds of cats. Hundreds and hundreds of cats. Cats as far as the eye can see! They want cat stories? They got a cat story!'

45

'This is a press call, is it?' says Jacqui.

See? They get there in the end. Takes time, but it makes them feel clever.

'Right. So here's the battle plan. Shireen: all the Sunday picture desks. Go through the list. Put them on to me. Jacqui: catsuits, and all the TV animal suppliers. Liz: you and me'll do a press pack. On the cover – kitten looking through a keyhole. Headline: A Cat May Look at a King, dot dot dot.'

'I don't . . .' says Kevin.

'You don't know what it's looking at? Nor do they. They'll find that out on Saturday. Our own little state secret, Kevin. Just like Christmas. Pair of bedsocks – who wants them? Wrap them up in shiny paper and Auntie Lil can't wait to rip it open.'

'I don't . . .' says Kevin.

'You don't understand? No, nor does Jacqui, nor does Liz, only they're waiting for someone else to say so. Chorley-wood, Kevin – the Permanent Under-Secretary at the Home Office lives there, when he's not hidden away in his office together with the report on what happened to Mr Hassam.'

'I know,' says Kevin.

Oh, he knows. Full of surprises, old Kevin, if you can wait long enough to hear them. Pity he has to start out from square one again every time he opens his mouth. He could have got a lot further in the world if he could just manage to pick up where he left off.

'And if a cat may look at a king, Kevin, like it says in Magna Carta, then it may certainly take a peep over the front hedge at a Permanent Under-Secretary. Let's drag the buggers out into the light and see what they look like.'

'Yes, but I don't . . .' says Kevin. He still don't! Don't what, then? 'Don't understand what's going to happen if we let four thousand beloved family moggies loose all over Hertfordshire? Is that it, Kevin? In that case, Kevin, you're dead right – we'll never see them again. I'm dead wrong, and I thank you for pointing it out.'

Because it's only just occurred to me. I haven't thought this one through at all, have I. Don't matter – I'm doing it now. Thinking aloud, everyone pitching in together – that's the way we do things at OPEN.

'OK, change of plan,' I tell them. 'Scrub the cats, Jacqui. Cat masks. That's what we need. Cat masks for everyone. Get on to the party novelty wholesalers – and make sure we get a wholesale price. Cheshire cats – Cheshire cheese – Cheshire Cheese Producers' Association – annual dinner-dance – any bits and pieces left over that we could use? Well done, Kevin.'

'Yes,' he says, 'but I don't . . .'

Don't know when to stop! That's Kevin's trouble.

'. . . don't understand . . .'

Oh, don't understand. I'll kill Kevin one of these days! I will – I'll strangle him!

'. . . the logical force of the analogy.'

Oh. Yes. Well. The logical force of the analogy. Whatever that is. Right. It takes him a long time to get off the ground, old Kevin, but once he's up in the air . . . up in the air he is, good and proper.

'No, *I* don't understand the logical force of the analogy, neither, Kevin. But then I don't understand the logical force of beating yourself to death in the nick. I don't understand the logical force of stopping you and me knowing about it. I don't understand the logical force of letting the buggers get away with it. And I don't understand the logical force of not using every daft trick you can dream up, if you think it might just possibly do a bit of good.'

47

That'll shut them up. Logical force? I'll give you logical force, my dear sweet boys and girls! It just so happens that today I got logical force coming out of my earholes.

'Right – Shireen. First tell the Mad Lady of Dorset to tie herself up in her corset. Oh, that's nice! And if she says no, then tell her I'll go . . . down there myself carrying a large club, and I'll think of something else that rhymes with Dorset when I get there. Then run out and get sandwiches for all of us. My treat – work as we eat. Oh, listen to that! It's all coming out in poetry today. OK, let's get down to it.'

And down to it we get. Logical force! I don't know where we'd be in this organization if we let ourselves get pushed around by logical force.

'However . . .' says Kevin. Because he's still here, still wobbling about the room on his poor old string legs, knocking bits and pieces off Jacqui's desk with his poor old string arms.

'Come on,' says Kent. 'They don't want you messing about in here.'

'However,' says Kevin, 'I can appreciate . . .'

I give him a nice friendly squeeze.

'That's all right, Kevin. You don't have to appreciate.'

'. . . the analogy of Joshua and Jericho.'

Oh, right. But the thing that's puzzling me is Liz. I put my head back in the library.

'How did you know about me meeting Hilary, Liz? You run into Roy somewhere? Not in the Pic, was you?'

But Liz just laughs, and shakes her hair about. Another of her little mysteries.

Bit of logical force missing here somewhere. Never mind. We all got the right to a few little mysteries.

*

What a day! Come seven o'clock I'm good and done for. We're winning, though, we're winning! Feeling tired and feeling good – lovely state to be in.

They've all gone off looking pleased with themselves. Shireen on the Piccadilly back to her mum and dad and four brothers and seventeen cousins in Hounslow. Kent on the Northern Line to his mum in Stockwell, and who knows what evildoings with the local girls. Kevin on the District back to *his* mum in Gunnersbury, if he don't wobble off the platform somewhere on the way. Liz on the Bakerloo back to 'us' in Kensal Rise. Who's 'us'? I think it's a girl called Chrissie. OK by me – I've no prejudices – so long as I don't know any more about it than that.

A slight inconsistency in my philosophy here? Another little shortage of logical force? I don't think so. Got to keep public life and private life separate, just like Roy says.

And then there's Jacqui, still sitting on the other side of the desk, trying to get the newsletter away in spite of everything. No, she's looking at her watch, then yawning and dropping the old sky-blue shutters for a moment. She's packing up. Poor old love. She works harder than any of us. Never done a stroke in her life before she met me, that's the funny thing. Thirty-nine years doing nothing but go to the hairdressers and paint her eyelids blue, then one day she's standing in the doorway of a tobacconist's shop in Chancery Lane waiting for the rain to stop, and there's this great yob waiting next to her, ex of the Thames lighterage, and her feet haven't touched the ground since. Poor old girl.

Or lucky old girl, one of the two.

'Come on, then, missis,' I tell her. 'I'll just splash my face and put a clean shirt on, then I'll take you out and buy you dinner, once-off, *ex gratia*, no precedents established.'

She smiles. Only it's not all warm and cheerful, her smile,

like a nice shaded lamp being switched on over a corner table at the Pic or Mr Muggs, the way you hope it's going to be when a woman smiles. It's more like security lighting coming on. A bit white and meaningful. Carrying a definite suggestion not to come no closer.

'It's Tuesday,' she says. 'It's my mother.'

Oh, yes. And she's got a right to grin about it. I'm getting a bit out of touch.

'No reason why you shouldn't come with me, though, darling,' she says, looking straight at me, still got the bright white lights shining.

'You know what Roy says, love?' I ask her. 'He says we got to keep public life and private life separate.'

She don't say nothing to that, just switches off the Amstrad and goes up the corridor to the toilet. Bloody hypocrite, she's thinking. Preaches one thing all afternoon, then turns round and does the opposite in the evening.

Well, I don't see it like that, my love. I know what I mean, even if you don't.

All the same, by the time she's gone, and I've had a slash and a splash myself, and put on a nice soft clean white shirt (no tie this evening, it's not that kind of evening), I'm missing her. Missing someone, anyway. Someone to talk to about what a great day it was, someone to sit with while the machinery runs down.

Tina and Donna are bedding down in the doorway as I come out, sharing a roll-up and drinking coffee out of paper cups. 'Hello, Terry,' says Tina – sweet smile, not quite the shaded lamp, but then it's a raw evening. 'Where you off to, somewhere nice?' For half a moment I think I'll invite them along – take them to the Pic, give them a square meal. Big-hearted Terry. Everyone whispering, 'Where on earth did Terry find that pair of scrubbers?' Quite a comic turn, and no one'd ever forget it. And if it'd just been Tina I really think I might of. Chirpy little thing. But Donna never says nothing, and she's got sores over her face. Not her fault, poor lass, I don't suppose, but there it is. A question of moderation once again. I'm not Jesus, never claimed to be. So I give them two quid each instead, and go on up the street.

Two quid each? What am I on about? I haven't got money to chuck around like this. I'm going to be completely skint by the end of the month.

So I'm a little inconsistent, am I, about what's public and what's private? All right, so I'm a little inconsistent. Anyway, I'm not too sure what Roy's going to say about our Cats demo, now I come to think of it. It may be legal, for all I know. But then again it may not, in which case I don't want to know until afterwards.

'Oh – hello.'

Someone speak? Who? Where? Empty street!

'Listen, I'm sorry about yesterday evening . . .'

I stop and look round. Oh, yes. Behind me. Wrapped up in her quilted overcoat. She's stopped and looked round, too. I must have walked right past her. Well, that's the sort of girl she is.

'Oh, hello, Hilary.'

'It was a slightly awkward occasion. I'm sorry.'

It's a slightly awkward occasion now, by the look of it. She's fiddling about with her hair. Her and Roy and Liz – they're all the same. There's something about having brains that makes you want to grab hold of your hair. Pressure on the roots maybe. Anyway, there she stands, looking like a kid of fourteen. Which for some reason reminds me.

'You like cats, Hilary?'

'Cats? Why?'

51

'I think there's going to be some good cat pix in the Sunday papers.'

'Oh,' says Hilary. She waits, to see if there's some more to come on the subject, but there isn't, because that's *our* little secret. All she's getting is the teaser. 'Anyway, I'm sorry,' she says, for the third time, and she turns and goes on her way.

'He's not there, Hilary.'

Because there's nowhere else she can be going, down Whitchurch Street this time of night. It's a dead end. No one here in the daytime but us and Parchaks and a few other no-hopers. And at night Tina and Donna and about a hundred black plastic bags of rubbish, though where they come from I don't know.

She stops. 'No,' she says. 'I just thought . . .'

Just thought what? I wait to hear, but it's not forthcoming.

'He don't often come into the office, Hilary. Never in the evening.'

Don't she know that? Of course she knows that, as well as I do. So what, just come along on the off chance, has she? Things are as desperate as that?

'No,' she says, standing there, not knowing which way to go. 'Well . . .'

Poor kid. Passed all her exams, spends the day sitting up in that great concrete bunker, like Hitler, making life hell for immigrants and prisoners on remand, then comes out at knocking-off time and she's not Hitler at all, she's Little Orphan Annie. Nice kid. She just shouldn't ever have got mixed up with Roy, that's all.

'So what, Hilary – you're not going to get anything to eat this evening?'

'Oh . . .' she says, waving her hand about in the air as if

it was something not very nice she'd found in the street. The thought of anything as coarse as eating, she's saying, has never so much as crossed her mind.

I go back and put a welcoming hand on her elbow. 'Come along, then, Hilary. Two birds with one stone. Famine relief for you – company for me.'

She takes her elbow away.

'I've got to meet somebody . . .'

'He's not there, love! Not unless he's hiding in them plastic bags!'

'No, somebody else . . . a friend . . .'

She looks obstinately away down the street. I shouldn't have mentioned the plastic bags – she's going to go and look inside them all.

'I shouldn't go down there, love. There's people sleeping in the doorway. They might get funny.'

She's hesitating. Bit of the old logical force getting through to her at last.

'Anyway, don't worry, Hilary, we're not going to the Pic.' Because maybe this is what's worrying her, all them fancy people, and all that fancy food. 'There's a little place round the corner I know. No one famous. No *nouvelle cuisine*. Spaghetti and chips, if you like.'

Whether it's the spaghetti and chips or whether it's me I don't know, but she gives in, and we walk silently up the street together. Though I can't honestly say she's any more enthusiastic about the prospect than she was last night. Because I'll tell you what she reminds me of – me being taken out of Maidstone by the screws for transfer to Armley.

We go up the steps to the Strand and cross over.

'Anyway, Hilary, I don't know what you was apologizing for. I was the one who was shouting the odds last night.'

'Yes.' Very terse.

'And *I'm* not apologizing.'

'No.'

Oh, dear. Maybe I've overdone the milk of human kindness. I should let her go and camp out on the doorstep with Tina and Donna. Learn a thing or two about the world she's boss of.

Here we are. Fifty yards up from the Strand. La Bella Napoli. Been here forever. Was here when Covent Garden was still a market, and the street was just a mush of squashed cabbage leaves.

'OK, Hilary? Not too glitzy?'

She looks round suspiciously. Shaded lights over the tables – yes. But champagne by the glass? – Forget it. A nice Italian accent from the proprietor? – Gino wouldn't have the nerve, not for me at any rate. The dockside at Barking's the nearest Gino's ever got to Napoli. 'Hello, Terry, love,' he says. 'Haven't seen you in here for – stone me – how long?'

I'll tell you exactly how long. Or rather I won't. Because it's not since the Doctor of Philosophy. Number of sessions in here we had, the Doctor and me, getting the politics of pressure groups sorted out over the bolognese where no one'd interrupt us. Some lovely evenings we had, me and the Doctor.

Hilary, though. How am I going to cheer *her* up? No need to worry, after all, because it turns out that *she's* going to do all the talking. No sooner has Gino gone off with the order than she turns on me and launches into me like something out of a safari park.

'Yes, you're quite right,' she says. 'I shouldn't say I'm sorry about last night, because I'm not, I'm actually very angry about it. And what I'm angriest of all about is that I didn't say anything. I thought it was a waste of time arguing with you, so I just sat there in silence and let you get away with it.'

My turn to be silent now. Not at all what I was expecting. And before I can get myself together she's off again.

'I should have argued back. I should have stood up for what I believe in. Because you don't understand, you see. I mean about confidentiality. Or you pretend you don't understand. I don't know which it is, and I don't know which is sillier, because either way your views about the Civil Service are frankly untenable. I'm sorry to be so blunt. I'm sorry to be so un-Civil-Service-like.'

But by this time I've got my breath back.

'What do you want to drink, Hilary?'

'Yes, and that's typical of the way you argue!'

'I'm not arguing, Hilary. I'm listening. But Gino's standing here waiting to know.'

'A glass of water. And by the way, let's get one thing straight before we start – I'm paying for my own meal.'

'OK, Hilary. Up to you. Pay for mine, too, if you like. So that's one glass of water, Gino, and one glass of the house white. All right, then, Hilary. I'm all yours. No more interruptions, no answering back. You tell me – I'll listen.'

It's not going to be quite the peaceful little supper I'd been hoping for. Never mind. Nice to get a surprise.

She's looking at the tablecloth, like she was in the Pic. I've silenced her. No, I haven't. She's off again. Steam coming out of her nostrils.

'I'm not just talking about last night,' she says. 'I've seen you on the television, I've heard you on the radio. You don't argue, you don't present a case – you simply put on a performance. You make it sound as if you're just being the plain reasonable man. But you're not – you're being completely unreasonable. You say a lot of funny things, but you're not funny, you're very aggressive, and very destructive. It makes me so angry.'

I wait. No performance. No funny things.

'Look,' she says. Got that from Roy, hasn't she. But no need to tell me, because I *am* looking, Hilary. I'm looking straight at you, like I always do. You're the one who's not looking. You're telling all this to a packet of breadsticks.

'It's the same for us as for everybody else,' she says. 'I don't know why you can't see that. We *all* have to be free to discuss things frankly in private. We've *all* got to be able to say what we truly think without hurting people's feelings or destroying their reputations. If the Civil Service was different, if our debates were open to the public like Parliament's, then we'd have to have the same sort of immunities and privileges as Parliament. It would create the most monstrous injustice. Not for us – for everybody else. And we've got to be free to disagree with each other in private, and then to present a common front in public. I don't agree with all our decisions, of course I don't, and it would be ridiculous if I couldn't say so while they're being made – and equally ridiculous if I undermined them by telling anybody else about my reservations.'

And so on. All good points. All very nice and reasonable. Does she think I haven't thought of them for myself? Haven't heard them all put to me by nice reasonable people on radio and television, by nice reasonable kids in university debating clubs up and down the country? Does she really believe that being reasonable's what it's all about?

'In any case,' she says, 'if you ever did manage to find out what went on inside a Government department you'd discover most of it was so dull you wouldn't be interested. The case you were referring to yesterday isn't typical. And when something like that does go wrong then we've got to have some privacy while we investigate, or we'll never find out what happened, and we've got to avoid saying anything that might make the situation worse.'

The food comes. I tuck into mine – she don't touch hers. Funny, because the food's what she's looking at, and what I'm looking at still is her. She's getting worked up again, which I find rather interesting – a lot more interesting than all her nice reasonable arguments.

'It's hard work,' she's telling me now. 'No one knows what it's like, that's one of the difficulties. And yes, some of it's distasteful, though you'd think it very unfair if anyone looked down on dustmen and sewage workers for doing distasteful work. And no, it's not nice being unable to talk to people about what you're doing. It's rather painful. I suppose you're thinking, Then why am I having a relationship with someone in your campaign?'

I wasn't, as a matter of fact. But, all right, I will. I'm thinking it now.

'The answer is that it doesn't make any difference, because (a) I couldn't talk about my work with him even if he weren't in your campaign, and (b) the person I'm having this relationship with happens to be someone who knows how to keep work and private life separate. He's not putting on some kind of aggressive performance all the time.'

She looks like a clown in the circus – she's got the same comic red blotches in her cheeks she had last night. Well, better to get worked up and come out in blotches than to sit there like a fish on a slab, all cold and white and not feeling nothing. I got the wrong impression of Hilary when she walked in the door of the Pic last night. Looks like a Civil Servant, yes. But inside there's something else going on altogether, I don't know what. Some kind of underground nuclear test.

Policy and Management – Staff and Finance – Roy's committee. That's why he couldn't bring his report round. And if I know that then so does Hilary. It wasn't Roy she was looking for when she come down Whitchurch Street tonight, then. And I don't suppose it was Tina or Donna.

Slow, aren't I? Always was, tell you the truth. Bit of a handicap in some ways, but I'll tell you something – it's also got its advantages. Everybody else in the world knows the answer to everything already – they always did – it's no surprise to them. Suddenly I tumble it as well – and it's like a bomb going off. I'm amazed, I'm indignant, I'm over the moon – I'm *something*.

I'm something about this one all right, I can tell you. I'm *incredulous*.

I gently rub this little pink thumb of hers with my large rough cold-blooded one. Just have to put the idea to the test, then, won't we, see how it stands up. OK, here we go:

'Done all you're going to do with that chicken salad, have you?' I ask her. She nods, still not looking up. 'Come on, then, I better show you what you people are up against. I'll give you a tour of the office, OK?'

She don't even throw me a funny look. Just nods, slides back her chair, and picks up her handbag. And there it is again – the old tingling in the tum. Always a moment when you feel it. You get on the plane, it starts up, it trundles along over the ground, it stops and waits, it trundles on again. Then suddenly you're going down the runway, faster and faster, and then you're off, you're away – and there's the old funny feeling inside you once again. Never fails.

Nothing's happening in life, nothing's happening ... Then suddenly it's all happening at once. A bit fast, in this case, for a man who don't fly much these days. More like being on a rocket than a plane.

A bit *too* fast, now I come to think about it. Haven't got my seat-belt fastened.

'Hang on a moment, Hilary.'

I go and ask Gino for the bill, then dodge into the Gents. No secret what I'm looking for, but there isn't one. I dodge out again.

'OK if I slip out through the kitchen a moment, Gino?' I murmur. He gives me a funny look, and so does the chef as I pass, and the washer-up and the old lady doing the books in the corner, I think she's Gino's old Momma from Napoli. But I happen to know there's a pub across the street. As soon as I run into the bar it's 'Hello, Terry!' 'What are you doing here, Terry?' 'Come on, Terry, what are you drinking?' Sorry, lads, I tell them, bit of a rush on, and I shoot into the Gents, leaving much laughter behind me. OK, they got a machine, and ten seconds later I'm going back through the bar again, to even greater amusement. 'Cor, Terry, that was a quick slash!' 'Fast worker, old Terry!' I just give them a wave and run. You get a hide like a rhinoceros in this game.

Gino grins as I sign the chit. He's twigged. All these clever buggers the world's full of.

Hilary's waiting by the door, gazing sombrely through the glass into the darkness outside. I think she's forgotten she was going to pay for her supper.

'Had to see a man about a dog,' I tell her. 'Come on, then.'

And off we go, across the Strand, down the steps into the dark little streets behind. Not a word from her, not a word from me. Still prisoner and escort.

I'll tell you what I like about women: you never know what they're up to.

And I'll tell you what women like about me: they always do.

7

'No flowers tonight, Terry?' says this voice out of the darkness underfoot, as I step into the doorway. I jump right out of the doorway again, straight back into Hilary. I don't know what I was thinking about, but it wasn't Tina and Donna.

'Oh, you got company,' says Tina. 'That's nice.'

'This is Tina,' I explain to Hilary. 'And watch where you're putting your feet, because that's Donna under there.'

Up we go. Past Parchaks, past InterGalactic, past Jaypro.

'Sorry about that, Hilary. Should have warned you.'

Should have apologized sooner, too, before we got up this far and she heard how little breath I got left. No, that's a daft way to be thinking. Not going to start holding my stomach in and dyeing my hair for her. This is the way I am, she can take it or leave it.

Clunk of the key, click of the switch, and I can have a bit of a blow while she takes a look round. Which she does. Stands in the middle of the room, and gazes thoughtfully at the desks, at the Amstrad, at the coatstand, as if she's going to give me a price on them.

'What do you think, Hilary? Bit smaller than your place? No secrets, though. That's the difference. Look at anything you like. Open the drawers, pull all the files out, help your-self.'

Lot of things I wouldn't want her to see actually – all the stuff for the Cats campaign, for example, which is lying open on top of Jacqui's desk. Tell people they can look, though, and of course they don't bother. Beats me why they haven't managed to think of this simple idea over in Hilary's part of the world.

Anyway, Hilary don't look at nothing she's not supposed to look at. Only one thing she wants to look at when she's finished examining the furnishings, and that's me. She just stands where she is in the middle of the room, in front of Jacqui's desk, and watches me like a cat as I walk round giving her the guided tour.

'I got a little office in there,' I tell her, opening the door and showing her. No reaction. I close the door and pass on.

'Though most of the time I'm out meeting people, or else I'm in here, walking round the room like this, making a general nuisance of myself.'

Nothing. She just leans back against the edge of Jacqui's desk, as if she's all set to wait for a long time. And looks at me. Funny – first she won't look at me at all, then she won't stop. No sense of moderation, Hilary, I said so all along.

I think it's the plans for the Cats campaign she's got her behind parked on.

I open the library door. 'This is where Liz works, filing everything away, looking everything up. Find all your White Papers and Government reports in here, Hilary, plus all the dirt Liz can dig up from the newspapers and journals to make a monkey of them.'

I go and lean back against the edge of the table opposite her, where we keep the Nescafé and the mugs. She looks at me, I look at her. Our knees are almost touching. Don't need to look down to see – I can feel the radiation in my kneecaps.

'The desk you're sitting on,' I tell her, 'that's where Jacqui works. She does the accounts, she does the newsletter – plus anything else that turns up. Anyone in your office go to finishing school in Switzerland, Hilary? No, well, that's where we got the drop on you.'

I lean forward and slip her overcoat off her shoulders. She don't need an overcoat in here.

'Then we got Shireen behind that window, on the switch. Nice girl, always smiling, no brains, but then if she'd got any brains either she wouldn't be on the switch or else she wouldn't be smiling.'

Shireen's window's behind her. She don't turn round to look at it. I hang up her overcoat. Then I take her jacket off, while I'm about it, and drape it neatly over the back of a chair.

'Window behind me – that's the copying-room. Got Kevin and Kent in there doing the mail-outs. Dozy pair. One's white, one's black, but they both start with K, so people are always mixing them up.'

All she's got to do to see the copying-room is look just past my right ear. But she don't even do that. So I unbutton her shirt, make her feel more at home. Now you can see her throat. It's longer than what you'd think. I put my lips against it. Softer, too. And buzzing my lips like a torch battery, because she's saying something. I straighten up in surprise. First words she's uttered, so far as I can recall, since we was sitting in the restaurant.

'What?'

So she says it again. 'There are no blinds at the windows.'

No blinds – it's true. No call for them in the ordinary run of events. I go and turn the lights off instead, best I can do. Now you can see the yellow world outside the windows. Brick gables on the other side of the narrow street, blind dusty attic windows, a bit of yellowy darkness where the sky is. Inside the room, the gleam of white paper here and there, darkness in the middle. I go back and perch on the edge of the table again, opposite the darkest darkness, and feel my way back to where I left off.

'I'll tell you how we got the Campaign started,' I say, to keep her entertained while I negotiate the next lot of fastenings. But I never do tell her, because she's got there before me, and I suddenly find I've got two soft warm naked heaps of darkness filling both my hands.

And she sighs. I don't know which stirs me up more, what I'm feeling or what I'm hearing. Either way I think my guided tour of the office has come to an end. I don't think I can speak.

Time goes by, the way time does, and by the dim yellow lightness from the windows I start to make out various shapes and shades in front of my eyes. I can see the faint yellow lightness of her cheeks, six inches in front of mine, and the blackness of her mouth . . . Now the gleam of her eyes, looking back into mine from just two inches away.

No rush. Let the time keep ticking quietly on – you need plenty of it for thinking. And what I'm thinking is this: these are the best moments in the world. And then I'm thinking, supposing time stopped. Supposing I had to say when, and choose just one moment out of all of them, to last forever, which would it be? Would I pick this one, when I've got my tongue touching her teeth, and her teeth are beginning to part to let it in . . .? Or this one, with my hands on her knees . . .? Or this one, an inch above them . . .?

into the pale darkness above me goes the great face, then the hardness of his rib-cage and the solid softness of his stomach. The last little bit of him slips heartbreakingly out of me. Oh . . .!

By the time he's found a switch I'm up and wrapped in my overcoat. We both frown and grin in the light.

He is huger than ever, and more absurd, because he is still wearing his shirt and socks. Rising out of the socks and vanishing beneath the shirt-tails are two absurdly massive, absurdly hairy pillars.

'Hungry?' he says. 'Well, you're a silly so-and-so, aren't you, my sweetheart. You should have eaten your supper.'

Supper? Oh, yes, supper, No, I didn't eat it, did I. I remember it with a terrible pang of regret. How about lunch? What did I have for lunch? I can't think about anything except food! Lunch, though . . . 'I didn't have any lunch, either,' I tell him.

He gives me an odd look, eyebrows sardonically raised. He thinks I'm telling him that I've been working myself up all day to the events of this evening.

Was I? Perhaps I was. Being too busy to stop for things like lunch or thought, that's all I can remember about the day.

'You can't do this kind of thing on an empty stomach, darling. All you're going to get now is Nescafé and office biscuits.'

He unplugs the kettle and takes it out to some unseen tap. I walk slowly round the office in my bare feet, holding my coat round me with one hand, picking things up with the other. His suit, old and dark, and full of the smell of him. The files and papers that we seem to have scattered all over the desk and floor. Then little things like rulers and pencil-sharpeners and scissors. I just hold them for a moment and feel them. They have a curious solidity and rightness, some quality that makes you want to hold them, like little baby animals. I run my hand over the plugs and cables that my head was pressing against. They are attached to the back of a small word processor. Even the plugs and cables have some quality of being absolutely and simply themselves.

The socks have come shuffling back with the kettle. They're a strangely satisfying royal blue. I watch their complex and perfect evolutions around the table with the coffee cups on it. They stop, sideways on to me. I look up. The big red face is watching *my* feet.

'You're going to get splinters, my love,' he says. 'I better get you some slippers.'

He opens a door. I follow him into a little office almost entirely filled by a desk and a camp-bed. He opens a filing cabinet and rummages under a heap of underwear. I kneel down in front of the camp-bed and run my hand very slowly over the sleeping-bag. It's also blue, sky blue, and made of some slippery artificial fabric. What comes to my mind as I stroke it, for some reason, is a cool and cloudless morning in early summer.

'No room for two in there,' he says. 'Just in case you're wondering.'

I step into the slippers he has laid out for me. The thin maroon leather has bulged to the shape of his toes. The uninhabited heels follow me a few steps across to the row of coatpegs in the corner where another old dark suit is hanging, much like the one I folded up next door. He must have very few worldly possessions if they are all contained in this one tiny room.

'What – comic way to live?' he says, watching me. 'You're probably right. I'll tell you something, though, Hilary – and more out of life than two walks a day with a paid companion.

What Jibs and Lalla would say if they could see where I actually spend my working day I shudder to think. I mean, this doorway, for a start. It's the same every morning – an absolute garbage heap of broken cardboard boxes underfoot. It's not that I mind those poor kids sleeping here – of course I don't. There but for the grace of God. What I cannot see for the life of me, though, is why muggins here should be expected to fold up their bedding for them and put it away. I don't expect *them* to come out to Sunningdale and make *my* bed.

And as soon as you move the cardboard boxes you've got old Coca-Cola cans rolling around your feet, not to mention soggy paper plates with the disgusting brown remains of I dare not imagine what congealed upon them. On two particularly horrible mornings recently the people concerned had obviously used the plates for another purpose altogether when they'd finished eating off them. I realize they've probably no access to toilet facilities, but honestly . . .

I'm trying not to think about that. But there's no way of picking the things up without getting stuff all over my fingers . . . If *I* can do it, though, if *I* can take everything down to the next doorway and pop it into one of these black plastic bags . . . Euch! Keep my eyes closed . . . Now where are my tissues?

Why shouldn't someone in Parchaks do it, for that matter? It's their doorstep, too. I'm not madly fussy or houseproud – God knows I'm not – but the doorstep *is* how we present ourselves to the world, and if we're reasonably clean and tidy inside then it's just plain silly to advertise ourselves with a heap of filth. Though one glance inside the travel agency place, or this firm on the second floor, what's it called ...? Jaypro, yes ... One glance inside when their doors are open and you know you're not going to get any help out of *them*, thank you very much.

I must get Terry to do something about this loose door handle. He's always rushing off to put in a new light-bulb for his wretched Linda person – and she's not dependent on the good graces of some little man like Mr Shirley – she's got maintenance people from the Council on tap at all hours – but he never notices what's happening to the office. And this terrible smell, I don't know *what* it reminds me of ... Actually there's something different about it today ...

'Oh, Jacqui,' says Shireen, sliding back the glass and smiling. 'Can you ring Mr Moody, and someone called I think it was Mac something. And the cats place rang, they said it's extra on Saturdays, or something like that, oh, and here's the post. Terry's out having a bath.'

Who Mac something is, and which cats place she's talking about, I have naturally not the faintest notion.

'Oh, thank you, my pet,' I say, smiling back. 'Wonderful. Lovely.'

Because you've got to keep a happy atmosphere in the office. I'm always asking her to clear the doorstep when she arrives, for that matter. 'OK, Jacqui,' she says eagerly, lovely friendly smile. So next day I arrive and the doorway's ankle-deep once again. Lovely friendly smile from me. 'I thought you were going to clear up the doorway for me this morning, Shireen?' Another lovely friendly smile from Shireen. 'Oh, sorry, Jacqui, I forgot.' She doesn't notice, she doesn't think, all she ever does is smile. Terry simply doesn't back me up on this, it's hopeless. I try to keep the office running for him, but I can't do it if people know he's not behind me.

Kent, of course, is standing in the copying-room gazing

into space. He knows perfectly well what he's supposed to be doing this morning – and it's not what he *is* doing, which is frankly disgusting. Every morning I have to bang on the glass like this and smile at him ... Yes, I'm here! Yes, I'm smiling at you! Yes, I'm going to go on smiling at you ...! It's like Poops getting Pippy started when he's in one of his bloody-minded moods – sheer heels and will-power.

No sign of Kevin. Just check he's where I think he is, if possible without taking my eyes off Kent ... Yes, the usual little grunting and splashing noises coming out of the loo. What he gets up to in there, and why it always takes him half the morning to get up to it, I cannot imagine. Nor am I ever likely to find out, since Kevin's problems are something we never notice.

I *assume* Liz is in. Put my head round her door.

'Hello, my sweet!'

'Hello, Jacqui.'

'All right, my pet?'

'Fine.'

Although she *wasn't* in yesterday – it was nearly ten o'clock before she came wandering along, without a word of explanation – and actually it's a miracle she ever finds her way here at all with her hair over her eyes like that.

Right, switch on the Amstrad. Yes, I'm safely sitting at my desk, Kent, my precious, but I'm giving you another nice smile, so you can see I haven't forgotten you!

Now, what are we doing today ...? Cats, right ... Talking of which, I don't suppose for one moment that light-bulbs are the only things that my dear Terry's putting in for poor Linda. Oh, I've no illusions about Terry. I may have had once. But not after five years. I try not to think about what he gets up to during the week. I simply happen to believe he's a great man, that's all. No reason to change my mind about *that*.

'Oh, so brave of you, Jacqui, darling!' said Jibs, the first time she looked in on a Sunday morning and found him sitting in the kitchen in his vest, with his feet up on the sideboard. And Lalla: 'No one could say you haven't got the courage of your convictions, Jacqui.' I also know what they say about him behind my back, because Poops told me. But I've watched them talking to him, and I know they wouldn't mind having some great man of their own sitting in their kitchen. I've heard him telling them some of his frankly unbelievable stories about working on the river, and being a bookie's runner, and all the rest of it – and I've watched them giggling and looking at one another and egging him on. If I wasn't there I have a feeling he'd run through the ladies of Sunningdale like a knife through . . .

I've just realized why the Amstrad isn't coming on. The screen's unplugged. Odd . . .

And where are the disks? The disks have gone!

'What in heaven's name . . .?' I cry.

Liz appears in the doorway of the library, holding her hair out of her eyes.

'What?' she says.

'My box of disks! It's vanished! I keep it *here* . . .'

'Aren't these the disks?' says Liz.

Yes, they are. And no wonder I didn't see them, because they were on the table with the coffee things . . . Hold on, though – *everything's* in the wrong place!

'That's not where the stapler lives . . . And where's my address book? Why are all the pencils upside down?'

'Someone doing a bit of tidying up?' says Liz.

Tidying up? This makes me laugh. Or it would if I weren't so cross – I can't *bear* having my things touched, as Liz very well knows. I think the best I can manage is a slightly sardonic smile.

'My precious,' I say, 'it's Wednesday, so it's not the cleaners, and no one else ever tidies anything up in this office except me.'

'Well, and me,' says Liz, smiling as well, and looking right, left, and centre all at the same time, in that maddening way she has.

'Oh, yes – and you.'

Smiles, smiles. And back she goes to work. Offended, I suppose, but I can't keep everyone happy. Anyway, I'm the one with a right to feel aggrieved in this situation, surely.

So who was it? Shireen? I turn round and look at her. She's in a world of her own behind the glass in there, with her headset over her ears, smiling and chattering away to someone, probably some friend of hers, no wonder the phone bills are so horrendous.

Kent? He's folding subscription reminders behind the glass in front of me, with that terrible vacant look he keeps on his face just to let us all know that the use of his mind is not included in his contract of employment.

Kevin? He can't be thought about just at the moment. Though now the loo's flushing, and a few moments later he appears in the copying-room. At once the look on Kent's face changes. He's turning to talk to Kevin, with his face half-hidden behind his hand. He's laughing, and I can imagine what he's talking about, because Kevin's looking through the glass in my direction, with a kind of dreadful smile hanging around his open mouth. They're as thick as thieves, those two.

I wonder . . . No point in marching in there and challenging them, though – Kent wouldn't know anything and Kevin wouldn't be able to speak. Well, I suppose it will remain a mystery. One of the minor mysteries of office life, of which there are so surprisingly many. Put it out of my mind. Like so many other things.

To work. I reach for the folders I was using yesterday . . .

Oh, no! They're all buckled and creased! And everything inside them is mixed up and upside down . . . What's happening? And the print-out of the Cats material . . .! It's all *rumpled*, like a badly made bed! And some of the pages are torn! This one's got what looks like a footprint on it . . .!

Right! This I am *not* standing for! Tidying up? This is a piece of absolutely flagrant sabotage . . .!

'. . . Anyway, don't worry, that's lovely . . . No, no trouble at all, it was nice to have a chat about it, and I'll ask Terry to ring you back as soon as he comes in . . . Bye, then . . . Oh – and did you say your name was . . .? Oh.'

I don't know, I wouldn't mind staying on the switch, only Jasna keeps going on at me. 'You've got to get off that switch, Shireen!' she says, 'you've got to do audio!' Only I quite like being on the switch, that's the thing. It's no good telling Jasna that, though. 'Don't be silly, Shireen!' she says. 'I know what it's like. You've been with that lot over a year now, and you're not getting anywhere, are you.' No, but if I like it . . . 'Oh, come on, Shireen, you *don't* like it! It's boring, nothing ever happens!' It's no good arguing with Jasna, she just goes on and on at you. And maybe she's right, I don't know. But I think it all depends. In a small friendly office like this one . . .

'Hello – OPEN . . . Oh, lovely, I'll send you our Schools Information Pack. It's got everything in there, it's very interesting. Oh, hold on – who shall I send it to . . .?'

. . . In a small friendly office like this one it's quite interesting. It's wonderful working with Terry – he's just like you'd imagine, really nice and ordinary. You know – 'Hello, Shireen. How are you doing, sweetheart?' And all rampaging round the office, saying funny things, making the sparks fly. And Liz is nice. Jacqui's a bit, you know – always going on about things – but you get used to it. 'Shireen, my pet, this, Shireen, my precious, that.' Like the doorway downstairs – she's got a real thing about it. But I don't take it too seriously, I know how to handle her. Then one of the boys in the copying-room is always hanging round, but I don't take any notice of him . . .

You can't have any music on if you're on the switch, that's true, so some people would go mad. Like Mum, she's addicted to it, though I don't know how she ever hears it where *she* works, what with the noise of the machines. But there's usually something going on here on the other side of the glass to keep you entertained, it's like watching TV sometimes, only with the sound turned down. If it's not Terry storming around, it's Jacqui blowing her top. Jacqui's having a great go about something now, I can see her rushing in and out of the library, waving bits of paper about. Oh, no – here she comes! What's got into her this time?

'Shireen, my precious, you haven't been touching the things on my desk, have you?'

'Oh, Jacqui, no, what's happened?'

'Only someone systematically destroying my files, that's all!'

'Oh, no, how awful! The boys might have noticed something – I think they were in there earlier.'

And off she goes to the copying-room. No, she's all right, you've just got to be nice and sympathetic. They're all all right, really, and I agree with what they're doing, I think it's a very good thing. And you're in your own little cubby-hole, so you don't have to be more involved than you want to be.

'Hello – OPEN . . . Hold on . . . Liz, it's that woman in that, you know, college place . . . OK . . . Putting you through . . .'

And people ring up, they tell you their stories, about how the Government won't give them the information they need, things like that. Some terrible things you hear – it really makes your blood boil. They want you to help, and you have to know whether to put them through to Liz or Jacqui, or sometimes you can just give them an address of something or the name of someone yourself.

She's really giving the boys what for. She hasn't stopped talking since she got into the copying-room. What did she say they'd done? Mucked up something on her desk? That'd be Kent. Or Kevin. They're as hopeless as each other, those two.

And then you get all television people ringing up, all interviewers and chat shows and people like that, and you get to know quite a lot of them, and it's all 'Hello, Shireen, my love!' – 'Hello, Jimmy, how are you?' – 'I'm going to ask *you* on the show one of these days, Shireen, my sweetheart.'

Also it's not as if you don't ever get out of the office, because you do. I'm always running downstairs to get sandwiches and mineral water and things for people. I know some girls don't like doing it, but I think it makes a nice break, also you meet girls from other offices and you all have a bit of a moan together.

And you never know what's going to be happening next. Some days that light's flashing all the time, you're going mad. Everyone's saying 'Get me so-and-so, get me this, get me that.' Other days – well, take today, for instance . . .

'Hello – OPEN . . . Oh, hello, Mr Donaldson, how are you . . .? The where . . .? Oh, the Ritz, yes. Well, I can't tonight, Mr Donaldson . . .! Well, because I'll be down the club with my friends . . .! Yes, well, we'll just have to see, won't we, when next week comes . . . Oh, it's really Terry you're after, is it, Mr Donaldson . . .? No, he's out. I'll tell him you called, Mr Donaldson . . . You, too.'

So cheeky, some of them, but at least they're the other end of the phone, and you can't help laughing . . .

Yes, other days you've got time to think your own thoughts. Which I enjoy. I know it's not something everyone likes, having a little think to yourself, but I do. It's lovely – here you are in your own little room, you don't have to share it with your sister or anything, and you've got a few of your own bits and pieces round you, and you can just sit here thinking. I sometimes wonder what it is I do all this thinking of mine about! What am I thinking about now, for instance? I don't know – I'm thinking it's lovely, here I am in my own little room, and I don't have to share it with Jasna, I've got some of my pictures Blu-Tacked up, and I'm thinking . . .

'Now all my slimbreads have gone!'

I nearly had a heart attack. Jacqui's standing there with the glass panel crashed back.

'They're on the table with the coffee things, Jacqui! I saw them this morning! Where they always are! Look . . .'

Headset off, and out I come. I'd better find them for her, she's in such a state.

'I'm perfectly happy to buy some for other people as well,' she's saying. 'All they've got to do is come and ask me. But to find someone's eaten the lot, when as it happens I haven't had any breakfast this morning . . .'

'Here they are, Jacqui . . .'

But – oh, no – the box is empty! First everything's mucked up on her desk – now the slimbreads!

You think, Oh, today's going to be a nice quiet day.
Then suddenly something interesting like this happens.

It's like poison-pen letters. I saw this film on TV once.
There was this woman and she seemed quite nice – she was
a bit like Jacqui – but then she started getting these poison-
pen letters, and you found out that everyone in the village
had some reason for hating her. So they were all under
suspicion, and there was this priest sort of person who said
how this happy community had been turned into a nest of
intrigue, and they suddenly found this other woman hanging, I think it was the woman in the post office, only I don't
think it was her that had written the letters.

Anyway, it must be Kevin who did this. Or Kent. I don't
like to say anything to Jacqui, I don't want to get them into
trouble. I just have a look through the window of the
copying-room at them, to see what they're doing. So does
Jacqui.

'Hey, Kevvy!' I go. 'You know what you are? You're a dirty
little devil, Kevvy!'

'It wasn't . . .' he says. 'It wasn't . . . It wasn't . . .'

Look at him, the daft monkey! Grinning away to himself
all over his daft monkey-face! He loves it, he loves it! I
mean, OK, we're banged up together in this copying-room
all day long, me and Kev – we got to pass the time somehow,
right? We got to fool a little, we got to have a laugh or two.

So, no worries, I keep after him. 'It was, Kevvy,' I go.

'It wasn't . . .'

'It was. It was you.'

'It wasn't . . .'

'I saw you, Kevvy. Going through her things. Feeling all
her things. You dirty little devil!'

'You didn't . . .' he says. 'It wasn't . . .'

Look at that filthy grin! Wicked! He can't get enough of it!

'Putting your disgusting great hairy fingers into all her little doodads!'

'It wasn't . . .'

Cause this is what really gets him going, right? Me telling him he's a dirty little devil. Don't know why. 'No, no,' he says, 'I didn't . . . I never . . .' Gets so excited he can't get the words out. Twists himself up into a knot and giggles like a little kid. There he goes – dropping letters and envelopes all over the floor, don't know what he's doing. Down on his hands and knees, scrabbling after them, still grinning. Wicked, wicked.

No, here's why he likes it. Cause he *is* a dirty little devil. He'd love to have his fingers in the jam, and the nearest he gets to it is me telling him he do. He knows he don't, and I know he don't, but when I tell him he do he kind of thinks he do. And here's what makes me laugh – I kind of think he do as well.

Got to get through the day, right?

OK, look at him. He's picked all his letters off the floor – he's straightened up and nutted the bottom of the table – he's put his little heap of mucky letters on top of the rest – only there's one of them's hanging over the edge – so now it's fallen off again – he's got back down on the floor to pick it up – only he's got his foot on it, so it tears in half. So now he's sitting there with his mouth open waiting to see what's going to hit him next, and I'm standing here pissing myself.

No, I'm not. I'm not doing nothing. I just seen Jacqui out there on the other side of the glass with Shireen, and they're clocking us. Nothing to clock, though, is there, cause I'm putting letters in envelopes, aren't I, good as gold. OK? No thoughts in my head, nothing.

'What?' says Kev, cause he's not as daft as all that, he knows there's something up. Only he's too late, he's always too late. Time he looks round, Jacqui and Shireen have gone into the library to see Liz.

OK. So, what's going to hit old Kevin next?

I know: 'She's old enough to be your mum, Kevvy!'

'No, she's . . .'

'It's like, inside your head, you're messing around with your mum.'

'No, she's . . .'

'If you're not careful, Kevvy, my son, you're going to end up in Broadmoor.'

'No, she's . . . forty-four.'

'Oh, so you been checking her out! You really got plans for her, haven't you, you dirty old man.'

Great screwed-up grinning knot he's in now. So chuffed he don't know where to put himself. Now what? I know, I know!

'I'll tell her, Kevvy.'

'No . . .! No . . .!'

'I'll tell her I looked through the window and seen you. I'll tell her you wasn't in the toilet, you was out there going through her desk.'

'No . . .! Don't . . .!'

'OK, show us what you got in your bag today, then.'

Because we haven't done the old bag routine yet this morning. And here we go again. He shoves out his hand to save his bag, and down goes another stack of letters.

'No, I don't . . . I don't . . .'

Don't want to show me. But yes he do want to show me. He do, he do.

Wicked, that bag of his. Dirty green canvas thing, come out of the old War Museum. His mum's written his name and address inside the flap in big letters, case he gets lost on the way home. He don't like no one looking inside it, so he always keeps the straps done up. Come lunchtime and he wants his sandwiches, he's struggling away for like an hour to get it open. 'Here – I'll do it,' I tell him. 'No! No!' And when he gets it open he still can't eat his sandwiches, cause he's got to get it strapped up again first. 'Come on, Kevvy – let me do it!' – 'No . . . no . . .' – 'I won't look, honest I won't!' – 'Yes . . . you will . . .'

Even takes it to the toilet with him. Only chance I get to look inside's when Jacqui calls him out of the room for a minute. Don't bother me – I just want to see if he got anything new, cause every now and then he goes up Soho after work and gets a fresh load of stuff. Why's he carry the old stuff round with him? Simple – he don't want to leave it at home for his mum to find.

All old stuff today, I know that. But he don't know I know!

'Come on, Kevvy!'

'No . . . no . . .'

'Just one.'

'Well . . .'

'A good one, though, right? Not the rubbish you was showing me yesterday.'

So then there's all this squirming and giggling and struggling with the buckles, and a lot more letters falling on the floor, and in the end he's holding one of his mags under the desk in the dark, and I can just see this tart, and this fellow's got her down over a Harley, right, with her great wobblers all like hanging over the handlebars . . .

Other thing I can see is Jacqui. She's back there clocking us through the glass again, got Liz with her as well as Shireen, and she's coming this way. Don't worry me, cause all I'm doing is putting letters in envelopes.

'What?' says Kev. Smart, right? Knows there must be something up if I'm putting letters in envelopes.

'What? What?' he says, and he looks through the glass. Nothing to see out there, though, is there, cause by this time Jacqui's round behind him, coming through the door.

Him trying to get his dirty book back in the bag! Scramble struggle stumble! I'd laugh till I bust myself only I got nothing in my head but letters and envelopes.

Wicked!

'I haven't . . .' I explain.

'So you keep saying, Kevin, my precious, but *someone* has.'

'I haven't . . .' I start again. The strap won't go into the buckle, the words won't go into my tongue.

'I'm not accusing anyone, Kevin, my love. It might just as easily be Kent here. He's keeping very quiet, I notice, he's got his usual know-nothing look all over his face. But the simple fact is that the box was half full yesterday and it's empty today.'

I want to make one thing absolutely clear to her. I leave the strap, and fold my arms round the haversack while I concentrate on the words. 'I haven't . . .' I say.

'It's the principle of the thing, you see, my pet. That's what I'm concerned with. You must see that we can't have an office where people go round tearing up documents and stealing other people's possessions! We can't live like that!'

'Yes, but I haven't . . .'

'So you keep saying, my precious, but you obviously *have* – you have *something* – you've got it hidden inside that bag!'

This is outrageous. I cram the flap down over the bag more tightly still and hold it as far away from her as possible. Now let's get this straight once and for all.

'I haven't . . .' I say firmly.

Taken your slimming wafers, I am going to explain, because in the first place I am not given to petty larceny, as you perfectly well know, but secondly because I shouldn't dream of burdening my digestive system with the kind of rubbish foisted upon us by those who trade upon human credulity in matters of health.

But she's changed the subject.

'And what are these letters doing all over the floor, my sweet?'

I get down to recover the letters – a task made more difficult by my absolute refusal to let go of my haversack – but I have no intention of allowing myself to be distracted from what I wish to say.

'I haven't . . .' I tell her.

Anything that is any concern of yours concealed in my haversack, I am going to say. But nor have I . . .

'Pick them *up*, my sweet! You're just sliding them round the floor! You're making them dirtier and dirtier! You can't do it while you're clutching that bag! Put it down!'

. . . But nor have I any intention of demonstrating this by letting you see the contents, since they include items of a strictly personal nature. In any case . . .

'Kevin, my love, if you want to be treated the same as everyone else, which I assume you *do*, then you must make a bit more of an effort to *behave* the same as everyone else! Look at these envelopes! They can't be sent out like this! I shall have to do them all over again!'

. . . I shall refuse to collaborate in any search as a matter of principle, because I believe . . . I can't get at those two letters if Kent persists in keeping his legs . . . Agh! Head again! This really is too bad . . . Because I believe that each of us has a moral obligation to resist the unjustified extension of quasi-juridical powers . . .

'Look! You're standing on one! Kevin, my sweetheart, what *are* we going to do with you?'

'I haven't . . .'

'Kevin, my darling, if you say that once more I shall scream!'

'I haven't . . .'

'But you *have*!' she screams. 'You have, you have, you have! Look, there's a footprint all over it! Yes . . . Where's the other footprint? The one over my printout? It's the same! It's your footprint!'

'I haven't . . .'

She doesn't have the elementary courtesy to listen to what I have to say, however. She's simply flounced out of the room – I can see her on the other side of the glass, snatching up the papers on her desk. She's showing them to Liz and Shireen, and pointing at me, in the most openly discourteous way. She wouldn't dare behave like this if Terry were here.

'Now you're for it,' says Kent.

Kent, yes. I haven't, I was going to say, any proper way to defend myself from these egregious accusations without implicating my wretched colleague. I can't explain that it was Kent who made me drop the letters. I can't point out, if this is something she refuses to see for herself, that it must plainly be Kent who is the culprit in all the other matters as well.

'I can't . . .' I tell Kent. 'I can't . . .'

I can't help feeling, I am trying to tell him, that he might have admitted responsibility. I can't help feeling the injustice of being shut up in this room with him day after day, of trying to treat him as an equal, even though I am a grown man – I'm thirty-two – I'm fourteen years older than he is. Of struggling to confide in him about personal matters, even though I am mocked for my efforts, of attempting to protect other members of the staff from his outrageous innuendoes – and then of finding that I am expected to take the blame for his misdeeds!

'I can't . . .!' I say, and I can hear that my voice is becoming very agitated.

'Here she comes!' says Kent. '*And* she's going to find those mags in your bag!'

'I can't . . . explain . . .'

9

'*Do* try to understand, Liz, my precious!' snaps Jacqui when I tell her I'll run out and get some more slimbreads myself – I'll print up the document again – it won't take a minute – anything to avoid a scene like this. 'It's the *principle* of the thing, Liz! I just don't see why I should be made a fool of! *Why* do you always take everyone else's side?'

And off she storms into the copying-room again with her empty slimbread box in one hand and her bits of smudged paper in the other. I go back to my table in the library, because I don't think I can bear to watch. And then at once I come out again, because I can't bear *not* to watch. It's like having a bad tooth. Even when I'm watching I'm not watching. I take one quick look into the copying-room, and there she is, waving all her bits and pieces about – and at once I look away. I look at the sky outside the window, I look at the copy for the newsletter on Jacqui's desk. I look at Shireen, but she's looking at the scene in the copying-room, so I can't look at her. I look back into the copying-room, and Jacqui's still there, banging the empty box about in front of Kevin. It's worse than seeing people kissing in public, and seeing Shireen watching it is worse than catching someone out watching them kiss – she's got the same awful hungry look on her face. I know what I've got on my face, too – I've got this terrible grin of mine. I know they're all suddenly going to look out and see me grinning at them, as if I'm amused by it all, so I run back into the library again.

What's happening now? Yes, she's still raving inaudibly on. Every time Kevin tries to explain he knocks things off the table, so now she's got him crawling round the floor again . . . He's still clutching that terrible old canvas bag of his to his chest – he looks the picture of guilt. Kent's gone completely dead in the head, as usual, so I imagine it was Kent who put Kevin up to it. Sometimes it's that blank look on Kent's face that sets Jacqui off, but today she seems to have forgotten about him completely. She's decided all her troubles in life are caused by Kevin.

What causes trouble, though, is the combination of Kent and Kevin. They're always playing silly games together in that copying-room – Kent trying to grab Kevin's bag, Kevin trying to swipe him with it. They obviously came rushing out here at some point and knocked everything off Jacqui's desk, then – I don't know – they started to eat the slimbreads . . . Or the slimbreads got broken and Kent made Kevin pick up all the pieces . . . What does it matter?

I can't think when all this happened. It wasn't last night, because Jacqui and I were still here when the boys left. And when Kent arrived this morning Kevin was already installed in the loo. But what does it matter, what does it matter?

Which reminds me . . . If Jacqui goes into the loo and finds that Kevin's left it in the state he sometimes does . . .

But when I get in there it's reasonably clean. The lavatory paper's somehow unrolled itself all over the floor, but otherwise . . . Otherwise there's just two coffee mugs draining on the shelf over the basin, in the middle of Terry's shaving things. This must be a bit of Terry's washing up – Shireen and I never get the mugs mixed up with the soap and the toothpaste. I suppose Terry made himself a cup of coffee last night . . . Or two cups . . . And then ate the slimbreads . . . No, not Terry, he wouldn't eat health food . . .

So, someone . . . Some friend of Terry's . . . Some woman . . .

Yes. Probably. Knowing Terry . . .

And so all the stuff getting knocked off Jacqui's desk was . . .

Oh, no! Don't be silly! No, no, no!

Well. Not impossible. Terry being Terry . . .

Anyway, be on the safe side – take them back to the office and put them where they belong before Jacqui sees them. I remember all the rows there were over that woman who was making the film about Terry . . .

'Roy!'

This is a surprise. Roy? At ten o'clock in the morning? I've never known him come into the office this early before.

'Oh, hello, Liz.'

He's sitting in Jacqui's chair, still in his overcoat, gazing at the performance in the copying-room with Shireen. He's like someone who's switched on the television halfway through a programme, though. Shireen's trying to explain the story to him, but he doesn't understand, and he doesn't much care. His eyes are on the copying-room – his mind's on something else.

'Anything I can do to help?' I ask him.

'Not really,' he says, not looking at me. 'I just wanted a word with Terry.'

And suddenly – I don't know what it is, whether it's the two mugs I'm holding, or the look on Roy's face, or just his being here first thing in the morning . . . or his mentioning Terry . . . or just all this undirected anger flying about – but suddenly I know exactly what's happened.

Hilary. *Hilary.* I might have guessed. Well, I might have guessed as soon as Chrissie said someone had seen Hilary having dinner with Terry in some restaurant. No, I should have seen what was coming six months ago – as soon as she first met Roy.

But here, though, on the desk that Roy's sitting at . . .

No, no! This is mad! It wasn't like that! It didn't happen! Of course it didn't.

'Excuse me,' I say to Roy. 'I must just go and . . .'

Go and what? I don't know – make it all somehow not have happened, make everything the way it was. That's my real function in this office – making things all right for everyone. I go blindly into the copying-room – I've still got the mugs on the fingers of my right hand – I don't know what I'm going to do. All I know is that it didn't happen, it didn't happen.

'And *I'm* not leaving this room, you see, my precious,' Jacqui's saying to Kevin, 'until you've opened that bag.'

'Jacqui,' I say to her. 'This is terrible – I've only just realized . . .'

I can't look at her. I know she's staring at me, furious at being interrupted. But all I can see is the copying-machine – the floor – the ceiling – the light-switch – Kent's left ear . . .

'I think it must have been me.'

Did I say that? Yes, I did. So – on I go.

'I was looking for something on your desk. I was looking for the scissors. This morning, before you came in. I've just remembered – I knocked some things on the floor. I think it may have been the printout. Yes, because I picked it up, and tried to put it back the way it was, and . . .'

She's staring at me, so far as I can see out of the corner of my eye.

'And the slimbread things,' I say. 'I knocked them off the

96

table, and they went all over the floor, so I very stupidly . . . put them down the loo.'

Kevin's staring at me as well. Even Kent has turned round to look.

'I'm sorry,' I say. 'I don't know why I didn't think of all this sooner.'

Because, yes, that's how it was. I remember clearly now. It was me all the time, it was my fault, it was me.

What am I doing here? I should be back in Chambers. I should be preparing to go into court later this week to fight a vitally important test-case against the Department of Health, which could change the life and prospects of several thousand patients with special dietary needs, not sitting here watching these people squabble over a missing packet of – what was it Shireen said? – high-fibre wholemeal slimming biscuits? Oh, God. Why do one's associates in good causes so often make one's heart sink?

Even poor Liz has got embroiled in it now. She's smiling, and pushing her hair out of her eyes, and looking profoundly embarrassed. Not surprising, really – she's the only one in the office with any real intelligence. Actually I think Terry's got more than he reveals, but it's difficult to know when he's putting on all that performance of simple-minded direct-ness. I'm not casting any aspersions on the two lads in the copying-room. I've campaigned long and hard myself for a genuine equal opportunity employment policy in Chambers – though locking your one disabled employee up behind glass with your one black employee does make them look a little like an exhibit in an equal opportunities museum. Still – here they are, that's the main thing. And at the moment almost all the rest of the staff is round behind the glass with them.

I don't know about Jacqui. I'm not quite sure what makes her qualify for employment. Some kind of inverse social deprivation, perhaps. At least Shireen is Asian. Though I can't help feeling it's slightly unfortunate, in an organization of this nature, to be employing someone as a receptionist who just happens to be female and attractive.

Or am I being a little naïve? Is Terry sleeping with her? Probably, from everything one hears. Perhaps that's why Jacqui's in such a temper.

Here is Terry, anyway, at last, huge in the doorway, still panting from the stairs, with the door handle rattling behind him. At once I'm filled with obscure irritation. Why is he so large and full of himself? Why doesn't he take a little more exercise? Why doesn't he get the door handle fixed? How have I got myself mixed up with him? Yes – and what am I doing here now?

'Oh, Terry,' says Shireen, 'Professor someone rang, could it be Jelly? And Mr Donaldson, and Peter, and Jane you-know at the BBC. And Jacqui's having a bit of a go at Kevin – he's messed up her things.'

But Terry takes no notice of Shireen. He's gazing at me, visibly taken aback, for some reason, at my appearance in the office. No jokes at my expense, no grasping of my hand or elbow or shoulder. 'Hello, Roy,' he says quietly, like a normal human being. His grey curls are wet, I notice. He's got a towel round his neck, and he's holding an open plastic box with a bar of pink soap in it. Perhaps he feels caught at a slight disadvantage, on the way back from his public ablutions. Or perhaps he recognizes for once that he went too far the other evening – even thinks I've come to remonstrate.

'I promised to bring in the final draft of the Government Agencies report today,' I remind him.

'Oh, yes,' he says guardedly.

'I haven't finished it yet, though.'

In that case, he might reasonably inquire, why have I come? But he doesn't. 'Right, right,' he says oddly, and looks away at events in the copying-room. I get the impression that he doesn't want to meet my eye. What's going on? One of his most irritating ways of asserting himself normally is to gaze straight into your eyes, and since part of my professional equipment is to be able to eye down witnesses in court I find it extraordinarily galling to be eyed down in my turn by a man who has only ever faced a court from the dock.

Some curious shift in our relationship seems to have occurred. I find this reversal almost as awkward as the original relationship. I have to look away myself after all, so as not to see his discomfiture. This is absurd!

So we're both resting our eyes on the little drama unrolling on the other side of the glass, like a television show with the sound turned down. There's been some further twist in the plot, and Liz has joined Kent – or Kevin, whichever it is – crawling about on the floor.

'I gather he's eaten all her special slimming food,' I explain.

'Oh, right,' says Terry, plainly not thinking about it. I get the impression he's still waiting to find out why I've come. But then so am I.

'Look,' I say, 'perhaps we need to have a bit of a talk about things.'

'OK,' says Terry. 'Right. Sure.'

'In your office, perhaps?'

He nods and leads the way, in a very uncharacteristically sombre silence. He perches himself on the edge of his desk, the towel still round his neck, looking like an old-fashioned boxer's manager. I sit on his camp-bed, just above floor-level. I don't much like crouching at his feet, and I don't much like sharing the bed with the memory of Shireen and all his various other triumphs, but there doesn't seem to be anywhere else.

He waits.

'Look . . .' I say. We both wait. 'I just wondered what you made of Hilary.'

So *that's* why I've come – to talk about Hilary. I suppose I knew all the time. I've got to say her name to *someone*! I've got to hear *someone* say it to me! Terry would be the last person in the world I should choose for the task, if I had any choice, but I don't, because he's the only one who's met her, the only one who knows about her.

For a moment he just looks at me uncomprehendingly. Oh, dear, he can't even remember her name.

'In the restaurant,' I explain. 'The other night.'

Now he's remembered, and he's changed completely. He starts to laugh. He throws his towel into the corner, on to a heap of old socks and underclothes, puts the soap in the filing cabinet, and sits down behind his desk. I think we're back to something more like normal.

'What I made of Hilary?' he says. 'Right. Yes. Well. What I made of Hilary . . .'

And he becomes very serious and thoughtful.

'Lovely girl, Roy,' he says, and at once all my distrust evaporates. I know he means it.

I see why everyone always falls in love with Terry. He's an absurd man, but his heart's as open as an open book. My sudden change of feeling is ridiculous, I realize that. I have to resist the urge to jump up and fling my arms round him.

'Yes, well, I think she's a somewhat remarkable person,' I hear myself telling him. 'I know you and she slightly got across each other in the restaurant . . .'

'Just kidding her a little, Roy. Just keeping the conversation going.'

'But that's because she's rather like you, in a totally different sort of way.' What *am* I babbling about? 'I mean, she's a very powerful personality, and so are you. I think you made a strong impression on her.'

'Look them straight in the eye, Roy. That's the secret. Don't need to tell you no secrets, though, do I. Sly old devil you are! I didn't think you was the type.'

'I'm not, I'm not! It's not like that, Terry!'

'Not like what, Roy?'

Yes – what isn't it like? What *is* it like, for that matter? I run my hand through my hair, trying to smooth down the thoughts within.

'I don't know how to explain . . . She's had a rather difficult life, that's the thing . . .'

And I find I'm sitting there at Terry's feet telling him everything. Not only about how she'd never known who her father was, but about how her mother had always suffered from depression, and how Hilary had been forced to look after her. About how she'd taken an evening job to keep the household going, and got up at five o'clock every morning to do her homework. About how she'd got a scholarship at Balliol, and how she'd hated it there because no one took life seriously.

Terry sits there, nodding and gazing at me, but for once not saying anything, just listening and obviously thinking about it all.

I explain to him about how she finds it difficult to express her feelings, and how she had a relationship with a man who turned out to have a wife and children already, not to mention a criminal record . . .

'What'd he got?' interrupts Terry.

'What? Oh – I think it was burglary and assault . . . Yes, I'm sorry – I didn't mean to imply . . .'

'No offence, Roy. Same as you, when they tell you about someone – nice to know what college they went to, what they was studying.'

Natural enough, I suppose, even if I can't for the moment recall what Terry was reading . . .

'Theft, false pretences, and actual bodily harm,' he reminds me unprompted. 'Though the actual was in rather special circumstances, more in the nature of re-educating the fellow concerned and fitting him to take his place in normal society.'

Oh, yes. Anyway, I tell him about how Hilary lived with another woman for a while, which seems to surprise him somewhat, though I explain that she won't talk about it. And I tell him how I feel I can't let her down again, after all the difficulties she's had in her life, but how I can't bring myself to tell Fenella about her just when she's got her first big fraud case, and she's up till two every morning studying the papers for the next day, with no end in sight for another five or six months at least.

'It's so difficult to know what Hilary's feelings are,' I explain to him. 'I mean, you saw what she's like. I'm sure she's *attracted* to me in some kind of way . . . At least, I think she is . . . Look, this is going to make you laugh – we've never even been to bed together.'

I laugh and he doesn't. He just goes on looking at me with that same disarming frankness. Then he nods.

'Good rule in life, Roy. If you're not sure what their feelings are – don't.'

'No, well, I know it's not the kind of thing that would worry you. I mean, from what one hears . . .'

I laugh. He doesn't. I'm surprised, as always, by how much more serious people are about these things underneath than they seem on the surface.

'It would certainly worry me if I didn't know what their feelings were, Roy,' he says. 'It'd worry me a lot. I like to know what their feelings are.'

'I mean, I shouldn't say I was abnormally slow off the mark in general. Well, Fenella and I, for instance – fine – no problems. Normally. Before she started on this present case. But Hilary . . . I don't think that's what she wants, you see.'

He waits patiently.

'She wants something out of me, I know that. But I don't know what it is – I don't think *she* knows what it is . . . You caught us at a rather bad moment the other evening – you probably realized.'

He nods. 'Sorry about that.'

'No, running into you was actually rather a good thing. Gave us something else to talk about.'

Yes, I told her one or two of the standard stories about his exploits with women, including various idealistic young followers who hadn't realized quite how thoroughly Terry was committed to freedom of communication until they came to work for the Campaign. But never mind that now.

'No, I'm very grateful to you,' I say. 'Things were really quite a lot better by the end of the meal. But then I don't know what happened, because last night she didn't show up at all. I completely missed Policy and Finance. I rang her this morning and she wouldn't even talk about it.'

Terry looks out of the window, and lets air hiss slowly through his teeth. I think he's going to give me some wise advice. What's more, I think I'm going to listen.

'One or two things I think I better tell you, Roy,' he says finally. And he starts to, but I can't hear what it is because the door's being flung open and there's Jacqui raging away worse than ever.

Her original complaint seems to have broadened out to include a mass of historical grievance about everyone else in the office, especially Liz, who always takes everyone else's side against her, and who now seems to be trying to create difficulties between herself and the unfortunate boys in the copying-room, with whom she can get on perfectly well if only other people don't interfere. She notices me and turns to explain it all to me without breaking her stride.

'I'm sorry, but she comes rushing in with some wild story about it being *her*, when what she actually means is that I'm being unkind to Kevin, but I *know* it was him, Shireen saw him, and you *have* to treat them just as you would anybody else, that's the absolutely basic principle, and if she doesn't agree then why doesn't she have the courage to say so, and then we can have the whole thing out and *talk* about it, instead of all this nonsense about putting things down the loo?'

Or words to that effect. I shouldn't like to be required to give an account of it in the witness-box.

Terry says nothing. He simply puts his arm round her shoulders and squeezes. The next patient of the day for treatment. She pauses for a moment, then resumes, at a slightly more moderate pitch, still talking to me.

'And yesterday she was giggling away with Shireen when I came in, I don't know what the two of them are up to, and of course she lives with this woman friend of hers, and I can guess what *that's* all about, though naturally Terry doesn't want to know, he never wants to think about things he doesn't want to think about, whereas I *have* to think about them, I have to be involved, because I'm dealing with these people day after day, he's no idea what it's like, and I suppose *I* have to get the door handle fixed, do I?'

This last grievance is I imagine addressed to Terry. He preserves his masterly therapeutic silence, though – just rubs his hand over her shoulder and gazes down at her. She resumes her complaints at an even lower pitch.

'And how can I get on with the Cats thing,' she says, 'when everything on my desk has been systematically disrupted and destroyed?'

'So that's the trouble,' says Terry. 'Someone messing around with your desk.'

'They've also eaten my slimbreads.'

'Oh, dear,' says Terry. 'You can't trust no one these days.'

'Not that I care, if only they'd simply admit it. If they'd simply say the words, that's all I mind about.'

He holds her by the nape of her neck, like a kitten, and gently shakes her. I have a distinct feeling that my treatment has been postponed *sine die*, and that I should withdraw and leave him to complete the current consultation in private. He winks at me over the top of Jacqui's head as I go out, and all my old misgivings about him come back. You can't help seeing what a terrible old charlatan he is as soon as you watch him exercising his skills on somebody else. He catches me up at the top of the stairs, the door handle rattling behind him.

'Sorry about that, Roy,' he says. 'She's got her problems, though, poor love, me among them.'

Now he's going to go back and distract her from all these problems of hers by telling her about mine. He really is a rather dreadful man.

I wonder what he was going to tell me when Jacqui

Because I didn't think about it at the time. Because I'd got other things on my mind. If only we could foresee all the consequences of our actions . . . we wouldn't enjoy them half so much.

But if it hadn't all gone out of my head I'd certainly have nipped round to the health food first thing and got Jacqui a new box of sawdust delight. Anything I could have done to spare her anguish I'd have done, and if I'd spared myself a bit at the same time I wouldn't have said no.

So there we are, we got Jacqui calmed down – then we've run after Roy, make sure all this with Jacqui hasn't put no bright ideas in *his* head – then we gone tearing back to Jacqui, to keep up the good work on *that* front – then naturally in walks Liz. 'Oh, sorry!' – grin, grin – eyes everywhere – and back out of the room again like a trodden cat, because I'm standing there with my arms round Jacqui, pressing her lovely shiny blue eyelids into my clean shirtfront. Don't worry me, Liz coming in, don't worry Jacqui, the only one who's worried is Liz. Only now I'm starting to think, Yes – what's all this about Liz going round telling everyone she messed up Jacqui's desk and put all her whatsits down the karzy? And I don't have to think very hard, because I know what it is. She's sussed out what was going on, just like she sussed out the Police National Computer Organization (oh, no, I'm thinking – I didn't leave nothing around in the toilet that oughtn't to have been left around, did I? – I done that before now) and she's very kindly doing her best to make sure Jacqui don't suss it out as well, only being Liz she's going about it in such a way that it won't be just Jacqui who susses it, it'll be the entire building.

As the day goes on, though, I realize that's not really what I'm worried about, people finding out. What I really mind about is that I done wrong. Never thought of it like that before, but I can see now – I gone too far. We got an agreement between us, Jacqui and me, and I stepped over the line. It's an unspoken agreement, true, so I don't know quite what it is we've agreed, I don't know where the line's been drawn. But wherever it is I think the top of Jacqui's desk is definitely beyond it. I can see that now, and I'm sorry. It won't happen again.

Things are getting back to normal by the end of the day. Or they are until I open the front door downstairs, and there's Tina and Donna sitting up on their busted boxes sharing an early evening roll-up and a polystyrene of coffee, blocking the doorway like a couple of security guards. I'd forgotten about them.

'Oh, hello, Terry,' says Tina, as I squeeze between them. 'All right?'

And she gives a little laugh. 'All right?' – that's new. So's the little laugh. Smile, yes. Laugh – I don't like the sound of that too much, specially seeing that Jacqui's squeezing her way through behind me by this time.

'Oh, hello,' says Tina to Jacqui. Different tone altogether, and no name, because no one's ever told her.

'Now listen, my precious,' says Jacqui to Tina. 'Every morning I have to fold up your cardboard boxes, not to mention clearing away all the old tin cans and disgusting plates of congealed food, and I'm absolutely sick of it.'

Oh, no. This we don't need.

'Come on, love,' I say to Jacqui.

'But I can't see any earthly reason why they shouldn't do it themselves,' says Jacqui. She's standing there shaking the collar of her coat clear of her scarf in a way that seems to me rather unnecessarily noticeable. It's a cashmere scarf, though hopefully Tina and Donna may not be able to see that in the dark. It's also a fur coat, though not the kind

they needed cruelty to get away from the animal that owned
it, because Jacqui's very careful about cruelty to animals,
only whether there's enough light for Tina and Donna to
see it's not that sort I'm not too sure. I put my hand in my
pocket to feel how much change I got for them. But then I
take it out again. Don't want them getting no ideas in their
heads about payments for keeping their mouths shut. Don't
want Jacqui getting no ideas in her head, neither.

'All right, my sweet?' says Jacqui to Tina.

'All right,' says Tina, and gives another little laugh, fol-
lowed by a quick look at me, as much as to say I see why
you get up to tricks.

Donna don't say nothing, but then she never does, and
maybe she was asleep last night and don't know what this is
all about. If she don't, though, I'm pretty sure Tina's telling
her as soon as me and Jacqui's walking away up the street,
because I can hear them both laughing. Next thing I know
Jacqui's going to start getting daft ideas into her head about
me and them two. She wouldn't put it past me in the mood
she's in at the moment. Because I don't need a Freedom of
Information Act to discover what's happening inside the
Ministry of Jacqui today. One look at her and I know: she
got a feeling there's something going on somewhere, and
the something's bad news, and the somewhere's me. I can
tell by the way she's walking one pace ahead of me, and
pulling her coat tight around her, as if it was one of them
anti-chemical-warfare suits, and I was the chemical warfare.

I'm not complaining. I was wrong, and I'm sorry. Only I
can't tell her I'm sorry without telling her I was wrong, and
I can't tell her I was wrong without telling her what way I
was wrong, and I don't think that would be reasonable
behaviour. Moderation, moderation.

But she's thinking: why's he coming down to Sunningdale

with me, when it's not the weekend? Why's it Friday all of a sudden when it's only Wednesday? – Simple answer to that. It's because her desk got messed up and her chunky chews got eaten, poor love. Because she got in one of her states, and it's high time she had a bit of love and reassurance. OK? Reasonable enough for you?

Yes, I realize that, she's thinking. But my desk didn't get *that* messed up. My health food didn't get *that* eaten. All right, I got in a state. But only the kind of state that normally gets treated with five quid's worth of chrysanths. Now suddenly – major surgery. What's going on?

What's going on is this (I can't tell her, but I don't mind telling you, whoever you are):

I'm being specially nice to her just to make totally clear there's nothing going on, because she knows I wouldn't be specially nice to her if there *was* something going on, owing to the fact that this would immediately make her think there was.

Understand that, can you? Oh, good. You can explain it to me, then, because I can't make no sense of it at all.

No, look, put it another way. If she got it into her head that I was up to no good in town then I'd have to go down to Sunningdale with her just to show her I wasn't. So of course she'd immediately realize I *was*. OK so far? The consequence is that she knows I'd *never* go down to Sunningdale with her if I *was* up to something, so if I *am* going down to Sunningdale with her then she knows I'm *not*.

Even I can understand that.

Though why I got to go showing her I'm not if she never thought I was in the first place – that I *don't* get, but then I left school at fifteen.

Particularly since the result of all this is that she thinks there *is* something going on.

111

Reasoning all this out for myself's as good as a Walkman – the train's arrived at Sunningdale before I've arrived at the end of the tape.

Got another tape to keep me going on the walk from the station. Very solemn and uplifting piece of music on this one. Goes like this: the whole thing is yet further proof, if proof was needed, of what we at OPEN are saying. Because if Jacqui and me never had no secrets from each other then none of this would be happening. I shouldn't be walking along all these cold empty streets with nothing to look at – no shop-windows, not even anyone lying in doorways. I shouldn't have fourteen great carnivorous carthorses jumping all over me and thrashing me round the kneecaps with rubber truncheons as soon as she unlocks the door. I shouldn't be stood here telling lies, which is bad enough, and telling them to poor dumb animals that are too stupid to know whether you're telling them lies or not, which is even worse. 'Hello, Whatsit!' I tell them warmly, and 'Come on, then, Doings!' I rub their ears and scratch them under the chin – and it's all lies, because I'm not feeling hello and come on and rub and scratch, I'm feeling piss off and a sharp boot up the backside.

No, if everything was out in the open between Jacqui and me, I shouldn't be here at all. I should be sitting quietly at the Pic, with the little bursting bubbles from a nice glass of champagne tickling the end of my nose, looking at people getting up to all the things that people given half a chance get up to. I should be finding some strange smooth knee in my hand, then a second knee as strange and smooth as the first. I'd be discovering a little gap between the knees that somehow no one had ever noticed before . . .

Did someone speak? – Oh, sorry, love, I was a bit distracted. Thinking about the Cats campaign. Yes, lobster bisque and chicken cordon bleu'll be fine. No – great! Wonderful! I'll switch on the microwave. Leave it all to me – I'll get it on the table. You listen to your messages.

'It's me, at 9.07 am on Wednesday,' booms this big important voice off the corner of the dresser. Her ex, and trouble coming, by the sound of it, but all I can think of when I hear that great red-faced voice is the private drawer he used to keep locked in the bureau that he and Jacqui shared, which turned out to contain, one day when she found he'd left his keys behind, a well-chewed ivory teething-ring, a tube of jelly for preventing premature ejaculation, a photograph of his mother, and a loaded revolver.

'I've just been rung by the school,' he tells her, sounding as if he'd go off like the revolver if it wasn't for the jelly. 'Apparently Poops was found crying in the changing-rooms, and when they asked her what the trouble was she said it was because I had refused to send a cheque for her to go on the school nature study trip to Florida. Now, point one: this is the first I have heard about any nature study trip to Florida. Point two . . .'

It's the last I've heard about it, though, because by this time I've discreetly removed myself from the kitchen. 'You don't have to go out of the room!' shouts Jacqui after me. 'There's nothing secret about this.'

Always cross, Jacqui, when I don't want to know what goes on between her and her ex. If I let her keep a bit of her life to herself, she thinks, it's because I want to do the same with some bit of mine.

Six foot two, her ex, same as me. Big red face, big idea of himself – just like me. Not much to choose between us, probably, except I haven't got a potato in my mouth, or any bits and bobs in the bureau drawer, or any dodgy little millions hidden away in foreign banks. What you see you get, in my case. One unused how's-your-father still tucked away at the back of my wallet, now I come to think about it, but that's about as far as it goes.

I sit down on the sofa in the living-room, next to a large heap of moulting cat, and turn on the seven o'clock, just in case she calls her ex straight back, and things get a bit noisy out there. The Home Secretary's answering questions on the Hassam case. He didn't just beat himself up, apparently, Mr Hassam – he beat up half the police force before minimum restraint could be applied to stop him. He come out of a chemist's shop holding a bottle of cough linctus, so far as I can make out, then, for reasons not yet established, stopped a passing special patrol van, dragged five coppers out of it, and set about all five of them simultaneously. Real social problem Mr Hassam must have been. So that's that little mystery solved.

On the news, though! Questions in the House! Riot shields and petrol bombs! I bet Mr Hassam never guessed what he was starting. Plenty of people before him have fallen down in the charge-room, plenty of people have blacked both eyes and broken all their ribs in the process, and they never got themselves on TV. Why's Mr Hassam receiving special treatment all of a sudden? So unfair! – That's what they're all thinking up there at the Home Office. We're just doing what we always done, and they drop on us!

I'm still holding the chicken cordon bleu on its little plastic tray, ready to go in the microwave, and one of the dogs walks over and rests his chin on my knee, gazing up at me with a trusting smile like some girl in the front row when I'm doing one of my college debating numbers. He's recognized the cordon bleu – I think he's a bit of an expert on deep-frozen *haute cuisine*. So now he's telling me Good old Terry! Course I support your campaign!

Even the dogs are at it, you see. Telling you one thing and thinking something else. Well, fair enough in this case, seeing I was doing the same to them.

Yes, and I'm doing it again! Can't even remember the bugger's name – is it Sticky or is it Sprouts? – and I'm tickling his stomach! So what am I after – his biscuits? His rubber bone? No – I'm trying not to hurt his feelings. Feelings, yes. Problem there. Don't know what we're going to do about feelings when we get to heaven, and all our skulls are made of glass.

We're halfway to heaven right here in Jacqui's house, now I come to think about it – windows everywhere. Pure glass from floor to ceiling, from one side of the room to the other. Only trouble is there's nothing to see out of them, just the garden. Sit here and watch the grass growing, if you like, but that's about as far as the entertainment goes. And here we are inside, totally exposed for all the world to see – only there's no one out there looking in. Beat yourself to death in full view here and you'd get clean away with it.

It's not the windows that keep you on your toes in this house, it's the other walls, because they're all covered in mirrors. Mirrors hanging here, mirrors hanging there. Whole walls made of mirror. I don't know what Jacqui and her ex thought they was up to when they moved in here, they must have been desperate. Always plenty going on in the mirrors. Lots of people to look at. Me and Jacqui, for a start. Then there's me and Jacqui again. Me from behind. Jacqui from the side. Here comes someone walking down the corridor towards me – very familiar face – seen him on television. 'Hello, Terry!' I say – because it's him, it's Terry Little, I'd know him anywhere. He's saying something, too – I think he knows who *I* am, wonderful memory for faces he has.

115

I turn off into the bathroom. Oh, he's going the same way. Funny place, the bathroom in this house. Concealed lighting, gold fittings, ankle-deep carpet, plus two baths, two bidets, and two toilets. If they're spending that much you'd think they could afford partitions between the toilets. But no – two bog seats side by side. So there me and Terry sit – two pairs of trousers round our ankles and four bare knees – and every now and then we look round and catch each other's eye. I know what he's thinking, because I'm thinking the same: if we hadn't both had eighteen months' practice crapping in front of the blokes we was sharing a peter with in Armley we'd both have died of constipation by now.

Now here we are in the bedroom, me and Jacqui and Jacqui and him, all four of us. We're all going to bed together. Not the kind of entertainment I go in for, and I don't think Terry neither, but that's what they seem to like out here in Sunningdale. So here's me and him sitting up in bed, trying not to catch each other's eye, watching the girls taking off their faces and putting on two more. They're wearing identical frilly nighties, look like clouds of pale blue steam, you'd think they was going to come on with ten more likewise and do a song-and-dance number. What are they looking at? Not at Terry and me. They're looking at each other. They keep giving each other little experimental smiles. Not sure whether they know each other or not. Then some very funny looks at each other out of the corner of their eye. Fancy coming on wearing an outfit like that at *her* age, they're thinking.

Now they're going round turning out the lights, until there's only a dim gleam left on the bedside table, and I'm on my own with a bed full of rustling dry bubblebath. Arms full of it, face full of it, mouth full of it. Which girl have I got, Jacqui or Jacqui? I know my friend Terry's got the other one, because I can just make out the bedcovers bulging and shifting on the other side of the glass. Jacqui's got her eyes shut, and I can't resist turning round and sneaking a look at how old Terry's getting on inside the wardrobe there. Know what he's doing, the silly sod? He's turning round to see how *I'm* getting on. I can't quite make out, but I think he's giving me a little grin and wink.

I don't know what that's supposed to mean, but I give him one back. Comic sight he is and all, with his great grinning face rising out of the bubbles. I know people think we're alike, but really we're chalk and cheese. Me – I'm all thinking this and feeling that – most of the time I don't even know whether I got a face on the front of it all or not. Him – he's just a big red face and nothing going on behind it.

Brain without a face – bit weird, haven't come across *that* anywhere else in the world. Face without a brain, though – that's just plain *ridiculous*.

'Cats!' I shout. 'Where are they? When are they coming? Where have we got to?'

'Oh, Terry,' says Shireen, sliding back the glass and smiling. 'Roy rang, and that man with the strange voice – oh, and hello, Jacqui, here's the post.'

Everything's back under control again. Jacqui's happy. I don't know exactly when all her nasty suspicions about why I come down to Sunningdale melted away, but it was some time between 2307, which is what the alarm clock said when she got into bed, and 2333, which is what it said next time I happened to look at it. And there's nothing she loves more than walking in through that door with me in the morning, Mr and Mrs, happy working couple. She looks in on Liz – 'Sorry we're late!' – slaps on the window of the copying-room with the stack of mail – makes sure they all know we've arrived together. And everything in the office is looking good. No one's done anything terrible to the top of her desk. The new packet of concrete crunch she bought yesterday's still on the table with the kettle and the mugs.

So we're right back to where we was. No, we're not, we're ahead of ourselves. We was on a down before, now we're on a real up. Funny, the way it goes. Suddenly everything's coming up roses. Even Jacqui's blast at Tina and Donna's done a bit of good – at least they folded up their boxes and stacked their plates. Unless it was Shireen. Or more likely Liz, dashing away with the smoothing iron again. Anything works in this office there's usually Liz at the back of it somewhere. Miracle we managed to do our stuff between 2307 and 2333 without any discreet help behind the scenes from her.

Good day for all of us, in fact, because there's a big brown Private and Confidential for me that Jacqui's handing over, with the name and address written in printed letters. Always nice to get, big brown Private and Confidentials with no identifiable handwriting or typing on them, because ten to one what's inside them is copies of documents we're not supposed to have copies of.

'Right, now listen, everybody,' I say as I open it. 'This is what we're going to do to put Cats on everyone's mats. Thought of this while I was talking to Jacqui's dog . . .' But what it is they never discover, because I can't talk with my mouth open, which is how it is when I see what I'm taking out of the envelope.

Stack of xeroxes, and I'm looking at page one. It's covered in very neat handwriting, with a reference number in the top righthand corner, and a little black circle in the top lefthand corner with a straight line through it. I know what it is because I seen them before, but not nearly as often as I'd like. It's a copy of a minute written by someone in a Government department. The black circle's where the hole is in the corner, and the line's the little tag thing they use to keep the pages together.

But what I'm looking at is the heading. *Mr K Hassam*, it says.

Fellow in Armley with me had won £10,000 once at roulette. He said when they call the number, and you know it's yours, it's like as if time stops for a moment. It's like you're on the edge of the waterfall, or you're just about to come. It's only a fraction of a second, but it lasts forever, because you're outside the world, you're in a place where no one gets old or dies, where nothing changes. You've gone to heaven. Then you get this great rush of blood through your veins, and it's wonderful, you're over the edge, you've come, you feel good. But that first moment, he said, is the best of all.

Mr K Hassam. I think they just called my number.

Out of nowhere. *Mr K Hassam.* Funny, the way things turn out.

'What?' says Jacqui anxiously. 'What is it?'

But I'm running my eye down the rest of the page, I'm coming down the waterfall. 'With reference to your minute re possible PQ . . . revised draft answer attached hereto . . . perhaps wiser at this stage not to mention . . . unfortunate timing . . . urges caution . . . any reference to the involvement of more senior officers . . . discourage unhelpful speculation . . . could successfully be argued that premature publication might prejudice any subsequent legal proceedings . . .'

And on page two, there it is – what the Home Secretary was reading out in the House on TV last night. Or something like it, because it's all covered in crossings out and extra bits written in. 'Is this necessary?' someone called AJF has noted against four separate bits, and apparently they aren't, because I can't remember hearing any of them. Across the bottom someone called MO has written: 'It might strengthen the Secretary of State's hand in presenting the department's case if he be briefed as sparingly as possible about those aspects of the matter which it could later prove to be an embarrassment to have been aware of when he made his statement.' Come again? Oh, I see: don't tell the silly bugger everything, because he won't act the part so good if he knows he's going to have to admit it was all lies.

In other words, by the time I've finished reading this I'm going to know more about the Hassam case than what the Home Secretary does.

And pages more to come. Faxes from the local Chief Constable. Report from the pathology lab. Hurried note from the Home Secretary scribbled round the edge of the menu for some big City lunch he was at. Memo from the PM's office . . .

We got the whole Hassam file.

Right, into action!

'Shireen, get me Mike Edwards, BBC News! He's in a conference? – get him out of the conference! He's on a plane? – get him off the plane! No, hold on. Let's think this out . . . Get Roy first! If he's in court tell him to get the case adjourned. Let's find out where we stand on this . . . I don't need to find out – I'll tell you where we stand. Knowing or having reasonable cause to believe that they're protected documents, and it's three months for not returning them if we're told to, it's two years for disclosing them. That's where we stand . . .'

Jacqui's gazing at me – she knows this is the real McCoy.

Or has reasonable cause to believe so. Liz has come out of the library to see what's going on – she could feel the electric waves coming off of me. Something like this in your hands, and all the world's listening, waiting to know.

'Take a look at this!' I tell them, waving the papers about in front of them, so their two heads are dancing around like daffodils in the wind, trying to lock on to the target. 'On second thoughts, don't take a look at it,' I add, snatching them away again. 'All three of us banged up we won't have no organization left.'

'Is this . . .?' says Liz.

'Nothing. Don't ask. We don't want no more knowing or having reasonable cause to believe flying round than we have to. Let's just get it copied before anything happens to it. The fairies bring it – the fairies might take it away again . . . I'll do it myself. Get the boys out of there, OK? Don't tell them nothing. Send them out to the post or somewhere. And Shireen . . .'

'They're just looking for him, Terry!'

'Who?'

'Roy.'

'Oh, right. Listen, Shireen, anyone asks you, you haven't seen nothing, you haven't heard nothing.'

'OK,' says Shireen, smiling. Maddens me, that smile of hers.

'That's all very well, Shireen,' I tell her, 'but you won't be smiling when they take you down the nick, start asking you nasty questions.'

Just goes on smiling. 'Doesn't bother me,' she says.

'Put your headset back over your ears, Shireen. Nothing going on outside, nothing going on inside.'

Now here's the other pair, being shooed out of the copying-room by Jacqui.

There's a list of people getting copies at the bottom of the page, and one of them's an H. I never knew her name, but I do now – H Wood. That's her – I know it. I know it as sure as I know my own name.

I might get away with it – *she* won't. They know the distribution, they'll narrow it down. Then – very nasty. And it could end up with her getting two years. She's only a kid. No dad. Passed all her exams. Proud mum. Then this.

H Wood . . . Oh dear. Oh dear oh dear oh dear. What did I do? Showed her I liked her, that's all. What did I say? Nothing! Didn't spin her no yarns, didn't tell her no lies.

What – all that about the city of glass? I said that a million times! No one's ever taken much notice before! Not *that* much!

'You can trust me . . .' says Kevin again, as I retreat into my office, with Jacqui giving me one sort of funny look, because she don't understand what's going on, and Liz giving me another sort, because oh dear oh dear – I think she does.

'Going to have a bit of a think,' I tell them. 'Got to tread a little careful on this one.'

'. . . not to be garrulous,' says Kevin, as I close the door on them all.

11

'Hilary Wood . . .'

The same familiar name speaking itself, in the same matter-of-fact voice, every time I answer my phone. I find this rather curious. I have after all done a very surprising thing. I have done something that changes everything. Yet nothing about me has changed.

'Hilary Wood . . .' Again. Still her, still me. And still not the slightest tremor of shame or exultation or defiance or astonishment at being the bearer of this totally transmuted identity.

'Oh, Hilary,' says Tony Fail in reply. 'I just wanted a quiet word in your ear to see if we can coordinate our ideas before we get together with Michael and Penelope . . .'

'Listen, Hilary,' says Michael Orton. 'I've just had Tony Fail murmuring seditiously away at me. He hasn't been on to you as well, has he . . .?'

'Hilary,' says Penelope Wass, 'I get the impression from something Tony Fail said that you and Michael Orton have entered into some kind of understanding behind our backs . . .'

And what do I tell them in return? 'I think the best way to deal with any objections from Michael and Penelope would be this . . .' I tell Tony Fail. 'Yes,' I tell Michael Orton, 'he's had a go at me, too, but I think I managed to fend him off . . .' 'Not me,' I tell Penelope Wass. 'But I have a shrewd suspicion that a deal is being done between Tony and Michael, as usual . . .' And nothing about my voice gives any of them the slightest hesitation about my identity or my state of mind. Not even Jane Syce-Hill on the other side of the room, who has to overhear everything I say, gives the faintest sign of surprise or doubt when I name myself.

'Hilary Wood . . .' Here we go again. And almost every call is to do with the Hassam case. We're all still racing round with mops and buckets as ever more holes appear in the rotting fabric of the structure. 'Hilary Wood' has – I have – all kinds of ingenious ideas for shifting pictures and furniture in front of the bits where the rain is coming in. Meanwhile, someone has been setting a bomb underneath the building that will blow us all apart. She has. I have.

What I have done is the most surprising thing I have ever done in my life.

It's the most surprising thing, whether done by me or by anyone else, that I have personal experience of.

The worst thing that I am reasonably capable of imagining myself doing.

What does it feel like? I don't know. It doesn't feel like anything. A lot of the time I'm not even thinking about it. I can't, because I'm thinking about other more urgent matters, such as how to conceal or embellish the very information that he is at this minute taking out of the plain brown envelope . . .

Am I afraid of being found out? I haven't even thought about it. Of being tried and imprisoned? The prospect seems as remote and unreal as dying.

Why should I feel anything? There's not much to feel it about. How could I possibly be found out, or sent to prison? There's almost nothing that I've done. I scarcely noticed I was doing it. Nothing's happened. There's the file, safely in front of me on my desk. There's my briefcase on the floor beside my chair, empty, with no trace of any plain brown envelope waiting to be posted. Everything's back to normal.

'Oh, Theo, do you have a moment? It's me, Hilary, Hilary Wood . . .' Her. Yes. Me. As always. You see? Nothing's happened. Don't let's overdramatize.

And now there I am in the washroom mirror. I look exactly as I did yesterday morning, before I went downstairs to the copier on the seventh floor. I put my face close to the glass and look myself in the eye. Right into the deepest darkness inside my head. Nothing stirs there. Kate Margolis crosses behind me, and her reflection gives me a brief smile. My reflection gives her a brief smile back. Tomorrow, after the story has been published, Kate will be one of the people who'll find herself caught up in the internal inquiry. So will Tony and Michael and Penelope, and indeed Stephen Hollis, who always placed such personal trust and confidence in me. They're all going to be engulfed in the most painful anger from above, the most distressing embarrassment with each other, the most humiliating sense of being dishonoured and made impotent.

But what I'm thinking about is him opening the envelope. Turning it over in his hands first, intrigued, feeling its smoothness and bulkiness. Then slipping his finger underneath the flap . . . sliding it along . . . The sound as the smooth brown paper tears along the fold . . . The whiteness of the pages as they come slithering out . . .

'Did you see that programme last night?' It's Kate Margolis, now reappeared and washing her hands at the next basin. 'It was about that wretched Scientific Officer in the Ministry of Defence, the one who tried to cut off his own head, do you remember? Apparently he was involved with some Syrian businessman – no question of blackmail, he was simply besotted – and they think he handed over *everything* – every single document that crossed his desk. I suppose if it happened it happened. But I find it absolutely impossible to imagine, don't you?'

Just like that, this story comes. Out of nowhere. As if she somehow knew. Or had been unconsciously led into it by association because of something about my appearance. She's looking at me in the mirror, eyebrows raised in delicate disbelief, waiting to know how I react.

'I didn't see it,' I say blankly. No interest. Not a question I've ever thought about. I look at my own reflection again. There's nothing about my appearance that could have invited the story; there's nothing that has responded to it. Not so much as one blink too many or too few. Am I acting? I don't think I can be. I remember being forced to act in school plays. If I was acting my arms would be fastened to my sides, my voice would be small and strange, I should be longing to die. No, I think this is me as I actually am. A natural traitor.

Side by side Kate and I dry our hands. She is married to an economic historian. They have a four-year-old daughter who is said to be very gifted. Perhaps the story was nothing to do with me at all. Perhaps it was something inside herself that leapt out. If I had raised my eyebrows back at her, and smiled, and caught her eye for a moment in the mirror, she might have laughed and said: 'Actually I *do* sometimes have this strange feeling that I might suddenly go mad and, I don't know . . .'

We're all holding things in beneath our smiles and raised

eyebrows, our absorbing relationships with serious partners. We all have dreams and stirrings. Sometimes they break the surface, sometimes they don't. It's probably only a matter of inches either way.

'He tied his head to a tree, and then rode off on his motor bike,' says Kate. 'I suppose he was trying to get rid of his thoughts. He was found unfit to plead, of course.'

And back we go to our respective sections. She'll remember this meeting in the washroom when the pictures are appearing in the paper of Hilary Wood glimpsed through the windows of police cars, sketched in court, stony-faced and unrecognizable. 'I was talking to her about that man at the Ministry of Defence!' she'll say. 'She didn't say anything. I can't imagine what must have been going on inside her.'

They'll ask me why I did it.

Yes, why *did* I do it? A perfectly reasonable question, now I've thought of it.

Because I was fated to do it. Is that a reasonable answer?

I mean because my entire life has led up to it. Because I have become someone who can look in the mirror and detect no trace of any change even with hindsight. Because I can murmur 'Hilary Wood' so naturally into the phone still. Because I *am* 'Hilary Wood', a person of whom my increasingly unreal activities in the department are only the most disconcertingly natural extension. Because I have lived my entire life *containing* something, and containing it so successfully that I still don't know quite what it was.

Because a world where half the things you know are things you mustn't say is a mad world. And because a world where no one remarks on this is madder still.

Because listening to all those *contained* voices saying 'Oh, Hilary . . . listen, Hilary . . . Hilary, I wonder if it wouldn't

turn out to be a sort of glorified cocktail bar. I suppose he's got stuck with that campaign now – there's nothing else he can do. He's got stuck in those attitudes, like a child pulling a funny face when the wind changes. Not much of a life, when you think about it, at his age.

People you dislike generally dislike you back. That was the odd thing about meeting him in the restaurant – realizing he liked me. He looked at me, and he liked me.

Then he touched me, and he liked me even more. He liked the softness of my skin. He liked my throat, and the soles of my feet, and my breasts. He liked unwrapping me, and opening me up . . .

I can feel his finger even now, running along inside the envelope. No, he'll have opened it hours go. By now he's got the pages spread over the desk . . .

Anyway, that's all irrelevant, because it's over. We made it absolutely plain to each other afterwards that we had no intention of ever meeting again. That was what gave it such intensity and sweetness – its coming out of nowhere, and then going back to nowhere, its being so entirely improbable and inappropriate. He's old enough to be my father, after all. I mean, quite literally. He could actually *be* my father, for all I know . . .

No, he couldn't. My father was someone living on the same estate in Reading – Mum met him when she was working at the biscuit factory. Or so Auntie May said. Oh, come on, this is getting out of control! It just shows how unreasonable the whole thing is.

'Hilary Wood . . . By all means, Theo, but can I call you back?'

I've got something to do before I can think about Theo's problems. Because I've just realized that my notorious admirer might be interested to see the file we've got on OPEN.

It would give him another envelope to open tomorrow, anyway. I need head of section's authorization to draw Special Branch files – I know because I've had it out before. I ring Stephen at once. 'Stephen,' I say, 'it occurs to me that the freedom of information lobby might be interested in the Hassam case. I wonder if I should have another look at what we've got on them and make sure a few discreet tabs are kept.' 'Good point,' says Stephen encouragingly. 'If you like to look in I'll give you a signature for Registry. Thank you, Hilary.'

So I do it at once, just like that, with no more thought than blowing my nose. I smile at Stephen, I smile at Sandra Wing in Registry, and I take the file downstairs to the copier. It's so simple! I feel absurdly light-hearted at the sheer naturalness of the act. You lay the first page face downwards on the glass, and cover it with the lid. The machine's bright gaze scans it from top to bottom, from bottom to top, and searches out its secrets, and knows it. Another searching look, and page two has confessed. Page three . . .

'Oh, you up here again, Hilary?' says Ranji, arriving with an armful of work for the head of our section. 'Can't keep away from that copier, can you! No, seriously – would you like me to do it for you?'

Funny that it happens to be Ranji I've coincided with both times. She's probably the only clerical assistant in the building who'd notice me and remember – certainly the only one who'd offer to do the copying for me. I shake my head and give her a nice smile. She'll remember that smile. 'She was just standing there, copying it all in front of me!' she'll tell everyone in the section. 'And, you know, like smiling to herself!'

If I don't accept the disciplines of the job, it strikes me as I turn the pages, and the bright frank gaze of the machine goes back and forth, then I should resign. I should *have* resigned! Why have I not thought this simple and obvious thought before? Another simple thought comes hard on the heels of the first: if I'd resigned I shouldn't be here copying this file. The logical thing, if I want to set files like this free, is to remain at my post until I'm caught.

I wonder how much longer I've got before the end comes? Days? Weeks? Hours?

I smile at Ranji again. 'Oh, you're very cheerful today!' says Ranji. I laugh, because it's true, I am.

'I said to her,' she'll tell everyone, '"Oh, you're very cheerful today!" I said. And she laughed . . .'

I'm still light-hearted and light-headed when I leave the building at the end of the afternoon. I post my plain brown envelope – the address once again printed in the same big ingenuous childish characters – quite openly in the box just across the street, but I don't go on down into the Tube. I think I'll walk to Charing Cross, since it's a dry evening, and save having to change. Does this mean, I wonder, that I'm going to walk down Whitchurch Street and see if he happens to be walking up it once again? No, it doesn't. I'm doing what I often do – walking to Charing Cross and getting the Northern Line direct. The very thought of going to Whitchurch Street makes me smile, because it's a thought that has never even come into my head.

What? I can't help smiling again at the thought of smiling at a thought I have never thought. But the faintest notion of going to Whitchurch Street is ludicrous. That's all over and done with. I have in the past occasionally met someone who quite simply wanted to go to bed with me, and thought I'd quite simply like to go to bed with him, and done quite simply that. (With *her*, on one reckless occasion which I haven't thought about for years, and which I don't propose to think about now.) A cup of coffee in the morning, and then Chrissie's golden rule applies: Stop now! Or else it may turn into a *relationship*, and the rule with relationships is the same, only with relationships, as Chrissie says, it should have been applied a day earlier.

The idea of having a *relationship* with this particular man makes me smile to myself all over again. I'm in such a strange mood – my imagination leaps wildly ahead of me. 'Oh, Chrissie, this is my fiancé . . .' – and she doesn't know what to say or where to look. Now we're buying furniture together – I think it's a transparent gold cocktail cabinet . . . We're standing at the front of the church, and he's all distinguished grey morning suit and flamboyant grey curls . . . Everyone on my side of the church is whispering. 'I thought she didn't have a father . . .?' 'Well, she does now.' The father of my children, and it's my father . . .

I mean, theoretically, for all I know, since I know nothing about either of them.

Actually I know quite a lot about this one from when I drew the file on OPEN out of Registry before. It was just two days before I met him in that restaurant, as it happens. There was quite a lot of biographical material – we'd authorized a tap on their phones at one point, after they'd published a rather alarmingly accurate report on the operations of the Police National Computer Organization. He has a wife living on a Council estate somewhere down in the depths of south-east London. He also has a prison record, including a conviction for violence.

I wonder what other files he'd like to see while I've still got the chance. I suddenly realize that there are no restrictions on me now. I can do anything I like. I can do anything I *don't* like, for that matter. There are no rules at all for controlling what I'm going to do next, or even for predicting it. I have no idea what I'm going to do until I've done it. Or not done it.

For example, I'm walking down the steps into Charing Cross Underground station as I think this. That seems definite enough – but really it means nothing, it commits me to nothing, it determines nothing, because I could still turn round and walk to Whitchurch Street instead. Indeed I think I will!

No, I won't, because I haven't, and by now I'm on the escalator, being carried inexorably on down, away from Whitchurch Street. But there's nothing inexorable about it! I could force my way back up the escalator! 'Excuse me . . . excuse me . . .' I shan't do it, naturally, but only because I should be making such a spectacle of myself.

I could continue to the bottom, though, then quite simply cross to the up escalator, and no one would even notice.

Yes, that's what I'm going to do . . .

No, that's *not* what I'm going to do, I discover, because I'm walking on to the platform. This complete indeterminacy of the future I find intoxicating. But also very alarming, because I might do something quite reckless or embarrassing. I might sit down on the ground. I might begin to sing. I might speak to this man who's standing beside me with the tired face and the blue plaid scarf – might say something in a foreign accent to him – tell him I have been robbed by the man behind him – bark like a dog at him . . .

He's looking at me! Only I've turned away, because now I can feel the breath of an approaching train on my face. I suppose I might jump in front of it . . .

Oh, no! That's the one thing I *mustn't* do, the one thing I know I don't *want* to do . . . So how do I know I'm not going to do it? Wanting to – not wanting to – that won't tell me anything.

Here it comes . . . What's to stop me?

And this is terrifying, because I can feel my legs beginning to move me forwards . . .

But now here are the lighted windows passing in front of me and slowing. Here are the doors opening, here is me stepping into the carriage. So apparently I didn't jump.

Interesting. I wonder why not?

And now here we stand on the Northern Line, on our way to Kentish Town. Me, and all these things inside me that may be going to do themselves and then again may be going to remain undone . . .

I've just remembered what this is like. It's like being fifteen again and not knowing what sort of person I was, whether large or small, good or bad, nice or nasty. Not knowing, when I opened my mouth to speak to someone, whether words would come out, or nothing, and if words, what words. Whether all the forbidden words might not suddenly say themselves aloud, in the middle of the maths lesson, or over the kitchen table at Auntie May's. Because I could feel them all inside my head, shouting themselves aloud in there, hammering a hole in my skull to get out . . . And I can remember days at the beginning of summer when I walked round the streets naked and shameless inside my clothes . . .

Kentish Town. I get off the train and hide myself safely away in the press of people moving up the stairs towards the escalators. Yes, I did what I did because I was fated to do it, because I was always going to do it. Because it was going to happen sooner or later, and I just wanted to get it over with. I was a very capable and suitable Civil Servant on the outside, but I was never a Civil Servant inside, and someone should have realized. Someone should have stopped me. The examiners – the personnel department – the security division. That's what they're there for, to stop people like me. It's entirely out of my hands. I've taken responsibility for myself for long enough. I'm not going to take it any more.

Here comes the train. I wait to see the headboard. Charing Cross or Bank . . .? Charing Cross – fine. I get on, and find a seat with no difficulty at all.

As the doors close, and the train moves off, I begin to realize just how curious this emptiness is. It's usually packed at this time in the morning . . . But no sooner have I thought this than the whole shape of the world around me begins to shift in the most horribly disconcerting way. It's not the morning, is it. It's the evening – I'm on my way home, not on my way to work. I was arriving at Kentish Town last time I noticed what was going on, not departing from it . . .

So, I'm on my way to Whitchurch Street after all.

Now I'm beginning to feel frightened. This is getting out of hand. I have lost control. These things inside me are working me, thinking my thoughts, distracting my attention while they direct my limbs. And there is nothing I can do about it.

Except to get off the train at the next station, and get a train back to Kentish Town.

Which I do.

Right, I'm in command again. No more silly games. Back to normal. Nothing more's going to happen. Nothing *has* happened; it was all inside my head.

Those two plain brown envelopes are the only things that have escaped . . .

But if I don't think about them . . .

All right. Order has been restored.

Coming up to nine o'clock. I'm not thinking about those envelopes, or what he's done with them, which is why I'm not turning on the news. I'm pulling the front door of my flat shut behind me, and climbing the area steps to go for a stroll instead.

At every narrow, awkward house along this narrow, awkward street one flight of steps leads down to a basement flat more or less like mine, and another flight leads up to three more flats above. Inside each house I pass are four unseen television sets, some facing this way, some that, all speaking in unison like a chorus. They are making serious allegations about senior policemen, members of the Government, and my colleagues at work.

Or not, on the other hand, and in any case I'm not thinking about it.

Four more sets in this house. 'Blood group,' they are saying. 'Denial. Evidence. Involvement.' Four more in this house. 'Concealed. Dying. Dead. Alleges . . .'

Or they are saying something else altogether, and either way it's a matter of complete indifference to me.

Somewhere in London – Barnsbury, I think – Tony Fail is watching the news with his friend, whose name he never mentions. 'Nothing to do with you, though, is it?' his friend is asking sympathetically. 'Well, yes,' Tony's replying. 'As a matter of fact it is.'

Michael Orton's ringing Penelope Wass. 'But who had access to the file?' he's asking. 'I mean, apart from Tony and Hilary?' 'Well, me, for a start,' says Penelope. 'Oh,' says Michael, 'yes. And me, of course.'

And each of them is thinking, 'Tony? Hilary? Certainly not! You, then . . .? That's not possible! Is it . . .?'

In Clapham, Kate Margolis is saying to her husband, 'How curious. I was just talking to someone at work today about passing documents to people . . .'

Rather grander houses here, as the ground begins to rise towards Highgate. Somewhere in the street I'm now walking along, I think, lives an Assistant Under-Secretary in the department called Pelling. I don't suppose the television set is actually naming him, but he'll know who's being referred to when it talks about a senior official who authorized the removal of various items from the records of the local hospital's casualty department.

By the time I get back to my flat the news is safely over. Everything's exactly as it always was. The books in the bookcase, arranged in Latin alphabetical order between the ceiling and the fifth shelf down, in Greek between the fifth shelf and the floor. The vase of white dried honesty exactly halfway along the runner bisecting the small gate-leg dining table, with its two oak chairs, and two more waiting in reserve on either side of the bookcase. The wing chair with the Indian shawl thrown over the back, and the pool of light from the standard lamp falling over the open book waiting on the little table beside it. The small portable television set on the sideboard, grey-faced and silent . . . Whatever disturbances are going on elsewhere in the world, my reasonably sensible, reasonably orderly life is still living itself in here just as it always has.

Yes, I think I have proved fairly convincingly that I'm back in command of myself. I begin to recall various routine obligations that I've forgotten about for the last few days, and phone Chrissie to find out if she's all right. She's not, needless to say, and I feel increasingly impatient as she goes on and on about all those endlessly ineffectual people she knows with names like Cis and Liz and Ros. I realize I'm just waiting for her to say, 'Did you see the news? There's some terrible thing going on in your Home Office place, do you know about it . . .?' I suppose this is why I rang her, now I come to think about it. But she doesn't, and by the time I manage to extract myself from her it's just coming up to ten o'clock. I should have rung my mother instead and asked her how *she* was, I think, as I turn on the television – she never misses any reference to the Home Office . . .

The television? On? What am I doing? Not going to watch the ten o'clock news, am I . . .? I simply wasn't thinking . . . Mad to walk all the way round the nine o'clock, only to turn on the ten o'clock . . . Still, now it's on . . . Though I suppose I could turn it off . . . I got off the train that was going back to Charing Cross . . . I can't walk round the neighbourhood for another half-hour, though . . .

But before I can settle the question the commercials finish and the titles start.

Also the doorbell rings.

The doorbell? No one ever comes to call at ten o'clock!

It's *him*. I know it with absolute certainty.

There's one other thing I know with absolute certainty, too – that it's *not* him. Why should it be? How *could* it be? He doesn't know where I live, for a start. He probably doesn't even know my surname . . . But by this time I'm out in the passageway, opening the door.

It's not him. Nor is it the police, whom I identified with a third shock of certainty even as I turned the latch.

It's a man running his hand awkwardly through his hair, with a face beneath it as tiresomely familiar as an old saucepan, and a voice emerging from the face as tediously unsurprising as the rattling of the saucepan's lid. For a fraction of a second, indeed, his identity is so flatly obvious that I can't actually quite locate it.

'I'm sorry,' the voice is saying. 'I did ring – I rang six or seven times. First there was no reply, then I kept getting engaged . . . I'm sorry.'

Oh, yes. My *relationship*. I'd completely forgotten about it.

'I did say I was going to ring . . .'

141

'Yes, yes.'

'I thought I'd better come round in case your phone was out of order . . .'

He waits to be asked in. I wait for him to go away. For some reason I can't bear the idea of his being in the room while the television is parading its shameful intimacies about my department. No, there's a perfectly good reason why I'm reluctant, now I come to think about it. I realize he must have spent the day with his fingers in these very intimacies – his hands full of them, his head buried in them. He's part of the Campaign, after all – they must have consulted him at once about the legal position, about how to proceed. He must have guessed immediately that I was the source. He must have talked to *him* about me . . .!

I start to close the door. I don't want to speak to him. I don't want to look at him. He puts his hand against the door, as alarmed as I am about the possibilities, and as desperate to discuss them as I am not to.

'What?' he says. 'What's going on?'

'I'll phone you.'

He's trying to see over my shoulder, in the narrow gap between the door and the frame.

'You've got people here?' he says.

'People?'

I can't even think what he means. *People*? What are these things called *people*?

'I can hear voices,' he says.

Oh, those things that have voices. Yes.

'The television,' I say, and we both strain, for our different reasons, to hear what it's saying.

'Oh, yes,' he says. 'Sorry. I thought maybe . . .'

Thought maybe what? I don't know – I'm not sure *he* does, either.

'Look . . .' he says, and runs his hand distractedly through his hair again while he thinks what words to try next. I remember him making exactly the same gesture the first time I met him, at that party given by Chrissie's political friend. 'Look . . .' he said, running his hand through his hair, disarmingly rather than distractedly then, while he tried to think what sort of invitation might catch my interest. 'I don't know what time you finish work . . .' He'd just explained he did a lot of work with OPEN, and suddenly there did seem to be something rather piquant about having a meal with this man who was committed to discovering all the secrets I was committed never to reveal. And, yes – it was just a week or two after I'd taken so strongly against his director.

'Look . . .' he says now, 'we've got to sort things out.'

Sort what things out? Knowing about my disclosure, presumably. Knowing I know, but knowing I don't know that *he* knows, and all the rest of it.

'I'm sorry about the other evening,' he says. 'I know that's when it all began to go badly wrong . . .'

The other evening? He's not talking about current events at all. He's talking about some remote historical era that everyone's forgotten about.

'I'd obviously no idea Terry was going to be in there . . .'

Oh, *then*. Was Roy there, in the restaurant? I suppose he was. Yes, of course he was. How strange.

'I know what you think about Terry – I realized it was going to be a disaster as soon as I saw him sitting there . . .'

How can he still be worrying about some minor social difficulty in the past, when this huge more recent event stands between us, as thick and unmissable as the half-closed door? He runs his hand through his hair again, in search of further words. How does he manage when he's in court, I wonder, and he's got his wig on?

'Look,' he says. 'I know it's a bit awkward, my working with Terry. But we've got to be able to keep our professional lives and our private lives separate . . .'

A bit awkward? Professional and private lives separate? A suspicion is beginning to form in my mind that he *didn't* immediately guess that I was the source of their wonderful leak. I don't believe the possibility has ever crossed his mind. I find this really rather stupid – and also obscurely offensive.

But if he doesn't realize I'm involved then he must surely be feeling just a little concerned about the fact that he and his colleagues are in the process of betraying me and my colleagues. I'm not sure he is, though. There is altogether a strange lack of congruence between the conversation and reality. What's he saying now?

'All right, he's a bit of a rogue, he's a bit of a chancer – he's got a rather aggressive manner. Though when you get to know him he's . . . well, he's not as awful as you might think . . .'

He's still stuck in the restaurant! But a more radical explanation for this amazing obtuseness has just suggested itself.

'He was tremendously taken with you, you know – he told me so . . .'

Yes. He's not mentioning my disclosure because he doesn't know about it. They didn't tell him. Terry didn't even bother to consult him.

'Anyway,' he says, 'you won't have to meet him again, I promise you . . .'

I don't think he's even seen the news. His total failure to know or guess or understand suddenly seems absolutely characteristic. All right – this time it's final: stop now!

'I'm sorry,' I say, 'but this is all rather beside the point. I think it would be better if we didn't see each other again.'

He gazes at me, stunned. The only resource he can find is to run his hand through his hair yet again. But only one word can he find there.

'Look . . .' he says.

'I'll write to you,' I tell him, and get the door shut.

I go down the passageway and run myself a bath to drown the sound of the doorbell, ringing again and again, ringing on and on. I feel suddenly light-hearted once more. I've disposed of him! A little job about the house that's been waiting for six months or more to be fixed – done at last!

And by the time I turn the taps off . . . Yes, silence. The doorbell has stopped. He's given up and gone away. It's all over and finished with.

The muffled sound of a voice through the wall becomes dimly audible. Oh, the television! But by the time I get to it the only news left is that half a dozen fried eggs are dripping incomprehensibly over a map of Britain.

The weather. Well . . . good. This is another thing that pleases me – my absolute firmness in not watching the news on either channel. I make myself a cup of chocolate and drink it in the bath, in peace and luxury. Then I go to bed, and fall into a sweet and untroubled sleep. Which lasts until eleven minutes past four, when I am woken by an insupportable anguish that occupies every corner of my mind and body.

I have done a terrible thing. I have done the worst thing that it was in me to do. And now, for the first time since I took the original batch of documents to the copier, I truly know that I have.

What I have done can never be undone.

I thought I hadn't changed. I have – totally and irrevocably.

My life is over.

12

Stupid girl. Stupid girl! Passes all her exams, so she thinks she knows everything – and she don't even know right from wrong.

Turn over on to my right side. Soon as I get there I remember why I gave up on the right two minutes earlier – because it's made of iron. Back on to my left, then. That's worse. Over on to the right again and look at the clock. Quarter past four. Camp-bed? You'd get more sleep in the average undertaker's casket. Though I can't remember what sleep's like, whether it's got two legs or four.

I don't know what I think I'm doing. That stuff should be rolling off the presses all over Dockland by now – it should have been coming out of every TV in the kingdom last night. And where is it? In its envelope still, on the edge of my desk next to the alarm clock. I'm never going to forgive myself for this.

If she'd had a dad it'd be different. He might have walloped a bit of sense into her. Oh – I'm her dad, am I? Is that it? Is that what she's telling me? She's trying to please me, get a pat on the head?

I don't know what all this about being her dad is supposed to be. I wasn't her dad the other night! I hope!

Maybe that's why she come looking for me, though. Find a dad. Turn to dad. Ask old dad what to do.

I don't like these thoughts. I don't like them at all. Real four o'clock in the morningers. Real killers.

'But *you* do it, Dad – *you* nick stuff!' This is what she's telling me. 'If you got your hands on something like this, you'd knock it off fast enough! I'm only doing what you'd do!'

Well, if she can't see the difference between nicking stuff off the other side and doing it when it's your own lot then she's even stupider than what I think she is.

So what am I saying? I'm saying I don't want people in Government departments spilling me the beans? Certainly I want them spilling me the beans! I want beans busting out all over! I got a beans factory to run!

People have sent me stuff before. I haven't sent it back to them. I done good things with it.

Certainly I want them to send me stuff. But not like this. – Like what? – This.

It's still there, next to the alarm clock. What am I going to do with it?

That stupid girl – she's really gummed me up. Got me back in dead shtuck with Jacqui for a start. Sat in the office here for an hour or more last night we were, me and Jacqui, after everyone else had gone. 'But *why* won't you let me see it?' – 'Because there's no reason for us both to get ourselves put away, my love!' – 'But I've seen all the documents people have leaked to us in the past!' – 'That was different.' – '*Why* was it different?'

I wanted children? All of a sudden I got two of them nagging away at me!

Fair enough question, though. All right, let's think of an answer. Why was it different? Because the other stuff wasn't sent round by some nice young kid. By some nice young kid with a mum who's proud of her, and no dad, and no idea what she's playing at. Some kid I happen to know personally. Some kid I may have come on a bit strong with. Who may have got the idea that I was someone she could trust.

Only I don't tell Jacqui none of that. '*Why* was it different?' And the best I can do is, 'Because. That's why.' So off she goes home to Sunningdale in a huff as big as a house.

Hilary. Yes. I'd forgotten her name till I saw 'H Wood' – I'd forgotten all about her! I'd just got everything nice and normal again. Meanwhile, she's sitting up in that great concrete tower of theirs, and she hasn't forgotten about nothing – she's working herself up into a great state. What about Cats, for a start? Can't make a proper job of Cats when I'm worrying about this business! She's gone and mucked Cats up, and all!

Stupid, stupid girl! One kiss and she goes bananas – it's ridiculous! I know I'm saying she's a kid – but she's not a kid! She's a grown woman!

A grown woman. That's right. No good my saying she's a stupid girl. That's just me being Dad. She's just as much in charge of herself as what I am of myself. She takes her own decisions, just the same as me. She knew why we was going back to the office, just as clear as what I did, and if she agreed then that's her responsibility.

So if she decides she's going to risk everything she's got and send me that stuff, then that's her responsibility, too, and it's no good me wagging my finger at her. I got to respect her decision.

Right. I'll do her proud. I've lost a day, but it's still not too late if I set to work this morning. I'm going to get that stuff on both sides of TV and in every paper in the country.

Hold on, though. No need to rush to extremes. Bit of

moderation called for here, as always. Bit of negotiation and compromise and pragmatism. What I'll do is, I'll have a word with her first, talk it over, make sure she knows what she's let herself in for, tell her what two years in the nick is going to be like, because she certainly don't know *that*, exams or no exams.

Slight question of *how* I have this word with her, though. What – I walk into the Home Office? 'I've come to see Miss Hilary Wood. What about? Oh, about some documents she's leaked to me . . .'

No, OK, ring her up. 'Can I speak to Miss Wood? Who's this? Terry Little . . . No, not *the* Terry Little, the one that you may or may not discover tomorrow has published a great batch of documents leaked to me by someone in your department whose identity I am guarding with my life. A different Terry Little, that's selling double-glazing . . .'

All right, let's have another think. Ring her at home – catch her before she leaves for work. Get the number from Roy. 'Oh, Roy, that girlfriend of yours. What's her phone number . . . ? No, no funny business, Roy – I thought I'd just pass on a few handy household hints . . .'

No, all right, scrub Roy. Directory Inquiry, then. 'Can you give me a number for H Wood . . .? No, I don't know the address, and I may have got the surname wrong . . .'

OK, skip it. I know what she'd say, anyway. She knows what she's doing, and she's doing it because she thinks it's right. Yes, but wait a minute. Since when does she think it's right? She told me she thought I was completely up a gum-tree. Got very excited about it. Broke all her breadsticks into little pieces. If she thinks it's right it's because I talked her round. It's still all down to me, whichever way you look at it.

What am I going to do, though, what am I going to do?

149

Moderation? There's no moderation here. It's either publish or not publish. Yes or no.

Try sleeping on my left side, that's what I'm going to do. No, on my right . . . On my left . . . All right, then, let's have a compromise – on my back . . .

What am I doing? If there's one place I can never sleep it's on my back!

But what a turn-up for the book! What a funny kid! I knew there was more there than met the eye. I knew there was something going on. Never guessed this, though.

Daft thing is, I can't remember what she looks like. Looks nice, that's all I can remember. Like someone you might be walking down the street with, and you'd tell all the people you ran into: 'Oh, and have you met my daughter?'

Daughter, daughter! Give it a rest! Daughter's just exactly what she isn't! Not on the desk next door she wasn't! So give over!

No, but I'll tell you what I really feel about what she done – I feel proud of her. Got the same old lump in the throat I had when I was seventeen and Charlton won the Cup. One tear running out of my right eye and away over my nose. Another out of my left eye running straight on to the pillow.

Be the end of her, won't it. Two years of her life spent with scrubbers and drug-addicts and child-murderers, and no job to come back to, no family, no nothing. And all because she happened to walk through the door of that restaurant.

Be different if me and Linda had had kids. Everything'd be different. I wouldn't be here, for a start – Linda wouldn't be there. Biggest regret of my life, no kids, I've always said so. And mostly down to me again, I have to admit. First I didn't want the bother, then by the time I thought I wouldn't mind she'd decided I was right. Well, she'd got her own life by this time. I'd got mine. We'd missed the boat.

Yes, I was running round all over the place by then. I suppose there might just possibly be someone somewhere in the world with the same curly hair as me, now I come to think about it. I wasn't the responsible citizen then that I am now. Didn't always think out quite so carefully what I was going to do. Wasn't always around afterwards to find out what the consequences was.

How old's Hilary? I mean, not that I'm thinking she could be. I'm not that barmy. I'm just thinking theoretically, for the sake of comparison. I'd guess she was twenty-eight, twenty-nine. What was I doing twenty-eight, twenty-nine years ago? No idea. Let's see, how old was I . . .? Not that much older than what she is now. I was retired out of the lighterage by then – I was running wild all up and down the Estuary, from Woolwich to Whitstable . . .

So theoretically . . . I don't mean that's what I'm actually thinking, even at the back of my mind, even at four o'clock in the morning – I mean *theoretically* . . .

Theoretically . . . Because she's only about seventeen. She's standing there in the church, all dressed in white, and the brass band's playing. I'm giving her away, and I'm so proud of her. I'm giving her away to Parchak & Partners, and in return they're taking off her white train and giving it to me. More and more of it they post to me, all made of paper, soft white paper, it's a special sort that goes in the photocopier, until my arms are full of it, and it's so soft, it's so soft, so soft and warm, smiling up at me so trustingly, this is terrible, I feel so bad about this, so bad and so good, my heart's going to burst . . .

And it's daylight. I look at the alarm clock on the corner of the desk. Half seven, and I haven't slept a wink all night.

I get up, feeling like what someone in a horror movie must feel like when they rise from the tomb, and go along the corridor for a slash. I got one thing straight inside my head, though, after all my night's thinking, and that's what I'm going to do with the plain brown envelope next to the alarm clock.

'You're early this morning, Terry!' says Tina, as I step over her and Donna. 'Don't worry – we'll clear up before your friend gets here. She give us a right slagging-off last night, didn't she, Donna. I don't know what you been doing to her, Terry.'

I give them a couple of quid for breakfast. How old's Tina, I'm thinking, how old's Donna? What was I doing nine months before *they* come into the world?

I just check the inside pocket of my overcoat, make sure the plain brown envelope's still there. At least it won't be lying round the office, if by any chance the filth come calling on us, like they done before when things have gone missing in Government departments, I can't think why. Or for that matter if Jacqui starts getting any ideas in her head.

Daft thing I'm going to do with it, I'm starting to think, now I'm out in the open air. But that's the beauty of my idea, because the filth won't have thought of it.

I don't think even Jacqui will have thought of this one.

'Hilary Wood . . .'

This is me, is it, sitting here at my desk, answering my phone, using my name? The people at the other end still seem to think it is, I notice. 'Oh, Hilary,' says Tony Fail. 'In view of events in the area last night, Stephen thinks we all need to refresh our memories about arrangements for police-MOD liaison . . .'

Or is it me who's drafting the minute on the desk in front

of me? It's addressed to this same Stephen who is concerned to remind me of departmental secrets I may have forgotten, and it begins: 'I'm afraid I must ask you to accept my resignation, with immediate effect . . .'

This doesn't feel any more like me than the other one. But Jane Syce-Hill is gazing at me absently as I write, thinking about something she's writing herself, and there seems to be nothing about me that she finds in any way unusual.

I have a feeling of complete unreality. I'm not a person, not even two people. I'm a department of state which is pursuing one policy for the outgoing government, even as it prepares its opposite for the incoming one.

'Hilary Wood . . .' says one of us.

'Listen, Hilary,' says Michael Orton, 'the Secretary of State is going on the one o'clock news and Stephen thinks we should brief him on the positive aspects of police–community liaison in the area, just to help put the casualty figures into some perspective . . .'

But I can't be both people at once! I can't think out advice to my masters and simultaneously think out explanations as to why I am ceasing to do so. 'My conscience will no longer permit me to conceal information which ought to be publicly available', I write in my minute, then turn to note on the piece of paper next to it: 'The past record of liaison between police and the Asian community in the area is not all that helpful to the case we are trying to present, and it might be wiser to lay more stress on the community's very positive involvement in staffing the hospitals where the casualties are being treated . . .'

I feel as if I'm in one of those dreams that one has with a high fever, when one's fingers are simultaneously as thick as sausages and as thin as matchsticks . . . Hold on – here we go again. 'Hilary Wood . . .'

'Hilary, I've got that stuff you wanted on holdings of CS gas in the area . . .'

Penelope Wass. Why don't I tell her I'm resigning? How can I, though, before I've informed Stephen himself? But how can I inform Stephen, when I'm listening to Penelope Wass?

And how can I keep my mind on either, when I look at the other item on my desk?

Nothing. This is the other item on my desk.

By which I mean all the daily newspapers, purchased in increasingly improbable batches at various newsagents between Kentish Town and here, and nothing in any of them. Well – arson, deaths, talk of civil war. But nothing originating from the first of my plain brown envelopes.

I've betrayed nothing. Everything is as it was. It's just not real any more, that's all.

All the drafts of my resignation that I composed in my head during the night have become irrelevant. 'I realize that I have betrayed the confidence placed in me', I minuted in the darkness. 'I regret that I had no alternative . . . I have no regrets . . . I am deeply saddened . . . I rejoice . . . I will of course cooperate fully in any inquiry you may order . . . I will of course decline to answer any further questions . . . I accept . . . I reject . . .'

Now what do I say? 'I realize', I write, then stop. *I* realize, but *they* don't realize! Perhaps the envelope has simply taken two days to get there – is on his desk this morning – is being opened even now . . . If I make them realize what has happened they will have time to find ways of stopping it, and all this madness and fever will have gone for nothing.

But I can't sit here and let them all continue to trust me!

'I must tell you at once that I have found myself compelled', I write, and cross it out. 'I must tell you at once that', I write, and cross it out. 'I must tell you', I write, and cross it out. 'I must', I write.

Perhaps the envelope hasn't arrived at all – perhaps it's lost in the post. Then, if I am to make any sense of what I have done so far, I must copy the file again and send it off once more. In which case . . .

I screw up the minute and throw it into the waste-paper basket.

'Drafting problems?' says Jane. I give her a rueful smile. Even the smile is a *suggestio falsi*.

Or the envelope did arrive, and he didn't find what I'd sent him interesting enough to make use of. Perhaps I simply misjudged it. I've lost all sense of what's what in the world! Has he seen it or hasn't he? What's he doing with it? I must know! Until I know what's happening I can't say or do anything, I can't live, I can't breathe . . .

I pull the pad towards me again.

'If you can just get the first word right,' says Jane, 'you're halfway there.'

'I', I write, and cross it out. 'I', I write, and cross it out. 'I', I write, and cross it out . . .

The phone rings. 'Hilary Wood . . .' says a voice at this end.

'Look, I'm extremely sorry about last night,' says a voice at the other end, which for some reason brings nothing to mind but the picture of an old saucepan running its hand through its lid. 'I thought we just couldn't leave it hanging in the air like that . . .'

I can't think of anything to say to this. 'I', I write, and cross it out.

'Hello?' says the voice in my ear, anxiously. 'Are you there? Look, I'm sorry to phone you at work . . .'

155

'I', I write, and cross it out.

'Are you there . . .?' says the voice. 'Hilary . . .? Is that you . . .?'

I don't know the answer to these questions. *Am* I here? *Is* it me?

I put the receiver down and screw up the minute. Then I get up and fetch my coat from the stand.

'Going out?' queries Jane. She sounds rather surprised. I suppose I don't usually go out in the middle of the morning.

'Oh,' I tell her, 'there's a couple of questions I need to do a bit of research on.'

When I come out of the office this morning I was a tall man, I was six foot two. By the time I've got off the train at Woolwich and walked up to the estate I'm three inches shorter, I'm the same as everybody else.

Happens every time. Soon as I get anywhere near home I can feel myself shrinking. Home? What am I saying? This isn't home! I left nearly thirty years ago. This estate wasn't even built when I was here. I've lived in Gravesend and Gillingham and Dartford and Whitstable since then, plus that fort in the Thames Estuary, not to mention Sunningdale and the corner of my office in Whitchurch Street.

Is this home? Down to five foot eight by this time. Feels like home.

Couple of women go by with push-chairs, looking at me sideways. 'Oh, Christ, it's Terry,' says one to the other, when they're behind me. That's a bit of a lift, anyway. Put an inch back on me at least.

Or maybe they just know me, like anyone knows anyone. Home ground, after all. Worse than not recognizing me, in that case, and I shrink two inches. Shrink another two as I reach Wilkins House, and walk up the unflushed gents' urinal to the access deck. Five kids doing nothing together over by the bins look round at me rather thoughtfully, wondering whether it might break up the day a bit to murder me. I press one arm against my overcoat, checking the bulge of the envelope inside without letting on there's anything there. If all this stuff goes running off up the access deck under some kid's bomber-jacket I'm going to be in even worse trouble. Some of the kids round here, I wouldn't put it past them to ring the Home Office and demand a ransom.

Or else send it all to Terry Little. *He'll* know what to do with it.

I almost walk past the door, because some helpful so-and-so's tried to rub out the old familiar National Front flash on the wall next to it, and some other helpful so-and-so's sprayed a lot of other stuff up I never seen before. I press the bell. Bing bong! – and I lose another inch at the sound. Silence. She's not in. Maybe she's on the morning shift now at that place she works. Well, that's all right, because it was a daft idea, anyway ... No – slip slop, slip slop ... Here she comes – and there goes another inch of me. Silence again. I know what she's doing – she's looking at me through the little spyhole. I know what I'm doing, too – I'm going down like an old balloon. It's a wonder if she can still see me. By the time I've heard all the keys turned inside, and all the bolts go back, and the rattle of the chain being taken off, I'm about four foot six, I'm scarcely out of short trousers.

Oh, but she looks so old! Her hair's sat down and given up. All frizzed up still, last time I see her – looked lovely. She's three years younger than me, and somehow I'm fourteen and she's ninety.

'Hello, love,' I say. 'You're looking beautiful.'

She don't seem surprised to see me, but then she never does. Don't seem pleased, for that matter, but then again she don't seem not pleased. I'm like the rain, as far as she's concerned. You don't expect it, but as soon as it starts it's been raining forever.

'Button hanging off your coat,' she says, stepping back to let me in.

Button, right, we're under way. Now, where do I go from there?

'Bedroom wall,' I say, because it's just come back to me, as I walked through the door. 'You got water running down it again.'

Button, she says, and what she means is Don't she do your mending for you, then?

Bedroom wall, I say, and what I mean is No, she don't, because I do my own mending, thank you very much, I learnt to sew in Maidstone, but I'm not saying nothing about *my* life, or we won't even get as far as the Nescafé.

'Give me your coat,' she says. 'I'll do it before you lose it.'

'You don't have to start sewing buttons on as soon as I walk through the door . . .'

But all she does is hold out her hands and wait. I take the envelope out of the pocket as I hand the jacket over.

'What?' she says. 'Something I got to sign?'

I don't know what all this is about. When have I ever brought her things to sign?

'No – work, that's all,' I tell her. 'Thought it might drop out . . . Same place as before, is it, the water?'

'Hold on, I'll just . . .'

She goes into the bedroom. Just make sure the bed's made, she means. Just check there are no pairs of dirty tights left out for washing, no pills by the bed, no signs of life stirring. I go into the kitchen and put the kettle on for coffee. What was she doing when she heard bing bong? Nothing in here, by the look of it. Everything's in its place, waiting, not doing. The cereal packet's on the table, waiting for tomorrow's breakfast. The tin of catfood's on the draining-board, waiting for the cat. The cat's in its basket, waiting for the tin of catfood. Was she doing something in the bedroom, then? In the toilet . . .? I don't know why I'm thinking about it! She don't want me in any bits of her life that haven't been laid out for me to see, and I don't want to be anywhere she don't want me.

She comes into the kitchen, holding my overcoat and a biscuit tin with a picture of Buckingham Palace on it. Buckingham Palace – that's where she keeps her sewing things. She's kept them there for thirty years and more. It could do with a bit of redecoration, the old Palace.

'I don't know what you think you're going to do about that wall,' she says. 'I've had the devils round three times. There's nothing can be done.'

She stays in the kitchen with the overcoat – I go into the bedroom with the envelope.

The leak's the first thing you see when you come through the door, because it's different from everything else in the room. Neat bed, all careful flowers, not too bright. Neat chest of drawers, with a lamp on it I bought in the British Home Stores on a Saturday afternoon in January, which January I can't remember, but I know it was January, and two brass candlesticks Linda's brother Laurence give us as a wedding present, not much else. And nothing going on, unlike some other bedrooms I come across. I mean no one looking at you out of mirrors, because there's no mirrors to look out of, only one on the dressing-table, and that's minding its own business, it's looking up at the ceiling. Window, yes, but it's got thick lace curtains bowing to each other all over it, so there's nothing to see outside, and no way the outside world can see in, even if it got up on a fire ladder or come abseiling down off the roof.

And then hanging over it all is this great rough wound where the world's come bursting in anyway, in spite of the lace curtains. In the whole of one corner of the room, from the ceiling down, the skin's peeled back to reveal the concrete panels behind, all dark and blotched with fungus, and oozing with pus.

She's right – I don't know what I think I'm going to do about it. I already been up there several times with the sealant gun and the fungicidal paint. I stuck the paper back – I repapered the whole wall last winter. But there's some fault in the structure of the building, and as soon as the wind's in the west and there's driving rain – in it comes again. And the wind's always in the west, it's always raining. Can't think what to try now except either rebuild the estate or shift it to the Costa del Sol.

I'm not too sure what I'm going to do about *my* leak, neither. Looks almost as raw and nasty as the wall, my envelope, now I fetched it here. I had a good clear plan in my head when I got up. Bit of a daft idea, I can remember thinking that, but a very simple and natural one. So what was it?

Well, I can't put it in so many words, because it wasn't that kind of an idea, it was more a kind of feeling. It was a kind of feeling that me and Linda might get together to look after it.

Yes, OK, put like that it don't seem too brilliant . . . I can see what went wrong. I thought I was awake when I worked all this out, but I must have been asleep. What I remember is seeing us standing side by side, me and Linda, and opening this drawer . . . Like this one here, say . . . And there's all these soft clothes in it, like this, and we lay the envelope on the clothes, like so . . . and it smiles . . .

Only it don't smile. It just lays there on top of Linda's nightgowns like a plain brown envelope. A plain brown envelope that's going to get up and grass you if you don't treat it right.

Slight confusion between being awake and being asleep, that's all. Got it straight now. OK – take the envelope out and close the drawer again, before Linda comes in and catches me, or she'll think I'm up to something very funny.

Just as well Mike Edwards at BBC News can't see me now, for that matter – he'd never take another story from me. Not to mention Jacqui. Be real trouble there. Or all the rest of them. Get your headset back on, Shireen! The boys can't hear through the glass, can they? Where's Liz?

And Hilary. I wouldn't want her walking in just at the moment, seeing old Dad making a fool of himself.

Oh, not all that again. Not in broad daylight.

But what *am* I going to do with it?

Take it back into the kitchen for a start. Hold on to it while I make the Nescafé. Linda's at the table with her reading-glasses on, still working away at my overcoat.

'Pocket coming unstitched here,' she says. 'I thought you liked to look smart?'

Button . . . bedroom wall . . . pocket . . .

'I'll have another go at the Council for you,' I say.

She looks up at me over the top of the reading-glasses, but don't say nothing. I know what she's thinking. Oh, she's thinking, the big man, are you? Yes sir no sir, soon as they hear your name?

I just look straight back at her, because all right – why not? Why shouldn't she get the benefit of it for once?

Then I look away again. Can't do my trick with her. Don't know why. Do it with anyone else in the world – the prison governor, the Minister of This and the Permanent Under-Secretary of That. Try it on the Queen if I got the chance. But it don't work on old Linda.

Funny. Dad when I got up this morning. Sonny Jim by the time we got to coffee break.

She goes back to her work on the pocket. I get the milk out of the fridge.

'You want me to look after that thing for you?' she asks. 'Is that it?'

The envelope, she means. She knows that's why I'm here. Reads me like a book, Linda. Always did. Maybe that was half the trouble.

Still, knowing I got this envelope on the brain is one of her less amazing feats of clairvoyance, because I haven't put it down all the time I been here. I got it tucked under my chin even while I'm struggling to open the milk.

'Oh, what, *this* thing?' I say. 'Well . . .'

Well what, though? I don't know what to say. Isn't going to bite *her*, though, not if she don't know, which she don't, not if she don't have reasonable cause to believe, which I'm not going to give her.

She holds out her hand for it. So what *does* she think it is? She don't think. Knows it's something dodgy, that's all, and has reasonable cause to believe I want a home for it. That's enough for her.

'All right,' I say. 'Why not? Save carting it back to town.'

She takes it out to the hall and pulls down an old suitcase with a broken handle from the top of the cupboard. As she opens it I get a glimpse of wide red and white stripes. My schoolteaching days. I had to stand around on the freezing foggy afternoons they used to have in them days and ref the football. She knitted me a scarf – Charlton's colours. Lot of my old things she keeps in that bag.

So there it is, safely tucked up in a cradle of old clothes, just the way I planned it.

13

So there it is, lying on the desk waiting for him. Private and Confidential, it's screaming once again, in the same big square printed letters as yesterday, on the same plain brown envelope. 'Oh, Jacqui, look, another one!' cried Shireen, waving it about in front of me even as I came through the door, and giving me her usual lovely smile, only what it meant today was: 'There's something tremendously mysterious and important going on, and you don't know what it is any more than I do.' It really does put us all in an utterly impossible situation. Here we are campaigning for openness, and suddenly we don't know what's going on in our own office!

We don't know what Terry's doing, for that matter – we don't even know where he *is*. Eleven o'clock, and still no sign of him. Shireen has to put all his calls through to me, which means I can't get on with any work. 'Sorry,' I have to keep telling all the people who want to know when he'll be in and whether he's remembered engagements and interviews, 'I don't know ... No idea, my precious ... Yes, it's our own official secret – hilarious, isn't it ...'

Meanwhile, there the envelope lies on my desk, facing the door so that he'll see it when he comes in, but still only too plainly visible to me every time I turn to answer the phone. 'I don't know,' I say for the umpteenth time. Private and Confidential, says the envelope likewise.

'Oh, Jacqui . . .' This is Liz, putting her head round the door of the library, and holding that great scruff of hair off her face so that she can see out. 'You don't happen to know where Terry is, do you?'

Absolutely incredible, isn't it. If she was so busy minding everyone else's business earlier in the week – I haven't forgotten her interfering between me and Kevin! – why hasn't she been listening in to what I've been telling everyone this morning? That great bird's nest has never stopped her overhearing everything before. I'd like to scream at her. Only naturally I don't. 'Not a clue, my sweet,' I tell her patiently, with a lovely friendly smile.

And then she spots the envelope – though I can't think *how*, with her eyes jittering away all over the place like that. Out she comes at once, and her eyes stop jittering, and settle on it like two butterflies gorging on nectar. I know what she's going to do next – she's going to read out what it says.

Yes. 'Private and Confidential,' she announces, and even manages to get her eyes settled on me for a moment to make sure I've grasped the implications. Oh, thank you, my darling. It's quite true, I didn't go to university like you, and I do have some difficulty understanding words of more than one syllable.

'What happened in the end about the first one?' she asks.

I only need very short words to answer this, and I've had a lot of practice with all three of them.

'I don't know,' I tell her.

She puts the envelope back on the edge of the desk, so that Kevin sends it spinning when he comes by to clear the waste-paper baskets.

'*Please* don't start knocking things off the desk again, my love!' I beseech him smilingly, but he's finished knocking it off. What he's doing now is picking it up and looking at it.

'Private . . .' he starts, so I simply give him another nice smile and snatch it out of his hands.

'What . . .?' he says.

'I don't know, my precious,' I tell him, before he gets any further.

'What . . .?' he tries again.

'I've told you – *I don't know*,' I explain to him patiently. 'I don't know anything, you see. I don't know what you're trying to say, for a start, but it doesn't matter, my sweetheart, because whatever it is the answer's the same: I DON'T KNOW!'

By which time my voice has become almost as loud and clear as the message on the envelope, and I'm bundling Kevin back into the copying-room. I turn round to find some anxious-looking young woman coming through the door.

'Excuse me,' she's saying to Shireen. 'Is . . .?'

'. . . Terry here?' I break in helpfully, because I'm not sure I can bear to hear anyone say the words yet again. 'No, he isn't.'

'Oh,' says the young woman, turning to look at me, totally disconcerted by this news. 'Do you know . . .?'

'Where he is? No, I don't. When he's coming in? Not the foggiest. Anything else I can tell you?'

'No,' she says. 'I just wanted to . . .'

Just wanted to what? She seems to have forgotten.

'Well,' she says, 'I just thought . . .'

But she can't remember that, either. I think she knows even less than I do. She's hovering uncertainly, fiddling with her split ends. One of the things she apparently doesn't know is whether to go or stay.

'Do you want to leave a message for him?' I ask her. 'Who shall I say?'

'Oh . . .' And more hair-fiddling.

Oh, come on, my love, I haven't got all morning! You must at least know who you are!

Though in her case, now I look at her, I suppose it wouldn't be very surprising if she didn't, because she looks exactly like all the other young women we seem to attract as supporters – ie, completely nondescript. No make-up, which in her case is certainly a mistake, nothing done to her hair, apart from all this fiddling it around her finger, which is definitely not sufficient treatment for the state it's in, and everything else covered up by one of those shapeless padded overcoats that young women of this sort seem to go in for these days.

'Oh . . .' she says again. I think she's also very slightly mad. Well, Terry can deal with her. I'm damned if I'm going to get involved. 'You want to wait for him?' I ask. 'If so, sit down over there.'

'Well . . .' she says. She looks at the chair. She looks at the door. She looks at her watch. Complete silence. She seems to be in some kind of trance state. Then I realize that this is because she's stopped looking at her watch, and she's gazing at something else instead, completely hypnotized. It's the envelope I'm holding. My God – a total stranger, and she's going to read out the words Private and Confidential to me! I move it away from her rather briskly.

'I'm sorry,' she says hurriedly. 'It was just . . . I was simply . . . I'm sorry.'

She's as guilty about being caught looking at it as Liz was the day I came in and found her looking inside Kevin's haversack.

And here *is* Liz coming out of the library to see what's

going on, then stopping dead at the sight of the young woman and me madly confronting each other.

'Oh, sorry,' she says, grinning and jittering worse than ever, and bolts straight back into the library. I suppose, given her leanings, she leapt to the conclusion we were just about to fling ourselves into a wild embrace.

But no sooner has she gone than she's back.

'I'm sorry,' she says again, but this time she's talking to our visitor. 'Didn't we . . .? Aren't you . . .?'

'Oh,' says our visitor. 'Yes, I think we did just . . . With Roy somewhere . . .'

Well, small world. Though she's exactly the kind of young woman Liz *would* know. But now Liz is jittering and flittering away worse than ever. She keeps turning helplessly first to our visitor and then to me, her hands held out, as if she were entreating us not to murder each other. But the only thing she can manage to say is 'Oh . . .' She keeps saying it. 'Oh . . .' she says anxiously to me. 'Oh . . .' she says anxiously to our visitor. She's gone into spasm. She thinks she's responsible for everything in the world, but then she always does. She's in the same kind of state she got into over Kevin and the slimbread.

But what's she worrying about *this* time? What's going on? I don't understand!

Or . . .

Yes. I think perhaps I do understand.

I have one of those strange flashes of lightning that come every now and then in life. Suddenly the night simply vanishes, and you see the whole landscape around you as bright and clear as noon. It's a bit like when I first met Terry, in the doorway of that shop in Chancery Lane. That was in a thunderstorm. Wave after wave of rain pelting across the pavement outside, and the sky as black as ink – and within minutes I knew with absolute certainty what I had to do, and where I was going in life.

What makes it happen this time? I don't know! I think it's something about the mention of her knowing Roy. I suddenly remember something about his meeting girls in Whitehall – and then the look on Roy's face the other day when he was shut away with Terry, and I came bursting into the room . . . Then something about the words Private and Confidential . . . the way they're written . . . the look on her face when she saw them . . .

I can't explain it logically, but it's like everything being plugged in to the same socket at once. There's a kind of short-circuit in my brain, and a tremendous blue flash . . . The great I Don't Know inside my head has disappeared like the pumpkin in the pantomime, and a shining crystal carriage has taken its place. I know everything there is to be known.

I know who this young woman is and why she's here.

I know why Liz is so agitated.

I know why Terry suddenly changed his mind about publishing the material in the plain brown envelope.

I know where Terry is now.

And I know exactly what I've got to do. The muggy haze of resentment I've been walking round under for the last few days has cleared, just like the air after a storm, and everything is as transparent as a raindrop.

'Listen,' I say, very calm and in control of things. 'Why don't we all sit down and have a nice quiet cup of coffee together while we wait for Terry?'

'Oh,' says our new friend, looking at the door. 'No, thank you. I don't think I can really . . .'

'Oh, dear,' says Liz, flittering her eyes anxiously first at me and then at our mystery guest. 'Oh, dear.'

I firmly give Liz the kettle to fill. She zig-zags uncertainly out of the room like one of those maddening insects that can never make up their minds which way to go. She's still giving little anxious buzzings, even as she goes through the door, but at least it's got her out of the way for a moment.

I offer Miss Mouse a biscuit.

'Thanks,' she says, 'but I think I'd better be . . .'

She can think what she likes – I've no intention of letting her escape.

'How about some of my own special stock of slimbread, then?' I urge her. 'Terry says it tastes like plaster dust, but that didn't stop Kevin scoffing the lot the other day while my back was turned.'

She gives it one glance and then looks hurriedly away, she obviously finds the prospect so nauseating. I take no notice.

'That's Kevin,' I explain to her. 'The one who ate the slimbread. On the other side of the glass. He and Kent do all the copying and all the postal work. You wouldn't believe how much of it there is in an organization like this. And they're such terrific chums – people are always getting their names mixed up.'

'Well,' says Miss Mouse. 'I've got to be . . .'

'My name's Jacqui, by the way. And that's Shireen. I think you said hello to her on the way in . . . You might as well have the whole guided tour, now we've started. Oh, don't worry, I'm always doing it. It's usually our local branches and sixth-formers. "Where does Terry work?" – that's what they always ask, and the answer's through there, though most of the time he's in here, prowling round like a caged tiger. And through *that* door is the library, where Liz works. I'll let her show you round in there herself, as soon as she's finished scattering Nescafé over the floor. All right, Liz, my sweet?'

Because Liz is back with the kettle, and she's busy grinning and knocking things over on the table where the coffee things are kept. I've never seen her in quite such a state. I'd be calling a psychiatrist if I didn't happen to know what the trouble was.

'Anyway . . .' says Miss Mouse.

'Yes, anyway,' I tell her, 'this desk you're looking at is the real nerve-centre of the whole operation, because this is where *I* do my stuff! No, but in fact it *is*, because Terry's always at work on it as well . . . Liz, just sit down and let me do it. You'll break something in a moment.'

I get our visitor sat down eventually, in spite of all Liz's snitterings and twitterings. Indeed I install her in my own chair, and I perch on the edge of the desk in front of her, sitting over her while she drinks her coffee, and making it very difficult for her to get out. Not that she makes any attempt to. I think she can sense my utter determination to keep her here – I think she can feel it surrounding her like a wall.

She's going to be my little surprise for Terry.

Things have been getting very scratchy between Terry and me recently. I think he still fails to realize quite how hurt I was yesterday when he refused to show me what was inside that envelope. If there are difficult decisions to be made I naturally want to help him make them. If there are risks then I should share them. I don't want to be sheltered and protected, he *must* realize that by now. I'm not some temp who's come round to do the filing – I founded this campaign with him! I'm also his wife, for heaven's sake! To all intents and purposes. A damn sight more like his wife than his wife ever was. Perhaps this will change his attitude a little. Any minute now he's going to come walking through that door, and he's going to discover that I'm not such a fool as he evidently thinks. He's going to find that I've worked out for myself what's going on. He's going to see that I can act just as calmly and decisively as he can.

The absurd thing is how obvious it all is once you've seen it. What else could Miss Bun be but a Civil Servant? One glance at her looking at that envelope and you know she's the person who sent it. One more glance and you know what's happened since. She's panicked. She's like a silly child with a firework. She lit it – she flung it away into the darkness – she covered her ears and waited for the bang. And nothing happened. There was no bang. So now she's crept out to see what's happened. Perhaps she's lost her nerve. She's decided she's not going to play with fireworks after all. It didn't go off, so she's going to pick it up and put it back in the box, and no one will know. Not until the whole box goes off, and the house is in flames, and half the street with it.

She's a very silly girl. All I want to do is to hand her over to Terry – 'I've found your little firework-thrower for you.' Then it's up to him to decide what to do with her. He might just possibly persuade her to give us all the rest of her fireworks for safekeeping.

Liz keeps vanishing into the library, then coming out again to make sure we're still here. She saw the whole thing at once, I'll give her that. But being Liz she just went into a hopeless tailspin about it.

So I guard my little offering like the Crown Jewels. Actually she doesn't need all that much guarding after a bit. I just keep talking – anything that comes into my head – rather the way I did when Poops used to get into one of her states. I tell her how the Campaign started – the whole story, from the famous meeting with Terry in the rainstorm onwards.

'It was a kind of miracle, you see,' I say, with my hand on her arm. 'I was at rock bottom – we both were. Me in the middle of this truly ghastly divorce – Terry absolutely on his beam-ends. I'd just been at my solicitor's – I couldn't find a taxi – when suddenly the heavens opened. So there we were, sheltering in the doorway of this shop, both feeling sorry for ourselves – and we simply looked at each other – and that was it. We started to talk, and we went on talking for seven hours non-stop. My precious, it was the Sea of Galilee all over again. I said, "You've just found your first disciple." And when we were starting the Campaign I wasn't only his disciple, I was all twelve apostles. One room, that's all we had then. Just the two of us, living on faith, waiting for the miracles to start . . .'

She's settled down by this time, just like Poops used to. She's stopped looking at the door and started gazing into her coffee instead. She's even lifted her eyes off the coffee and managed to look at me.

'My name's Hilary,' she says suddenly.

Hilary. Yes. Poor Hilary. She's not much more than a child, after all. If things had been different Terry and I might have had a baby girl ourselves. Perhaps she wouldn't have been like my lovely Poops. Perhaps she'd have been like this – all degrees and no make-up.

Perhaps she'd have been a Civil Servant, too. Perhaps she'd have fallen in love with some hopeless man, and thrown away her career for him.

Because that's what Hilary's doing. That's why she's suddenly started playing with fireworks. How could she be such a fool?

Terry guessed what had happened as soon as he opened that envelope. That's why he wouldn't show me what was inside. He thought it wasn't up to us to decide what to do. I don't think many men in Terry's position would have been so scrupulous. But he's right! If Hilary's sending us plain brown envelopes because she's infatuated with Roy, then we can't just simply take advantage of it. The first thing is that Roy's got to be made to face up to his moral responsibility. That's where Terry is this morning, I realize – talking to Roy about it.

The door handle rattles.

'Oh, Terry,' says Shireen. 'There's someone waiting for you, she didn't say her name, Jacqui's looking after her.'

Hilary's turned to look at him, all her agitation back at once. I put my hand on her arm. 'Don't worry, my sweet,' I tell her. 'You'll feel better after you've talked to Terry. He's a good man.'

Terry's stopped dead in his tracks. He's just standing there, looking first at Hilary, then at me, then at Liz, who's back in the doorway of the library again, squittering and skittering like a maniac. He knows at once that there's something going on.

What's going on in me is a terrific rush of feeling at the sight of him. I'm so proud of him!

I bend down and murmur in Hilary's ear. 'I'll tell you a little secret, my precious. He's a *great* man.'

I'm completely off the air for a few seconds.

One moment I'm walking into the office. Brass handle's jingling, nice old smell, Shireen's smiling, etcetera. Lovely to be back, it's the nearest thing I got to home, etcetera. That's funny, I'm thinking – here's me in *my* home office, there's Hilary up the road in *her* Home Office. I wonder what hers is like, I'm thinking, and what sort of person she is when she's there. What she's thinking about now? Is she thinking about me? Is she thinking about what I'm like when she's not there? Is she wondering what I'm thinking about? Etcetera.

Then – clonk. What's happened? I've lost the programme.

Well, I still got picture. I can see her face. I can see their two faces. I can see their two faces next to each other, turned to look at me. This one going all red and blotchy, that one smiling and whispering in this one's ear.

I can see Liz jiggering about in the background.

I just can't make no sense of it all. I've flipped channels – I've lost sound . . .

So what – a stroke? Legs have stopped moving. No words coming out. Always got my story ready, you know me, always give you a quote. And now – nothing.

Only lasts a couple of seconds. Then the old anchorman's back on the air again, nice and reassuring. 'Oh, hello,' he's saying. It's me – I recognize the voice. Sounds quite normal. Bit surprised, that's all.

'Terry . . .' says Jacqui.

Right. That's a help, because Terry's me, I remember the name. And Jacqui's Jacqui. OK. Liz is Liz, know her anywhere.

'. . . this is Hilary,' says Jacqui. And that's Hilary. Which of course I knew just as soon as she said.

'Yes,' I say, 'we met. In that restaurant, with Roy, if you remember.'

I'm there. I'm back. Voice, brain, legs – they're all up and running. The brain somewhat faster than Jacqui's Amstrad. 'Why what how not-me I-never,' it's going. Then – 'Apart. Get them apart! Questions later.'

OK, into battle. They're all drinking Nescafé. So I amble over, no rush, and fix myself a mug as well.

'Looking for Roy, was you, Hilary?' I ask. 'Never mind – have a look over the office instead. I'll give you the full guided tour.'

175

Get her into my office, I'm thinking. Library, copying-room, even – anywhere's better than in here with Jacqui.

'I've given her the full guided tour already, my love,' says Jacqui.

Oh. Right. Well . . .

'I think what she really wants to do is to have a little talk about things,' says Jacqui. 'With you. In private.'

'A talk?' I say. 'In private?' I'm losing the signal again.

'Why don't you take her into your office, my pet?' says Jacqui.

What? My brain's going fast, all right. Trouble is, the world's going faster.

Also Jacqui's got her special voice on, so I know she's telling me something that's full of significance, something that only I'm supposed to understand. On top of which she's got her back turned to Hilary, and she's giving me one of her special looks as well. I can't say it aloud, she's telling me, and you've got to work it out yourself from the way I'm saying the words and the way I'm staring at you with my head slightly turned on one side.

'Oh, right,' I say. Only I can't work it out. I can't work any of this out.

Never mind, we'll get all that straight later.

'Come on, then, Hilary,' I say. 'Let's leave Jacqui to get on with her work . . .'

I've sussed why Jacqui's got her back turned towards Hilary, though. It's because the special look and the special voice go with something she's showing me, that Hilary's not supposed to see.

And at once the old brain's gone again. Because what she's showing me is the plain brown Private and Confidential. I've just buried it in the suitcase with my football scarf at Linda's. Now here it is, accusingly shouting my name again in those same big blank printed capitals. It's come back from the dead!

'Would you like another cup of coffee, Hilary?' says Jacqui, leading the way into my office, and quietly putting Private and Confidential on my side of the desk for me. 'Hold on, my sweet – you can't sit on his dirty underwear! Honestly – men! You know he sleeps in the office, Hilary?'

By the time Jacqui's shut the door, and me and Hilary are sitting facing each other in silence across my desk, with the envelope lying between us, I've tumbled it. It's not the old corpse – it's a new one. Hasn't even been opened, this one. I don't know which is worse – having them rise from the grave in front of you, or finding there's ever more of them springing up behind your back.

All right, then, a little talk about things, just like Jacqui said. So Hilary's come to tell me something, has she? Fair enough. Only she's not telling me, is she. She's just staring at the desk, and frowning, and biting her lip. I got to kick off, then, have I? OK. I got a *lot* to say, because I'm just a little bit cross with her, now the first shock's worn off, just a little bit surprised and disappointed. I just don't know where to start, that's all, because I don't know what I'm crossest about, whether it's her sending me those letters, or whether it's her coming here. Or whether it's her doing one and then doing the other as well, which seems to me just about as stupid as you can get, and not what I should have expected from someone who's passed all her exams, from someone who's supposed to be running the country.

Well, we can't just sit here in silence.

'So what do you want me to say, Hilary?' I ask her, nice and gentle. 'Thank you?'

She lifts her eyes and looks at me, and – oh, dear, what can I do? She looks like a half-drowned kitten, all miserable and helpless. She don't know nothing about nothing. I'm not her dad – not now I'm sitting opposite her. That's all dreams, that's all nonsense. But I'm the one who's got to be responsible for her, that's still true. It's all down to me.

'I'm sorry,' she says.

'Never mind,' I tell her. 'No harm done. Yet. Don't worry. We'll get it all sorted out.'

'I mean about coming here.'

'Yes, well, I got a bit of a shock, Hilary, that's true, walking through that door. Only ten years off my life, though – don't give it a thought. What did you tell Jacqui, as a matter of interest?'

'Jacqui?'

'The one you was talking to. The one with the eyelids.'

'Oh – nothing.'

Nothing. No, I might have guessed. Just sat there looking half-barmy, while Jacqui went jumping to conclusions like a rabbit all round her.

'Jacqui, yes,' says Hilary, and I can see she's thinking about her. 'I suppose she's got a bit of a thing about you, has she?'

And she gives me a rather sharp look. I just look right back. Still works on Hilary, anyway. Two seconds and she's looking away.

'She told me about meeting you, and getting the Campaign started. She said it was like the Sea of Galilee . . . But then I suppose you get quite a lot of disciples trailing after you, one way and another . . .'

I just keep looking. Sea of Galilee? Give her a bit of a smile about that, maybe – not too much. Funny thought comes into my head – there's nothing about smiles in the Bible. What – they didn't smile in them days? Or they did but it got lost in their beards, and no one noticed?

'Jacqui . . .' says Hilary again, as if she's trying it out for size. 'I rather took to her, as a matter of fact. Though she was in a great rage when I arrived . . . That was *her* desk, was it?'

She shoots me another look. I look away this time, I have to admit. Just for a moment. Then straight back at her.

'Not worrying about it, are you, Hilary?'

'No,' she says. 'Are you?'

I can't help laughing. That's more like it. Bit of the old spirit coming back. Never mind about that, though. Let's get the main thing straight.

'What does Roy think about all this, Hilary?'

All this is the envelope. I'm holding it up to show her. She frowns. Can't even remember who Roy is, by the look of it.

'What, he don't know about it? That what you're telling me? Just for me, all this?'

'Oh . . .' she says. She flaps her hand. She's brushing a fly away, and I think the fly in question is one that wears a wig. Oh, dear – the fly-swatting's not down to me, too, is it?

'That's all over,' she says. 'I told you before. It never was anything.'

I look at the envelope. Those plain straightforward capital letters! They make it all look so simple.

'Anyway,' I say, chucking the envelope across to her side of the desk, 'good thing you dropped in, because you can take this away with you.'

She don't pick it up. Just looks at it.

'Number two, in case you're wondering. I'd have kept number one for you as well, if I'd known you was coming. Or if I'd known what address to put I'd have posted it back to you, but I didn't, so I've put it away in a nice safe place instead.'

Now she's looking at me. Very thoughtfully. I've shut my

179

eyes and jumped off the edge of the world for this berk, she's thinking, and what's happened? – I've landed on the bedside carpet and been tucked up for the night again.

'I'm sorry, Hilary,' I say. 'I can't do it. I wish I could, believe me. I wish with all my heart I could. That's what I'm here for, to get my hands on stuff like this. I don't know what's in this one, but there was things in the other one I could have blown up the whole of Whitehall with.'

She don't say a word. Just goes on looking at me. Oh, dear.

'I know what you must have gone through to do this, Hil. Don't think I don't. What about your mum, though? She's very proud of you. What's she going to say if you get yourself sacked? And never mind sacked, it's not just sacked I'm thinking about. Two years, Hil. Two years out of your life, and no life to go back to afterwards. And OK, forget that, too, if you like. Think about this, though – what would your mum say if she knew you was taking things from the people you work for?'

She looks down at the desk and smiles a little private smile. Must mean something – she's not much of a smiler. I only seen her smiling once before. Like me, in that respect. We should both have been in the Bible. I'm not smiling now, I can tell you. I got a tear in the corner of each eye.

'No more envelopes on the way, are there?' I ask her.

She shakes her head. Smiles another little smile.

'Yes, don't send us any more, Hil. If you get the feeling coming over you again, just bung us a small contribution to the funds instead. Always much appreciated.'

She gets up to go. I get up to see her out. There's nothing more to say. She's done the bravest thing she'll ever do, and it's over, she's back to earth again. I've had the biggest chance I'll ever have, and I've chucked it down the drain.

I'm a fool. Don't tell me. I've always known it.

I'm a saint, too, though, and I never knew *that* before. OK, so I won't get the windows round these parts glazed with golden glass. I'll just have to wait till I get to heaven, like all the other saints.

I come round the desk and give her a nice farewell hug. 'Take care, then, love,' I tell her. 'Wait till you're Permanent Under-Secretary. I won't give you no second chances then.'

She's stopped smiling, but she's still looking down at the desk. I don't think it's the envelope she's looking at – it's the throwaway for the Cats demo. Our little secret from them. Don't like to go snatching it away from her, though, in the circumstances.

'That's the present Under-Secretary we're getting at there, Hil. Your boss. Give him a bit of a tease. Best I can think of, without no nice Private and Confidentials to help us.'

What she ought to do, now she's found out, is tell him. And what *I* ought to do, now I've thought of it, is tell her to tell him. Oh, give over. Bit of moderation, if you please, even in saintliness.

She don't say nothing neither way, just looks serious and opens the door.

'You needn't worry about my being sacked,' she says. 'Or taking things from the people I work for. Or telling them about your plans. I'm resigning.'

And off she goes. No – she's putting her head back round the door. 'Thank you,' she says. 'I couldn't quite get it clear in my mind before.'

Oh, dear. I don't think my ticket's made out to heaven, after all. Now I look closer I think what it says is hell.

She hasn't even taken the envelope. But by the time I've got into the outer office there's nothing left of her but the jingle of the brass door handle, and Jacqui watching me from her desk, dying to find out what happened.

'Roy's new chum, I assume?' she says. 'It *is* her who sent them, isn't it? She *does* work for the Home Office?'

'Did,' I say. 'She's resigning.'

She goes on looking at me, waiting for the rest of the story. But there isn't no rest of the story. The story's over.

'What are you going to do with the things she's sent you?' she asks.

'Same as I did with the last lot.'

'What was that?'

'Gave them to someone,' I tell her.

She's still waiting. 'Gave them to who?' she wants to know. 'And what are *they* going to do with them?'

I just shrug. 'Up to them,' I tell her, and I go back into my office and shut the door.

Shrug – that's a lie. *Up to* – that's another one. *Them* – that's a third. Three lies in three seconds – I'll be getting the productivity bonus this week.

Few moments later the door opens. But by this time I've got Hilary's envelope open, and I'm deep in the Special Branch report on us.

'It's all very noble, her resigning,' says Jacqui. 'But what's the poor kid going to live on?'

'She'll just have to go down the Job Centre,' I tell her, 'same as anybody else.'

I don't even look up from my work. Me playing fathers is daft enough. Jacqui playing mothers as well – this is getting entirely out of hand. Anyway, I can't believe what I've got in front of my eyes.

'She could come and do a spot of work for us, couldn't she?' says Jacqui. 'She's the expert, after all. And I could absolutely do with some help. Liz, too.'

'I didn't know Liz was a Trot,' I say, though that's the

least of the surprises I'm getting from the stuff I'm holding in my hand.

'A lot of things we don't know about Liz,' says Jacqui.

And off she goes again. A lot of things we don't know about a lot of people, I'm beginning to think.

'We haven't even got a phone number for her!' I shout after Jacqui. For Hilary, this is. Because Jacqui taking her on in the office is the daftest idea I ever heard. Let's just crack on with Cats and forget about all that.

'She'll be back,' shouts Jacqui. 'You wait.'

14

We're all smiling, that's the rather bizarre thing. We've all got cardboard cat's faces sticking out of our sensible anoraks and scarves, and we've all got permanent smiles printed on us.

'You're not Stevenage, are you?' smiles a stout female tabby with a clipboard and walking boots. 'I'm Hilary Wood,' I smile back. The tabby smiles at her clipboard, scratching the grey hair behind her brindled right ear. She's got branches of the Campaign listed for Brentwood and Borehamwood, but she can't find Hilarywood. Of course not – it's a completely new branch.

We've been standing around in the road next to the coaches for at least half an hour, blocking the traffic, getting cold, and waiting for something to happen. Some of us are ginger, some of us black or tabby or tortoiseshell, but all of us are smiling. I suppose we're Cheshire cats, are we? We're a job lot that some wholesaler of party novelties happened to have left on his shelves.

Cars edge slowly past. It's Saturday morning, and we're making it very difficult for the citizens of Chorleywood to get to Sainsburys or visit their aunts. Mystified small children gaze at us through slow-moving rear windows. We wave at them, and wash our faces with our paws, and smile. They stare unsmilingly back. I'm smilingly surprised that there are no police controlling the traffic. I smilingly assume that we do have police permission for this demonstration.

We all begin to drift along the road, some of the younger cats capering about in kittenish ways, most of us wandering rather aimlessly along with our front paws in our anorak pockets. One small Persian pushes its way in the opposite direction, trailing an empty cat-basket and howling. We're passing houses with mullioned windows and double garages, half-hidden behind dank hawthorn hedges. No one comes out to look at us. I can't help smiling another small private smile to myself when I think that one of these cats is Terry. And then another smile when I think how *he'd* smile if he knew that another of the cats was me.

Because he likes me. That's what I can't get over. That's what I'm really smiling about. That's what we're all smiling about. How foolishly we're all behaving!

We seem to have stopped, and something seems to be happening. An inaudible amplified voice is addressing us. 'What?' we all smile to each other. 'What's he saying?' A hundred yards further up the road brilliant summer green and deep summer shadow come and go in the straggling autumn thickets on either side of a gateway as the photographers' flashes flicker. I suppose that modest complexity of mellow brick and whitewash just visible behind them must be where the Permanent Under-Secretary of my former department lives.

A cameraman on the roof of a car films the crowd. Some of us have placards to wave, some of us shout simple thoughts about Mr Hassam and open doors. The rest of us just keep smiling. I suppose we should really be snarling and spitting and showing our claws. No, it's better to be smiling. We're all embarrassed at being here, after all. We're embarrassed because we're being so silly and ineffectual – and also because we know we're right, and because we're giving up our Saturday morning to do something about it.

A very small police car noses cautiously through the crowd, and two young constables get out, also smiling with embarrassment. They should be setting dogs on us, firing tear-gas at us . . . Suddenly my heart jumps, because there, over the top of all the cats, as obvious as Nelson's Column, is a great red face and a mop of grey curls. No mask, no costume. He's talking to the policemen. He's gazing straight at them, and they're looking away and smiling and nodding. They think he's wonderful; they should go back and look up his record. Now he's seeing them back to their car, and all three of them are smiling.

Time goes by . . . There's no more red face and grey curls to be seen, no more photographers' flashes. People are starting to take their smiles off and talk among themselves and yawn. Now what? Go home again, I suppose. So these are my new friends, this is my new life. Well, why not? They're good people. No worse than my old friends, anyway.

And then everything changes.

Suddenly the air is full of urgent blaring noise, and I'm being pushed forward against the people in front of me. I turn round to see what's happening, but I can't, because someone's face is cracked violently against my nose. A star of pain radiates through my head, and my mask falls over my eyes. I can't get my hands free, because there are people all round me, crying out and shouting, pressing my arms to my sides.

I'm shouting as well by this time, to my surprise – I don't know what. I have ceased to be a cat among cats, and become part of one single monster cat, huge, terrified, and struggling. When at last I get a hand free to pull the mask down around my neck I glimpse the cause of this transformation – three white vans with revolving blue lights on top trying to force their way along the lane through the mass of bodies, compacting them against the people in front. The vans are being drummed by angry fists. One of them is rocking wildly back and forth on its springs.

Now there are police helmets visible among the crowd. I can see arms and heads moving about with astonishing violence. The vans begin to move forward again, and we're all swept helplessly away up the lane in front of them, our smiles discarded and trampled underfoot as we go.

There's one somehow familiar nervous grin left on a face over to the left of me, beneath a fuzz of shaking hair. 'Oh, no, no, no, no!' says the grin. Somewhere over to the right I catch a flash of alarmed blue eyelids. 'Jacqui!' I call to them, but she doesn't hear me. Now I'm flung up against the side of a parked car, some metal projection brutally hard against my ribs, and by the time I've managed to force myself away from it the helmets are just behind me.

I'm trapped. But also trapped, between me and the advancing helmets, is someone in a complete catsuit – a black cat from head to toe, but standing up on its hind legs and wobbling about in a funny drunken way. 'I don't think . . .' says the black cat indistinctly to the helmets, without moving its mouth, and a truncheon comes down on its head. 'I don't think . . .' says the cat, but there's something maddeningly slow and awkward about its voice, and something maddeningly ill-judged about the lovable look on its face, and something maddeningly ineffectual about the way it puts up its forepaws to defend itself. So they hit it again, and then again.

People are screaming at the helmets to stop. But the black cat goes on trying to explain, and the helmets go on hitting it.

'I don't think . . .' tries the cat once more, but its rear legs are just as maddeningly ineffectual as its front legs – one kick and it's fallen down in a silly heap.

'Pigs!' people scream at the helmets. One of the people screaming is me.

'I don't think . . .' says the cat, and they kick it again on the ground, then drag it away by its feet. Its black head falls off, and a strained white human face appears in its place, still saying something as it slides and bounces away along the ground in the direction of the vans. 'I don't think . . .' it says, '. . . that this is a commensurate response.'

'Pigs!' I keep screaming.

'The house!' says someone. The police have got one of their vans through to blockade the gateway, but there are gaps in the ragged hawthorn hedge through which half a dozen of us force our way. We trample through the blown flower-beds in the muddy November lawn, and peer through the small leaded panes of the windows. 'Pigs!' shouts a grey-haired woman in a sheepskin coat and green wellington boots. There are no pigs to be seen, though – only chintz furnishings, and heaps of books, and a home computer.

Something cracks against the glass, and a starburst appears in the pane beside my head. 'They're coming!' shouts someone. I look round, and there are dark figures running over the gravel in front of the garage. 'Round the back!' I shout, and lead the way. A rustic timber gate judders open as I fling my weight against it. Water is running out of a pipe in the wall into an open drain. I look through the window above it, and find myself face to face with a woman filling a kettle at a sink.

We gaze at each other for a moment, both of us startled and frightened. She looks rather younger than me, but not much. She has a serious, thoughtful face. She could be a daughter of the house – could for that matter be a colleague – could be myself. In that one short moment, before she looks awkwardly away, I know that we are indissolubly related members of the same class and species, and also that we are irretrievably on opposite sides of the glass. But only one word comes to mind to explain this to her.

'Pig!' I scream.

More succinct than most of my minutes, though possibly not quite as fully argued. And on we run into the back garden, with panting dark shapes close behind us.

'Hold on,' gasps one of them, grabbing the end of my scarf.

'Fuck off!' I scream back, yanking the scarf away from him.

He hangs on to the scarf like some huge bulldog, gasping and stumbling. But it's *my* scarf, and I won't let him have it, I won't, I won't!

'It's me!' he's saying. 'It's me!'

'Fuck off!' I'm screaming. 'Fuck off!'

I turn round and kick out at him, almost blind with pure anger, and only just able to take in that this towering mass of open dark tweed overcoat and coarse blue woollen sweater, bent over now to defend his knees and groin from my wildly kicking feet, is topped by a maddening red face and grey curls.

'Hold it, Hil,' he gasps, still hanging on to my scarf with one hand for support. 'Or we're going to have a nasty accident here.'

Oh. Him. I let him keep his hold on the scarf, and grab his flapping overcoat as well to reinforce the link, because now there are helmets coming round the other side of the house as well, and we're all doubling back and scattering towards the far end of the garden.

'Over here,' I urge him. I can see there's a place where the ancient grey hurdles in the boundary fence are sagging in their rusty wires, and I can kick them down, and we can scramble through into the next garden. Why not? If one garden, why not another? When I broke through the front hedge I seem to have breached some kind of barrier inside myself as well, and the way lies open to the entire world of private gardens. We are running through beds full of winter kale, and it doesn't matter at all. There's another garden beyond, too, this time hidden by a head-high board fence. But there's some kind of glazed seed-beds that offer a way up. I teeter along the edge of the frame, then haul myself up on to the fence and perch like a bird. A glass pane crunches underfoot behind me.

'All right?' I ask.

'Don't know,' grunts Terry.

Down into a heap of wet sand and builder's materials, and we're in a completely different kingdom – the muddled realm of a man with a pink baby face who suddenly appears through a beech hedge with an armful of sodden newspapers.

'Sorry,' I tell him, still running.

'Just a moment . . .' says the man.

'Security,' gasps Terry.

And already we're halfway up an unstable heap of shifting timber, then over the fence into the next kingdom. Different again – all whitewashed fruit-trees and mown clearings, and a dog bounding and barking towards us. But we're away and gone, over neat white rails into an untended wilderness of long wet grass and brambles . . .

Why are we running, though? We should be back there getting ourselves beaten and arrested . . . I stop – and realize I'm on my own. No sign of helmets, no sign of any house – and no sign of Terry. The dog barks on for a bit, then silence. I walk back through the brambles, suddenly aware, now I've stopped, that I'm scarcely able to breathe.

I find Terry sitting collapsed on the steps of an old wooden summerhouse which has foundered in the sea of brambles. His head is bowed between his knees. He lifts it for a moment and shakes it from side to side at me.

'Can't run no more,' he says.

I sit down at one end of the steps, with my back against the rotting balustrade, and watch him while I struggle to get my breath back. He's not so much out of breath as foundered and sunk, like the summerhouse itself. He's not just an older man any more – he's quite simply old.

Eventually he settles himself with his back against the balustrade on the other side of the steps, and we gaze at each other in silence. He looks straight into my eyes – his old trick – and I look straight back into his. He's an old man with a red face and grey hair, and his strength is going, and he knows it. I'm as firm and fit and alive and pink-cheeked as I am ever going to be in life, and what *I* know, at last, is exactly what I want.

I want this old man to lie on top of me.

I want him to put his weight on me. I want him to press down on my breasts and stomach, and to lie between my legs. I want him to do it here and now, in the openness of the open air, in the full light of heaven. I want it so much that my throat closes in excitement, and I can't speak.

But I know exactly what to do to bring it about, even though I have never done it before, have never even thought of doing it.

191

With my eyes still fixed on his, as I lie back on the damp wooden steps of the summerhouse, I slowly slide my feet back towards me. Then I carefully shift my left foot down a step and my right foot up a step.

I open myself to him.

His gaze never wavers, only becomes darker and more intense. Then . . . Yes. I was right.

And when the weight of him reaches my ribs and breasts I shout aloud at the pain. I must be a mass of bruises. I'd forgotten all about them. But before long I've forgotten about them again, and I'm shouting aloud for different reasons.

Afterwards I wonder about this. His eyes are still upon me even now, pale blue again, six inches above mine. What hedges and fences have I broken through today? What gardens of unknown knowledge have I found my way into, what jungles of overgrown feelings?

Perhaps this is why we were running.

'Logical force,' says Terry. 'I knew this demo was going to have bags of logical force.'

He gets up and pulls up his trousers. He's not as old as he was. Not as old, certainly, as the dear little, shrunken little, shrivelled little old man he's gently helping back to bed.

I laugh to myself. Where do these thoughts come from? Have they always been there?

'What?' smiles Terry down at me.

Shall I tell him? About the two old men I'm in love with, one big and one little? No, I can't tell him that. I just shake my head and jump to my feet.

'Right,' he says, 'I got to go and bail poor old Kevin. So you've slung your hook, have you, Hilary? You've asked for your cards? You're out of work?'

'Why?' I say boldly. 'Are you offering me a job?'

He looks at me thoughtfully.

'I don't know,' he says. 'Am I? You better come in next week some time and have a talk about it.'

I'm going to see him again, then. I'm slightly disconcerted by my own boldness. I find a piece of crumpled cardboard scratching against my ear. It's my smile, still hanging round my neck. I pull it back over my face.

'We'll see,' I smile at him.

Watford Magistrates' Court is where I am first thing Monday morning, watching nine of our supporters coming up on various charges ranging from affray to malicious damage. And when I get back to the office . . . I don't believe it! She done it again!

Because there she is. Sitting at the desk opposite Jacqui, just like she was before.

Smiles at me. Goes red, I'll say that for her. 'Hello,' she says. What do I say? Nothing. Still getting my breath back.

What did I tell her? Some time next week, that's what I said, not first thing Monday morning, not when I'm not here to keep an eye on things!

'She came about the job you're offering her,' says Jacqui.

'Oh, right,' I say. Oh, wrong, though. Because I'm not offering her no job. I been thinking about it all the way back from Watford, as it happens. I can't. It won't work. I can't have the two of them together in here.

'Yes, well,' I say, 'we're going to have to have a little talk about that.'

'We've had a little talk, my pet,' says Jacqui. 'I told her she could start whenever she liked.'

Oh. I don't even need to ask when that's going to be, now I'm looking at her properly, because I can see. She's got folders in front of her, she's got a pen in her hand. She's started already.

'OK, my love?' says Jacqui.

No, my love. Not OK. Far from OK.

'OK,' I say.

Because what can I do? It's out of my hands. Things have been decided. Fate's taken over.

That ghastly grin hovering nervously about in the background with no eyes above it, only a lot of hair, that's Liz, and she don't like this turn of events at all. She can see a lot of clearing up's going to have to be done sooner or later, and she thinks it's all going to be down to her, as usual. Never mind. The die is cast. So be it.

'So,' I say to Hilary, 'here you are, then. Welcome aboard the good ship *Titanic*. Looking after you, are they?'

'Yes, thank you,' says Hilary, keeping her eyes down on her work, and I should think so too.

'But what happened at Watford?' says Jacqui.

'Oh, set down for hearings on Thursday. So we got lots to do. Find them all lawyers. Get our supporters outside the court. All the media.'

I go and sit down in my office, and I can't help laughing. It's all a bit too good to be true, and it's not going to last. Nothing much I can do, though, except sit back and enjoy it while I can. Anyway, we need a bit of extra help just at the moment.

And there she is, right outside my door. I can't sit there. I go out again to see how she's getting on.

'Found you a coffee mug, have they?' I say. 'Shown you the powder-room, etcetera?'

'No, we're being absolutely beastly to her,' cries Jacqui. 'We're pulling her pigtails and no one's speaking to her. Isn't that right, Hilary, my sweet?'

You got to laugh, really. Jacqui's worse about her than what I am — she's fussing away over her like an old mother

hen. So are all the rest of them – they think she's wonderful!
It's not just me – they're all running out every five minutes
to have a look at her!

'All right, Hilary?' says Shireen, putting her head out of
her glass box, lovely big smile.

'Yes, thank you,' says Hilary. Getting quite good at smiling herself, with all this practice.

Liz hovers in and out of the library, grinning away. 'Anything I can do?' she says, meaning What's going on, has it
all come unstuck yet? But all Hilary does is shake her head
and smile.

'Like this at the Home Office, was it, Hilary?' I ask her.

Smiles. Shakes her head.

Even Kent comes out and joins in the fun. 'Hi,' he says,
and she nods and smiles, and he stands there for a bit
before he goes back. Well, there you go. No one's ever
heard Kent rabbiting on like that before. What, fancies his
chances, does he? The saucy bugger.

Now here's Kevin back for another go. 'Are you . . .?' he
starts.

'Yes, she is!' cries Jacqui. 'She's fine, she's wonderful!
Just leave her in peace, will you, my precious, and let her
get on with her work.'

Only no one's doing any work, because by now we're
conducting a minute-by-minute review of the battle on Saturday, and Hilary's the centre of it all once again.

'I suppose it's the same as in the Hassam case,' she says.
'The police panicked. I should never have believed what it
could be like, though!'

'Well, now you know,' says Liz.

'I've always known in theory. I often had to see the Police
Complaints Authority files. But to actually be on the receiving end of it . . .!'

We all feel lovely when she says this. Lovely about her, coming to see the way things really are. Lovely about our-selves, because we were right all the time. Here we are in heaven, or the nearest any of us is likely to get to it for a few years yet, and what the Bible says turns out to be true once again: there's more joy in heaven over one Hilary that repenteth than there is over nine-and-ninety Jacquis and Lizes. Unfair? Heartbreaking.

'But, honestly and truly, my sweetheart,' says Jacqui. 'When you started screaming at them like that! I could have died! "Pigs!" she goes!'

'You weren't there!' protests Liz. 'What – outside the window?'

'*I* was there!' says Kent. *More* words! We really got him going. What's this – love or battle?

'In the lane!' says Jacqui. 'When they were hitting Kevin, poor love.'

'"Pigs!" she's going.' Yet more from Kent. '"Pigs! Pigs!"'

Great state he's in. Great state we're all in. Even Shireen's come out of her booth. Standing there smiling away like Miss Bangladesh – and she wasn't even there! She don't know what we're talking about!

Only one who don't know where to look while all these medals are being pinned on her is Boadicea herself.

'Yes,' is all she says. 'Is Kevin all right?'

All she's thinking about – is Kevin all right? Isn't she lovely? And it's lovely to have her here, where we can all see how lovely she is.

'I'm reasonably . . .' says Kevin.

'He's fine,' says Jacqui. 'Aren't you, my sweet.'

'Well, I'm reasonably . . .'

I put my arm round Kevin. I'd like to put it round Hilary, but Kevin's better than no one.

'It's the poor old cat what Kev was inside of that got the pasting,' I tell them. 'Poor beast must have a real sore head. Wherever its head is. Because I get to the nick – there's Kev – is he feeling sorry for himself? Not a bit of it. He's playing hell with the buggers. No charges preferred, and no head neither, because they knocked it off and they don't know where it is, and he won't go home without it. "I'm not leaving without my head," he's telling them.'

'Anyway,' says Kevin. 'I'm reasonably ...'

'"Pigs!"' says Kent. He can't stop laughing. '"Pigs!"'

'Then,' I tell them, 'she went and got the idea *I* was a copper! I won't repeat what she said to *me*!'

'Why, what was it?' smiles Shireen.

'"Dash" and "damn",' I tell her. 'And even worse things.'

No, I think just possibly everything's going to be OK. It's all going to work out after all.

'I'll tell you what, though,' I say. 'We didn't half get some coverage out of it! More seconds of screen-time on Saturday night and more column-inches on Sunday than any demo this campaign has yet organized. Thank you, one and all. And bags more to come on Thursday, if only some of us would pull our fingers out and get it organized.'

Because the truth is we got a nice story going here with the Chorleywood Nine. Something we can really get our teeth into. Better for us, to be honest, than Hassam was. All out in the open, that's why. We know where we are. We know what the photo opportunities are going to be, and when.

'Anyway,' says Kevin, 'I'm reasonably ... well acquainted with the kind of sentiments that the officers concerned were expressing, even if not with the precise form that the expression on this occasion took.'

Whatever that may mean. That's why he can't get the words out – because they're all a yard long. But I'll tell you what we are in here this morning – we're a happy family. We all come through the war together, we all done well. Lovely new arrival in our midst, to complete the family circle. What a turn-up, when you think what it was like in here last week. Everyone at everyone else's throat. Can't even remember now what it was all about . . . Oh, yes, I can.

This very desk, where Hilary's now installed – that's what it was about. Bit funny seeing her sitting at it now, and Jacqui moving all her stuff up to make room for her, happy as a lark to be sharing it. What – I get some sort of kick out of it, do I? Not at all. There's just nowhere else to put her. Anyway, if you got a problem on your hands then there's only one place for it – out in the open. If I can't keep them apart then I'll keep them together, that's my instinct. I'll keep them under each other's eye all day.

What I'm most frightened of, tell you the truth, is that Special Branch are suddenly going to come waltzing in through that door. They been before – I didn't turn a hair. 'Previous convictions?' I told them. 'You don't even need to look on your computer. They're all here in our press release.' Yes, but that was before we had Hilary to worry about. That's why I keep running out of my office – make sure she's still there. Here I go now . . .

'All right? Good. Just checking.'

And that's why I'm so full of fun and games – because she still is there.

Anyway, calm down. *They* don't know she sent us anything, and if I got anything to do with it they never will. They certainly don't know she's here. No one knows that.

Jingle, jingle. Door handle! Out I run . . .

It's not the Bill – it's Roy. Shireen's yattering away to him, but he's not listening, because he just seen Hilary sitting there. 'Hello,' he's saying, in a kind of blank voice, like someone who's walked into the bank and found it's a fish shop. Should have told him – never thought about it. 'Oh, hello,' says Hilary just as blankly, like someone who didn't think it would be the rent collector at the door, only it is. All right, I *shouldn't* have told him.

'What are you . . .?' says Roy. He runs his hand through his hair. Doing here, I think he's trying to say, only it's the usual problem – he can't think without his head being under his little tea-cosy.

'She's working here, my love,' says Jacqui. 'We've taken her on.'

'Oh, I see,' he says, only he don't.

Silence.

'So it wasn't Hilary you was looking for?' I say, to help him out, because I don't think these two have got all that much more to say to each other.

'No,' he says. 'No . . . no . . .'

'What – Shireen? Jacqui? Me?'

'Well . . .'

Me. I knew it. I hold the door of my office open for him. He comes in and closes it behind him.

'Yes,' I say. 'I don't want old solicitors and I don't want solicitors with potatoes in their mouths – I want nice clean-looking young men who play soccer on Saturday and I want nice clean-looking young girls who go jogging – the kind of people who can talk to the telly on the steps of the court afterwards and everyone'll think they're normal human beings.'

'Oh, yes . . .' he says.

'Isn't that what you come in to discuss? Arrangements for

Thursday? Plus no doubt I'll be getting a summons in due course myself as organizer.'

He's not thinking about the Public Order Act, though.

'I don't understand,' he says. 'I go round – she won't see me. I ring up – she puts the phone down. Now I walk in here, and . . . I mean, listen, Terry – what's going on?'

I take my time, because I don't know quite where to start.

'You should have come to our little demo on Saturday,' I tell him.

He waves his hand. His heart's breaking, and they bring him demos. 'You know my feelings about that,' he says.

'I do,' I say. 'But do you know hers?'

'What do you mean?'

'She come to the demo.'

He stares at me. He frowns. If he don't do no better than this defending me the old judge'll have me back downstairs and doing a five stretch before he's got a word out.

'Hilary?' he says. All right, give him his due – he got there in the end.

'Hilary,' I say, 'that's the one.'

'Demonstrated against the Permanent Under-Secretary?'

'Told him he was a pig. Shouted at him in his own home. "Pig!" she said. Her word, not mine. So I said, "Come and work for us."'

'But . . .'

'She did work for them, yes. But she don't no more. Things change, old son, things change.'

And I look straight at him. Not just in my usual way, but in a special way that says Mark my words, because they got the answer to the mystery in them. Best I can do. I'm not going to go spelling it out for him. *He's* got feelings – *I* got feelings. I'm a human being, not a speak-your-weight machine. Frank – yes. Frankenstein – no. Moderation in all things.

I think he's beginning to get there, anyway. He looks at me for a bit, then he gets up sharpish, and goes out into the main office.

'So what grounds did you give?' he says to Hilary.

'What?'

'In your letter of resignation.'

He looks at her. She looks at me. Jacqui looks at him. Liz looks at Jacqui. What are we all thinking?

'Conscience,' says Hilary.

'Ah,' says Roy. And off he goes, without another word.

I know what *I'm* thinking. All that lovely golden glass – it's as fragile as soap bubbles. Anyone breathes and it'll be in pieces all over the floor.

15

'What's the matter, Liz, my sweetheart?' demands Jacqui, the third time I put my head out of the library. 'You're being an absolute jack-in-the-box this morning!'

I just shake my head and smile and try to stop worrying. We're *all* back in our own little boxes, that's the trouble. It's Tuesday – we've only got two days to get everything set up for Watford. So I'm in the library, drafting letters and phoning all our supporters; Kevin and Kent are shut away behind their glass doing all the mail-outs to the branches; Shireen's nothing but a headset and a smile and flashing red light; Terry's out all day doing interviews and having meetings with lawyers. Which leaves the two of them, Jacqui and Hilary, alone together in the main office, face to face across the desk.

I simply don't know what to do for the best. Even if I don't put my head outside I've still got the library door open as usual, and every time I look up from my desk I catch a glimpse of them sitting there. Working together, consulting together. Hilary asking Jacqui where everything is and how things are done, Jacqui telling her, calling Hilary her sweet and her precious and her love. They don't know. The only one who knows is me. I'm the one who has to keep the secret. I'm the one who must stop the words bursting out, must keep watch over every implication and inflection.

Or put an end to the situation once and for all. Tell them.

No! That can never be right! Can it?

Or at any rate help them to work it out for themselves. Give them some little hint . . .

I try to put it out of my mind. Once or twice I go to close the door so I don't have to see them, but they both look up at me as I stand there with my hand on it, and I think, They'll wonder why I suddenly want the door closed – they'll guess – they'll know. So I simply smile at them and leave it.

And they're not just working together – they're talking. Or at any rate Jacqui's talking. Telling Hilary all kinds of things about the office, about herself – things that don't need to be said at all. Suddenly she's got someone to listen to her, and she's being terribly knowing and confiding, when all the time she doesn't know one of the two crucial things about the world she's living in, and she's not confiding the other. I can't hear most of the words, just those over-emphatic swoops and swirls. 'You wouldn't *believe* . . . absolutely *wonderful* . . . absolutely *ghastly* . . . *total* nightmare . . .' She's got an audience, and her voice is flinging itself all over the room in front of it like an old-fashioned dance act. 'And then there's Shireen,' she says, '*sweet* girl, *sweet* smile – but I *have* to say . . . Whereas Kevin, poor lamb, nice boy, *not* his fault, *but* . . .' And what she's saying about them I can't catch, because as soon as she's mentioned their names she drops her voice. 'And as for *Liz* . . .' she starts, and I strain my ears not to hear the rest. I hope she's saying something really unforgivable about me, because this whole situation is my fault.

203

Isn't it? I saw Hilary looking at Terry when Chrissie brought her to that charity show six months or more ago. And then when Chrissie told me she thought there was something going on between her and Roy I had a strange feeling in my bones that it wasn't really Roy she was after. But I said nothing. I simply waited for it all to unfold.

Well, what could I have done? It was nothing to do with me! It's not for me to poke my nose in and mind other people's business for them!

I even told lies to stop Jacqui finding out. So it *was* something to do with me. I *was* minding other people's business for them.

Yes, because I didn't want anyone to be upset. I wanted to make everything all right.

Or did I secretly want to see what would happen? Did I want to watch it all going horribly forward, and be the only one who understood what was happening?

No one sees the evil things I do. I don't myself! I watch my hands working so hard to make everything neat and tidy on top of the table – I never see my foot moving underneath it to kick away the legs.

Anyway, they know about each other. They must do! They both know, and they're simply concealing it, like two opposing powers who know each other's secrets but never admit they do. This is even more horrible!

Or does Jacqui half-know? Does she have some tiny niggling anxiety she can't quite place? She's perfectly well aware of what Terry's like, after all – she's had trouble enough with him before. Is this why she's being quite so confiding? And what does Hilary think as she listens to all this? I can't hear her voice. Is she saying nothing? Is Jacqui's tone beginning to make her feel just a little uneasy?

What's Jacqui telling her now? I take my work across to the shelves behind the door. . .

Yes, it's nothing to do with raising money for the legal costs at Watford, which is what they're supposed to be doing today. It's nothing to do with the office at all. '. . . so Poops said to me, "Now, come on, Mums . . ."' Her daughter. Her home life. And that, naturally, means talking about Terry. So Hilary's going to find out about Jacqui soon enough – Jacqui's simply going to tell her.

'Now, you know what *Terry's* like . . .' I hear. 'So Terry said . . . but Terry, wretched man . . . so I said to Terry, "Listen, Terry . . ."' Each time I hear the word I feel that awful kind of tense buzzy feeling in my ears that you get when some child's playing with a balloon, and you're just waiting for it to burst. If Jacqui doesn't know about Hilary then there's no earthly reason for her not to talk about their life together. Any moment she's going to say something about him that will make Hilary realize.

Here she goes. 'Now, there are some things that Terry simply will not eat . . .' She's on to their domestic arrangements . . . And there's a sudden silence. Hilary is taking in the implications of what Jacqui has just said. Now Hilary's voice is saying something in its turn. I can't catch the tone of it. I can guess the sense of it, though. 'You do realize, don't you,' she's saying, 'that Terry and I . . .?'

She's stopped. There is an even more terrible silence. Jacqui's sitting stunned in her turn. Isn't she? I can't bear it! I put my head round the door and look at something in the main office – the door, the window, Shireen's booth – anything but Jacqui and Hilary. I'm grinning, I know I'm grinning, but I can't stop. Jacqui and Hilary have both looked up from their work.

'I wish you'd tell us what it is that's eating you, my darling,' says Jacqui.

'Oh, sorry,' I say. 'I just . . . Nothing . . .'

205

Back I go. And now they're talking about me again. Or rather, carefully not talking. Hilary's glancing at Jacqui, to see what she makes of this strange incursion. She's going to guess simply from the look on my face!

But no. Jacqui's smiling back and shaking her head, to assure her that my eccentricities are merely one of the amusing features of life in the office. Far from revealing the abyss between them I'm driving them closer and closer together, ever further out over the frail bridge that spans it!

And off we go again. 'I said to Terry just last night . . .' Here it comes, here it comes! Not listening! Buzzy buzzy ears. Keep turning over the pages of newspapers and making a noise. Hum something to myself, I don't know what, I'm making it up . . .

'Liz, my precious . . .'

What? I swing round. Jacqui's standing in the doorway.

'Happy in your work?' she says. 'Lovely, my sweet! I've never heard you singing before.'

'Oh . . .' I say. I can't think of anything else. I can't look at her.

'The papers on all our old court cases, my love,' she says. 'Where do you keep them? We're going to do a mail-out listing all the defendants in the past and what happened to them. One of Hilary's ideas. Terrific brainbox, that girl! I don't know how we ever managed without her.'

I get the files out and look through them, though she could perfectly well do it herself. She comes over and stands beside me, glancing back at the door. She wants to talk about Hilary! My hands move blindly through the papers in the file – I can't see what they're doing.

'Do borrow her, my sweet!' she murmurs.

What? I glance round at her. Her eyes are shining.

'I don't want to monopolize her,' she says. 'I told Terry

she could work for both of us. He wouldn't have taken her on otherwise. I had a terrible time persuading him!'

She persuaded Terry . . .? We're all willing this! It's not just me – we're all rushing the ship forward on to the rocks!

I know what she's like, with her eyes shining, and this excitement in her voice. She's like a woman in love.

I'm grinning again. I can feel the strain of it in my face.

'What?' she says. 'What is it, my sweet? You *are* in a funny mood today!'

Actually I've stopped grinning. I've got a hold on myself. 'Jacqui . . .' I say. I'm going to tell her. I've got to. It's my responsibility.

But she's not listening – she's balanced herself on her heel and she's revolving herself like a merry-go-round, as foolishly and unselfconsciously as a child.

'I think we're all in rather a state, as a matter of fact,' she's saying. 'I've never heard Kevin get so many words out all at once before. It's having a new arrival in the family.'

I shut my eyes. I've burned my boats. Now!

'Jacqui . . .' I say.

She's laughing. 'I don't know what you're doing with that file, my precious! You're just stirring it around like a pudding.'

'Jacqui . . .'

'Come on – give it to me. I'll get Hilary to do it . . . What's the matter, my sweet? You look most peculiar. Nothing wrong, is there?'

I shake my head. I've got my eyes open, I think. I'm grinning again.

Jacqui puts her head back round the door to me as she goes out with the file.

'And Terry *adores* her!' she whispers.

*

After the first few days I feel as if I'd spent all my working life in this place. Those bleak public service offices at Queen Anne's Gate have receded into some far-off grey time like childhood. Those bleak clever people have faded into pale smiling ghosts on the edge of an unhappy dream. Their very names have a strange emptiness and unreality. Tony Fail. Michael Orton. Penelope Wass . . . Queen Anne's Gate itself . . . Even Stephen Hollis, who always treated me with such kindness . . . They're as uninhabited as abandoned houses. Even that overhanging black cliff of decision that I climbed, with that terrible gulf of impossibility yawning beneath it, sucking me down, has vanished behind me, like the landscape flattening behind you as you climb a mountain.

I don't even know what's happened to the photocopies I posted. Is Terry going to use them, now I've resigned? The Hassam case has been somewhat overtaken by subsequent events. The papers are full of articles about the rights and wrongs of demonstrating against Civil Servants. Terry's out all day doing broadcasts and interviews. In the office the late Mr Hassam now has to share our reserves of indignation and practical concern with our own nine martyrs.

Terry says nothing about the photocopies, and I'm not clear whether anyone else here knows about them. Somewhere, presumably, they still exist, but in some kind of limbo, like the life I've left, just another bit of the past that has simply slipped away into the mist. How strange! Or how strange that it once mattered so much. The whole perspective has changed. I see it all from here now, not there. This is my home – this shabby muddled room, this rattle of the door handle every time someone comes in, these coffee mugs waiting to be washed, this dull good work, these dull good people, these silly touching my-sweets and my-loves, these little kindnesses, these endless poppings in and poppings out.

'Would you sit in for me a moment, Hilary?' This is Shireen, popping out, all good heart and smiles. 'Anything I can get you in the shops?'

'It's just . . .' This is Kevin, coming back from lunch, dragging something out of his ancient haversack, and laying it on the desk in front of me. 'It's just . . .' Something very roughly done up in a sheet of flowered gift-wrapping.

'It's just . . .' says Kevin. A present, yes. I'm very touched. Jacqui's smiling indulgently from the other side of the desk as I begin to unwrap it. Liz has popped out of the library to see what's going on.

'It's just . . .' says Kevin.

'A box of chocolate mints, yes, I can see.' I feel tears pricking. 'That's lovely! Thank you, Kevin.'

Ribald laughter. This is Kent, who's seen what's going on through the window of the copying-room, and who's popped round to join in.

'What? What?' This is Liz, popping in from the library at the sound of Kent's laughter, all anxious smiles and darting eyes.

'It's just . . .' says Kevin.

'All right, my sweet,' says Jacqui, like a mother shooing a child away from company before he outstays his welcome. 'Well done. Now leave her to eat them in peace.'

'It's just . . .' says Kevin.

'Come on,' says Kent, dragging Kevin forcibly back to-wards the copying-room, like an embarrassed elder brother. 'She don't want you hanging round all day.'

'. . . something to mitigate the shortcomings of the office coffee,' says Kevin, as he disappears.

'I think you've made a tiny bit of a conquest there, my love,' says Jacqui.

Which is just what she *would* say. Yes, Jacqui. There was

certainly no one like *her* at Queen Anne's Gate. I suppose I
should be maddened by her. I suppose I should find it like
sitting in the hairdresser's and having to listen to the radio
non-stop. She's like a weird combination of a disc jockey
and a soap opera – except that it's all done in this strange
archaic voice. But this is life! This is the way people are in
the great wide world outside the Council estates of Reading
and the colleges of Oxford and the austere high-minded
offices of Queen Anne's Gate!

We eat our lunch at our desk – I the sandwiches brought
in by Kent and one of the chocolate mints donated by
Kevin, she her special high-fibre health bars – and on and
on she goes. Everything she says is simultaneously outland-
ish and banal. It's like Religious Knowledge at school, that
didn't mean anything very much because you didn't have to
take an exam in it. I half-listen, half bored and half soothed.
Actually I could do an exam in Jacqui, now I come to think
of it. I know everything about her life and world. I'd happily
tackle a question on the relations between Poops and Pippy
– I'm even fairly certain now which of them is the daughter
and which of them is the pony. I could explain the shifting
balance of power between Bicky and Scrumps, in the face of
the perceived common threat from Moo. I might attempt
short notes on Mrs Turrell and Mr Shirley, not to mention
the little man in Virginia Water who looks after her lawn-
mower and the little woman in Bracknell who cleans her
upholstery – perhaps even a long answer on Jibs and Lalla,
with particular regard to the influence of Buddhist teaching
on patterns of consumer spending. I could do a special
paper on her ex-husband, and the contents of his secret
drawer.

The only thing I'm not certain about is her present domestic arrangements. 'We', she says sometimes. 'Us . . .

our . . .' Who is the other component, or components, of these plurals? Her daughter, possibly, or the whole domestic menagerie – perhaps merely the lingering syntactic ghost of her ex-husband. I have a shadowy picture, though, of some other person besides. A man-friend of some sort, I think, and one who comes and goes in a rather mysterious and not entirely satisfactory way. Not someone who shares much of the life she leads with her daughter and friends, I get the feeling, or even with Scrumps and Moo and the rest of them. Someone else's husband, perhaps. Or someone not quite suitable. Half her age, or the wrong class. The man from the local garage – the television repairman. A mystery, like the Holy Ghost in Religious Knowledge. From the hurried way in which Miss Tilt referred to it I knew it was not something I could ask about without mutual embarrassment. I feel rather the same about the third person in Jacqui's trinity. Once or twice she seems to be on the verge of confiding in me. 'I was just thinking last night,' she says suddenly, out of nowhere, lowering her voice, 'what absolutely peculiar creatures men are.' I wait. From her tone there is plainly more to come; we are about to move from the general to the particular. She looks at me speculatively for a moment, and evidently decides that I won't understand. Her voice returns to its normal level. 'Take Scrumps, for example,' she says, 'although I'm not sure he counts as a man because he's been *done* . . .'

And what do I tell her about myself? Anything she wants to know. Or, at any rate, anything she asks me about. What she really wants to know, I think, ever since she witnessed our curious confrontation in the office, is what my relations are with Roy. If she asked me I'd tell her. But she doesn't. She doesn't want to probe, only to offer me opportunities to confide.

211

'Is Roy keen on pets?' she asks. I could take the hint, and tell her about his feelings for the human creatures in his life, such as me, and about my lack of feelings for him. But I don't. 'I think his parents keep a goat,' I tell her.

'It must be a tiny bit intimidating,' she says, 'having rows with a lawyer.'

And I give her the same rueful smile I once gave Jane Syce-Hill.

What I ought to say is Look, Jacqui, you're asking the wrong questions! You've misunderstood the situation entirely. Not Roy, Jacqui! Never was! Never could have been! For heaven's sake, Jacqui – just look at him! How could it have been Roy?

Someone else, Jacqui, I should tell her. Someone you know. Someone you love and admire yourself. Someone we've talked about. Someone not fifteen feet from where we're sitting. Someone I couldn't possibly *not* be in love with.

Good God, Jacqui, I should scream at her, doesn't it shine out of me like light out of the sun? You *must* have thought it curious that I never talk to him, that I never talk about him. That I never look at him – that I don't so much as turn my head when he comes out of his office. You can't have thought I wasn't aware of his presence! Everything in the room is crackling with the charge between us! You must have wondered why I'm so careful to leave promptly at six o'clock every evening – before you, before Liz, often before Shireen – why I never hang around till after you've all gone, why I never seize the opportunity to stay and do the extra work I long to get on with. 'Good-night, Terry,' I call. 'Good-night, Hilary,' says Terry. 'Good-night, Liz, good-night, Jacqui.' 'Good-night, my sweet!' you call. Five, six, seven good-nights every night – and it never occurred to you that this was a demonstration, that I was underlining five, six, seven times a night my intention not to find myself here alone with him?

No? You mean, you really can't guess what happens when I walk out of that door each evening? That I go home to Kentish Town and move round my flat all evening in a kind of trance? That I come back at ten o'clock, stumble over Tina and Donna, and let myself into the office with the keys you can see I have in my bag here. That I lie naked and waiting inside the sleeping-bag on the camp-bed in his office until he comes in from the Pic or the Aerodrome or Mr Muggs? That I stay till seven, on the camp-bed, with him on the mattress on the floor beside me, half-awake, conscious at every moment of his harsh hairy skin beneath the hand I leave trailing down upon him? That at seven I wake, and lie with him again, and step over Tina and Donna, and go home to Kentish Town, and shower, or dream of showering, and breakfast, or dream of breakfasting, and come back in at ten, just after you and Liz? That it's only the end of my first week here, and that already we have a life as settled as the solar system? That I sit here all day in a kind of waking sleep? That all these my-sweets and my-loves, all these poppings in and poppings out, these stories of Bicky and Moo, of secret drawers and loaded revolvers, come to me from another world, as strange and familiar as dreams?

But she doesn't guess, and I say nothing. I smile my rueful smile, and let her feel sorry for the difficulties I'm having with Roy.

Liz knows something, I imagine, from the way she keeps nervously running in to find out what's going on, but then trying not to look and see. What will I do if she says something to Jacqui, and Jacqui asks me a direct question? Supposing she looks straight at me and says, quite simply: 'Are you in love, my sweet?'

Well, I'll tell her! As simply as she asked me. 'Yes,' I'll say.

And what will I do if she smiles and says, quite straightforwardly: 'And who are you in love with, my precious?'

I'll tell her that, too! I'll say his name. As straightforwardly as she asked me.

'Terry,' I'll say. 'Terry. Terry! *Terry*! TERRY!'

But she won't ask.

Why not? She won't ask because she doesn't want to hear the answer. She doesn't want to hear the answer because she knows what it would be.

I understand that. She has her own feelings about Terry, after all. She was his first disciple, as she made haste to inform me almost as soon as I walked through the door. She still sees him as a kind of father, I think, and she wants to keep him to herself. I respect her wishes.

She has feelings about me, too. Giving me a job here was her idea, as she made equal haste to inform me as soon as I arrived to start it. I'm another of her pets, a Bicky who doesn't need to be taken out for walks, a Moo who doesn't claw the upholstery. No, I'm more than that – I'm one of her creations – a kind of second daughter, to stand in for poor Poops while she's away at school.

Naturally she doesn't want to be told that she has been by-passed – that her father and her daughter have linked hands directly. She is even providing me with a little humorous attachment of her own as an alternative. I remember the way she looked when she told me I'd made a conquest of Kevin. She wasn't being arch – she was laying out a suitable dress for me to wear, demure and touching, whimsical and sexless, to spare us all difficulty.

I'll wear it, too. I'm wearing it already. I have little private talks with Kevin when no one else is around. I know two things about him that no one else does: what his passion in life is, and what he carries round in that greasy old haversack of his, apart from his sandwiches and his presents for me. It's books. And what they're all about is the fighter aircraft of the First World War. I'll go to the bookshops in Charing Cross Road one of these lunch-hours and get him a present of my own.

I suppose Jacqui will be forced to recognize how things stand between us all sooner or later. If it isn't tomorrow it will be next week. That doesn't disturb me at all, though, because tomorrow and next week don't exist. There's only today, and then today again, and then another today.

But I realize, now I come to think about it, that I don't say everything myself. I don't tell Jacqui about Kevin's books. I don't even tell Terry. I don't tell him, for that matter, about Scrumps and Moo – I don't ask him what's so unmentionable about Jacqui's man-friend.

Why not? Because I don't like to. They all have their feelings. Including Terry. He has his loyalty towards his oldest disciple. If he knows things about her that I don't then he must be allowed to keep them to himself.

Even in heaven, I am coming to see, every file has its own security classification. Even OPEN is just a shade closed. This is my conclusion as the week goes by.

Today, and then today again, and then another today . . . Today is Wednesday, and we're ringing round making sure there is transport for all our witnesses and supporters. Today is Thursday, and even Jacqui scarcely has time to talk, because we are running the office between us while Terry and Liz are out at Watford for the hearings. Today is Friday, and there's nothing left for us to do, since all our defendants were discharged or bound over, but sit in the office feeling flat, and trying to catch up on the week's routine. Chorleywood has slipped away into the past, like everything else, leaving nothing behind it except a file of cuttings. And me.

Now even Friday is finished. Kent and Kevin have gone, and once again it's coming up to six o'clock. 'Well . . .' I say, and I stretch, I sigh, I go to the lavatory, and I collect up my things. I have come to the end of the first working week of my new life.

'Off, then, are you, my sweet?' says Jacqui, taking my point as always.

'Unless there's anything else . . .?' I say. I first said that on Wednesday. I said it again on Thursday, and now I'm saying it on Friday. I can see myself saying it again on Monday, and on Tuesday, and on all the other todays until the end of time. One week, and already the rest of my life has taken shape, like the chick within the egg.

'No, no,' says Jacqui, smiling. She's got the desk in front of her covered in what look like accounts, but she's busy being mother smiling over the chores as daughter goes out dancing. 'Off you go. So lovely having you in the office, my precious.'

'So lovely being here,' I say, all smiles as well. And the loveliest thing of all is knowing that in a few hours from now I shall be back here waiting for Terry. And then . . . I don't know, we haven't talked about it . . . but the weekend together. It's enveloped in a shimmering mist of indeterminacy, too delicious even to be thought about.

I put my head round the library door.

'Good-night, Liz!'

'Oh – good-night, then!'

I look into Terry's office. He's on the phone.

'Good-night, Terry!'

'Hang on a moment, Steve,' says Terry into the phone. He

puts his hand over the receiver and moves his head upwards a centimetre or two. He means come a little further into the room so that he can say something.

'Been meaning to tell you, Hil,' he says quietly. 'Got to make a little trip tonight. Be away over the weekend. See you Monday. All right?'

He gives me a little smile and takes his hand off the receiver. 'Sorry about that, Steve . . .'

I can't take in what he's said. I cross the main office towards the door with no feelings left inside my body, not sure whether I'm alive or dead.

'Good-night, my precious!'

Oh, yes. 'Good-night, Jacqui.'

'Good-night, Hilary!' This is Shireen, smiling, and tidying things away inside the switch.

'Good-night, Shireen.'

'Have an absolutely super weekend,' says Jacqui.

I walk down the stairs. Did he say *Monday*? I don't think I knew there was even a name to designate a time so distant.

16

Half six, and I'm good and knackered. I put my phone down for the last time and have a listen to what's going on in the office. Silence. Nothing. Right – stick my head out of the bunker. Yes, perfect peace, they all gone home. No one left but Jacqui, still struggling with bills and columns of figures. I wish I knew why she won't use the software.

Still, that's the least of my worries.

'All right?' I say. What I mean is Come on, old girl, get your boots on, or we're not going to get to Sunningdale till midnight. I mean a bit more than that on top, only she don't know it. I mean She hasn't said nothing to put ideas in your head, then? You haven't said nothing to her to get her jumping to conclusions?

She yawns and closes up her folders. 'All right,' she says, and goes off to the lav.

And I think, from the way she says it, all right is what we are. Also all right, I think, was how Hilary took it when I told her about going away for the weekend. Been worrying about that – I could see a spot of trouble coming up there. But no, she took it good as gold. No fuss, no questions. Just nodded, and left it at that. Well, she knows I didn't drop out of nowhere. She knows I must have had a life before last weekend, and it didn't just stop and go away because she turned up. Same as Jacqui knows I got my life going on in London during the week, when she's down there in Sunningdale with the dogs. And what they also both know is that they don't want to know too much about it.

I never thought we'd get through the first week, tell you the truth. We have, though. We done it. And if we done one week we can do two. If we do two we can live forever.

The toilet flushes, and back she comes, pulling her coat on.

'All right?' I ask her again, I don't know why. Double-checking. Don't overdo it, Terry!

She nods. We're still all right. I go and have a slash myself. I can't help seeing some dodgy-looking devil in the mirror, also taking a slash and also thinking to himself, I don't believe it! We got through the week and we got away with it! We take a good look at each other, this dodgy devil and me, while we're at the basin afterwards, both giving our faces a bit of a splash, having a bit of a blow and a snort together. We're taking a rather more sober view of things, I notice, now we got to look each other in the eye. We can't get away with it forever, we both know that. We're not barmy. But then again, forever's still some time off. We'll surely manage to work something out before we get to forever.

Jacqui's standing in the main office, waiting to go, and watching me as I pull my overcoat on. Looking very thoughtful, she is, and I know what she's doing – she's working herself up to say something important. So I'm afraid it's not so all right, after all. I think we got to forever already.

OK – I better get in first. Say anything, don't matter what it is, just get it said before she says it herself.

'Listen,' I hear myself telling her. 'About Hilary . . .'

219

Oh, no. What am I going to say? I've no idea at all.

Never find out, neither, because Jacqui's giving me a little frown. What? She nods at the library. 'Night, Liz, my love!' she calls. And out pops Liz. Oh, I see, she's still here.

'Good-night, Jacqui,' says Liz, grinning away, looking at the floor and the window and the ceiling. 'Good-night, Terry. I'll lock up.'

Old Liz has sussed something, hasn't she, as usual, though I don't know how and I don't know how much. But I don't get a chance to think about it. I don't get a chance to find out what I was going to say about Hilary, for that matter, because as soon as we're out on the stairs, with the old door handle jingling behind us, Jacqui's saying it herself.

'Hilary, yes,' she says. She's lowering her voice, because we're going down the stairs, towards Jaypro's and Inter-Galactic, but by the sound of it she just can't hold it in no longer. 'I was just going to say. You know what she's doing every time she gets half a chance?'

Here we go, then. On the stairs, though! Well, why not? No worse than anywhere else.

'What's she doing, then?' I say.

'She's writing some sort of report for us about the way the Home Office works. I had a look when she was out of the room today. Terry, listen – she's putting in everyone's names – all the people she used to work with. She's saying what part they all played in the Hassam thing. She's even putting in the numbers of their extensions! Did you know about this?'

'No,' I say. I didn't, neither.

'Well, you're going to have to be very firm with her, Terry, and tell her you won't even read it. Because if you start ringing these people up . . .'

'Ringing them up?'

'Terry, my darling, I know exactly how your mind works! If you get hold of something like this you won't be able to resist, will you. I *still* don't know what you're going to do with all that stuff she sent us in the post. I know you think you're going to use it somehow . . .'

'Yes, well, don't worry, then . . .'

'Yes, but I can't *help* worrying, because, Terry, if we did anything that got her into trouble . . .'

We've stopped halfway down the stairs, and she's looking at me very close, with her hand on my arm. Jaypro's just above us, InterGalactic just below us, and she's still talking in not much more than a whisper, though there's no sign of life from either door.

'Honestly, Terry, she's scarcely more than a child. I look at her and I think, My God – Poops!'

'Now listen, my love,' I say, urging her on down a few more steps. *I'm* talking in a whisper, too – though I think this is more because I don't much want to hear what I'm saying myself. I don't know where I am in all this lot. 'I'm not going to do anything to make life difficult for her. I feel just the same as what you do . . .'

'Yes, but she's in a very strange state, Terry! I think she's probably had some truly ghastly bust-up with Roy – she obviously hadn't even told him she was working here! I've tried to get her to talk about it, but she absolutely won't . . . I haven't told her about *us*, by the way.'

We've stopped again, and she's giving me another good staring at. We're outside Parchak & Partners by this time.

'No,' I say. 'Don't go rushing at her.'

'I just feel a bit . . . I don't know . . . awkward about it. Do you know what I mean?'

'She's probably guessed, anyway,' I say. 'No need to go ramming it down her throat.'

221

'It's just that I can still remember the way Poops reacted when you first came out to Sunningdale. I don't think children want to know too much about what their parents get up to.'

Children? Parents? She's got all this nonsense into her bones, hasn't she, like a fever – she's as mixed up as what I am. I'm holding the street door open, waiting for her to go through. But she just stands there looking at me, and suddenly it all comes out in a rush.

'I expect she's a bit soft on you herself, you see, my darling,' she says. 'She's terribly careful never to look at you. Haven't you noticed? Well, even Poops has a funny thing about her father, I'm perfectly well aware of that, though she'd die rather than admit it to me. Anyway, all the girls still go a bit woozy when they see you, as you well know – and of course they do, because you're a very attractive man, and you're more than that, you're a great man, and everyone can feel it, and don't you forget it, and don't you take advantage of it, either.'

I don't know what to say to this. Specially since I just realized Tina's gazing up at me from her box in the darkness of the doorway, also waiting to hear what's coming next. Even Donna's listening for once. Mouth open – not so much as scratching her sores.

Jacqui turns to go in a great hurry, now she's said her piece, and walks slap into them.

'That's right, pet, you tell him!' says Tina.

Jacqui's stumbling about in a mass of cardboard and sleeping-bag, and she don't know where to look nor what to say.

'Don't worry,' says Tina. 'We wasn't listening, was we, Donna?'

I don't know where to look nor what to say, neither. And

that's another night I'm not giving this pair nothing just in case anyone gets the wrong idea.

Jacqui and me haven't gone more than ten yards up the street, though, when she turns back, and opens her bag. Tenner each, I can hear the snap of the notes.

'Funny old state *you're* in, my love, never mind Hilary,' I say when she comes back. And she is, she's all pleased with herself – she's glad they overheard all that lot. She laughs and takes my arm, which she hasn't done for a long time.

'I've always wished we'd had a child of our own,' she says softly. 'You know that.'

Yes, I do know that. I don't know much else, though. All getting a bit deep for me, this.

This is it – the Bella Napoli, though I didn't notice the name when I was here with Terry. What I recognize is the red check tablecloths, since I spent so much time then looking at the one in front of me.

'I must be psychic!' says the cocky little man inside as I come through the door. I'd forgotten him, too. 'I knew you'd be back! Look – I got the same table for you, love! Kept it specially! This one, wasn't it?'

I think it was, yes, but it's free simply because all the tables are free. It's still only quarter to seven, and the shaded lights over the tables are creating an intimacy which is so far achingly unoccupied. I have a sudden recollection of Terry's hand coming across these red checks, and his great broken-nailed thumb rubbing very softly against mine. It was stupid to come here, I realize that immediately, but I don't know anywhere else to eat in this part of London.

'Just the two of you, is it, love?' says the proprietor as I sit down, and he removes two of the four place-settings, which seems to gather the desolation a little closer around me.

'Just the one.'

'Oh, no! All on your own tonight? Oh, dear!' And one of the two remaining settings vanishes, like the last guest at an unsuccessful party. As long as he doesn't ask me about Terry!

'Where's Terry, then?' he says. This is the only reason he remembers me, because I was with Terry.

'I don't know.'

'I don't like the sound of that, love!'

I should be back in my flat. I don't know why I'm not. I started out. I walked up John Adam Street and Villiers Street when I left the office, heading for the Underground at Charing Cross, as I have every night this week. But my feet walked straight past it. They didn't want to get back to Kentish Town quite so soon, I imagine, when there were still sixty hours to kill before I could come back again. They walked me on to Leicester Square station, to use up a little of the time, then on again to Tottenham Court Road, to use up a little more. But at Tottenham Court Road they swung me away from the Northern Line, possibly because there now seemed to be alarmingly few stations left before Kentish Town, and headed me all the way across Soho towards Piccadilly Circus, then immediately back again past Leicester Square to Covent Garden. The next thing I knew they were walking me in here, and this little man was advancing on me through the wretched wastes of check tablecloth with his knowing grin, as if he'd been expecting me all the time.

Now he's back, and he's bringing me a tumbler filled with bright red liquid.

'Oh, no,' I say, 'I didn't . . . I don't . . .'

'On the house, love! Can't have you sitting there looking like that, it's bad for business.'

I suppose it's a kindly gesture, but it makes me feel even

worse. I can scarcely trust my voice as I order a chicken salad. The drink sits, untouched and reproachful, in the middle of the empty tablecloth. It smells like cough mixture, and the most desolate days of my childhood, and there's something about its fearful bright redness that makes me think of the heart's own blood, which in turn makes me think of . . . nothing, because that's what I'm sitting here thinking of, nothing at all. Except the feeling of that great rough thumb on mine.

The chicken salad arrives. 'I've given you a few chips as well,' murmurs the proprietor conspiratorially.

I sit looking at it for a long time before I can bring myself to take a few mouthfuls. Then my throat definitively closes, and I sit there with my uneaten food and my undrunk drink in front of me, from time to time picking up the remains of the breadsticks and breaking them into ever-shorter lengths. The proprietor stands behind the bar with nothing to do, being very careful not to watch me out of the corner of his eye in case I realize he's worried about me. He's tactfully taken off the tape of Neapolitan love-songs for fear they should reduce me to tears, and put on something quietly classical instead, which may sound more neutral to him but which is speaking to me of destiny and sadness and the heart's own blood . . . If I do succumb, I know, he'll be over here in seconds, even though he's not watching, and he'll be offering me a box of tissues.

Kind man, kind man . . . It's all this *kindness* in the world that's the worst thing of all. This is what's swollen my throat up so painfully.

But I'm not going to cry. There's nothing to cry about! I don't know what's happening to me! So Terry's gone away for the weekend. Why shouldn't he? I don't own him! I hope he has a wonderful time. He's got his life to lead.

Yes, and I've got mine! I've got plenty of things to be getting on with!

I straighten up, and instantly the proprietor is watching me. 'The bill, please.' And when it comes it's lying beneath two chocolate mints, two amaretti, and an artificial flower from the vase beside the cash register. But I'm no longer in danger; my mind's made up. I don't have to go home – I can go back to the office and work. It's the perfect opportunity to make a bit of progress at last with my report on how decisions were made in my old department.

'Next time there'll be two of you,' says the proprietor, squeezing my arm and ushering me to the door. 'Tell Terry – if he comes back here without you I'll kill him. I'll spill the spaghetti sauce down his shirt.'

What I'm thinking about, though, as I cross the Strand, isn't Terry at all – it's the decision-making process at the Home Office, and my own role in it. Strange how one's brain jams, then suddenly breaks free and begins to work with great clarity. I can see now how I knew fairly precisely, just as all of us in the department did, the kind of reservations and disagreements that could properly be expressed, and the rather more fundamental ones that could not. What I have come to recognize since I left is the existence of a third class of thoughts which were even more at odds with the prevailing philosophy, and which one could not formulate even to oneself – until they so to speak formulated themselves in the shape of unpremeditated and violent action. As I go back down Whitchurch Street I have a sudden picture of the same system re-establishing itself inside my head with respect to OPEN. Sooner or later I shall have to present suggestions for reforming the running of the Campaign. Already I know the kind of criticisms which I shall be able to make, and the kind which I shall have to keep to myself. Is a third level already beginning to develop, I'm wondering now, too deep inside me for me yet to perceive, which will one day come bursting forth in an eruption as violent and unforeseen as the last one . . .?

But before I can pursue this thought I become aware of a strange noise coming out of the darkness ahead of me. I stop. Yes – it's emerging from our own doorway . . . People singing . . . Oh, I see – Tina and Donna. But *singing*? I've never heard them singing before. I can't quite catch the words. It's something about being together and loving forever, and riding the freeway of dreams, and they're singing with a quiet, passionate intensity, in artificial American voices as devotional as the ecclesiastical tones of a clergyman. At the sight of me the song trails away, and they offer me the bottle they seem to be sharing.

'Never mind, pet,' says Tina. 'They're all the same. Fuck you and forget you.'

I decline the bottle. It's a rather expensive-looking sweet liqueur, with only a drop left in the bottom. I suppose they're both fairly drunk. Rather a change from their usual cans of Coke – I can't imagine where they got their hands on that much money. Not from Terry, I hope.

I pick my way between them and unlock the door. A soft Birmingham voice I've never heard before whispers next to my knee. It's Donna, the one who never speaks.

'You've always got us, pet,' she says.

More kindness! I feel reduced to the verge of tears all over again as I go up the dreary staircase, past the depressing doorways of the various hopeless enterprises that have washed up here. Even Tina feels sorry for me! Even *Donna*! And without knowing that I've any special reason to feel sorry for myself!

But I'm not going to give way. I'm going to work. I was

thinking some rather interesting thought about it as I came down the street. I try to remember what it was as I put my key into the door of our own office. But all I can think is that for some strange reason the key won't turn . . . Funny . . .

Then I realize there's a faint crack of light round the edge of the door.

Of course. The key won't turn because the door's unlocked already . . .

He's here!

I can't help laughing. It was a misunderstanding! A joke! A test! A dream!

The old brass handle shines and jingles like a toy shop bell as I shove the door open and go bursting in.

'You . . . *devil*!' I joyously, inadequately cry.

The only light in the room is from the shaded lamp on Jacqui's desk, and the green glow of the computer screen beside it. In the green shadows beyond the light, scrambling desperately to her feet at my entry, grinning with terror, eyes everywhere, chair tumbling over behind her and Jacqui's papers scattering out of her hands, is Liz.

A devil, yes. That's what I must look like to her, with Jacqui's papers in my hands, and this terrible grin on my face lit from below by the green glow of the screen.

I look at the papers sliding out of my hands – the screen – the door – anything except Hilary. Hilary looks at the desk – the floor – the papers – anything except me. Neither of us can get a word out for surprise. Neither of us can get a face on for embarrassment. Me at having been caught among Jacqui's things. Her at having caught me.

A devil. I know perfectly well she didn't mean me. I know perfectly well who she did mean. But it's me the

words landed on, and she's right – a devil is what I am. I'm
the devil who conjured her into this office in the first place.
I'm the devil who conjured her back here tonight, I don't
know how, to catch me green-handed.

'I didn't realize . . .' she manages at last.

'I didn't think . . .' I contrive in my turn.

'I thought . . .'

'I didn't know . . .'

She tries not to watch me as I go scrambling guiltily after
the fugitive papers.

'I was just going to catch up with a bit of work . . .' she
says.

'Yes,' I say, 'I was just . . . well . . . just . . .'

'Please . . . You don't . . . I don't . . .'

You don't have to explain, she means. I don't want to
know what you were doing.

But if that's what she thinks then I *do* have to explain.
Yes, I'm going to have to be the green grinning devil who
tells her the truth about this place. Except I won't. I'll just
tell her enough to let her work it out for herself. I'll just
explain why I've got Jacqui's handiwork all round me. She
may be a fool emotionally, but she's certainly not one intel-
lectually – she'll see the implications at once.

In which case, I won't – I'll say nothing at all. But I can't
say nothing at all! Not while she's sitting down in her place
on the other side of the desk, getting her files out, and not
being able to see what's written on them for the awkward-
ness of having me opposite her, up to the elbows in green
guilt.

'It's the newsletter,' I explain. 'She won't use the spell-
checker.'

I'm looking at the screen, settling to the work again.
Hilary's looking at me. Spelling! That's taken her by

surprise. I can't imagine what she thought I was doing, but she certainly hadn't thought of *that*.

'I don't know why not,' I say. 'And she hates anyone else looking at what she's done – I always have to go through everything when she's not here. It's so silly – she knows perfectly well I do it. People are funny, aren't they.'

I laugh. She doesn't. I look across at her. She looks away. She doesn't believe me.

'It can't go out like this,' I explain gently. 'Do you want to see?'

She shakes her head. All right. I work on in silence for a moment.

'This is her appeal for funds,' I say. 'Listen: "Come on all you affulent types . . ."'

I laugh. She doesn't. Not very nice, she's thinking, to laugh at Jacqui's little disability. But then she doesn't have to cope with it. Anyway, I'm not laughing at Jacqui. 'It's the word,' I explain '*Affulent* . . . I can just see them, all our affulent supporters in the local branches. At one of those lunch meetings that Terry has to go and talk to, probably. Somehow affable and flatulent at the same time, sort of burping benevolence.'

I can't help laughing, but I know I'm going too far now. I can hear that hard edge I get in my voice sometimes. Enough, enough. Let her think out the implications for herself.

'No commas, either – I think she's got something against them.'

I can't help just adding that last remark, because Hilary can have no idea from where she's sitting what a page of text with no commas in it looks like . . . And, oh, no, this is a classic!

'"Let's make next month's appeal figures a real *ban-asa* . . ."' I read out. '"Bonanza", I suppose. I had a wild picture of some sort of specially squashy banana.'

'You mean she's dyslexic?' asks Hilary. She's listening! And she's frowning. She's beginning to wonder why Terry employs a woman who's dyslexic to edit the Campaign's newsletter.

'Or *disexic*,' I tell her. 'That's what she said in one of her editorials. "Hold on to your seats chaps the poor old Ed's a raging disexic."'

I shouldn't have told her about that one. That was strictly for my private amusement. But now I've started I can't stop! I didn't know it was all bottled up inside me like this. But it's not surprising really, because there's never been anyone in the office I could say it to before now ... And, yes, she's smiling a little! I daren't look at her – I can simply feel it. *Disexic*. She likes it. I can feel the atmosphere in the room beginning to change.

'It's the same with the accounts,' I tell her. 'She won't use the spread-sheet, I don't know why. It makes Terry so cross! She does them all by hand, on little bits of paper. Then she takes them off to one of her *little men* down in Sunningdale. She's told you about her *little men*? It's like Snow White and the Seven Dwarfs! Anyway, her little man lays them out and makes them look all right – I don't know how – she never lets anyone else see them – certainly not me – I don't think even Terry – she keeps them under lock and key ...'

I pull at the drawer in front of me to demonstrate, and yes, it's locked. I look at Hilary to make sure she's taken this in. I think she's taken everything in. She's deep in thought!

'She's got some mysterious friend down in Sunningdale, too,' says Hilary. 'She never mentions him by name – never even refers to him directly ...'

Oh, no! She's going to get there! Well, *I'm* not going to

say anything! Not so much as a look or a gesture will she get from me! I don't know what my face is doing, though . . . Quick! Something to distract us both!

Wire coat-hanger, glinting on the hook behind the door. This is what I was grinning about all the time. I fetch it, and hold it up meaningfully for Hilary to see. She frowns. She's intrigued, yes, but she can't follow my line of thought.

'Haven't you ever picked a lock?' I ask.

I laugh. She doesn't. But she doesn't say anything, either. Just watches while I get on with it. Things are changing in here!

I can feel the bent end of the wire turn inside the lock with a kind of scrapy clunk. That's it! I look at Hilary. She's still watching, still saying nothing. We're doing this together.

I gently slide the drawer open . . . I don't like doing this, to tell the truth. I hate looking in someone else's things! I can feel my heart beating painfully, and the grin twisting up my face. I want to run out of the room, or else plunge my hands into this great private pudding up to the elbows. I don't know which is more confused, me or the contents of the drawer!

The first thing I pull out is a child's painting of a face. Blobs of poster paint for eyes and nose, a lopsided line for a mouth, a hoop of bright yellow for the hair, and underneath, printed in an adult hand, 'My Mummy'. I hold it up for Hilary to see. She gives a tiny smile. I'm grinning away like mad, I know. Aren't we horrible?

Then postcards, with messages from darling Poops at various ages. 'I'm having a brill time,' I read out. 'The food is yucky. Inez was sick in Fiona's ski boot. We all hate the French.' At least the child can spell simple words. What else? Two odd gloves . . . a Snoopy pencil-sharpener . . . a

miniature silver shoe off a wedding cake . . . four old pennies
. . . It's all rather pathetic.

'No loaded revolvers in this one,' I remark. Hilary looks
surprised. 'Oh, she tells everyone,' I say.

And inextricably mixed up with all this personal muddle
are receipts and unpaid accounts for stationery and the
office electricity, for printing, for the hire of halls . . . VAT
invoices . . . old-fashioned account books . . . I silently pass
a stack of stuff across to Hilary, and we both gorge like
schoolgirls.

'*Subs . . . covs . . .*' reads out Hilary. 'Subscriptions? Cov-
enants? There doesn't seem to be very much money coming
in . . .'

I've found the payroll, or what passes for it, in a spiral-
bound shorthand book. 'Do you want to see it?' I ask
Hilary. I can't help laughing. 'Do you want to know what
we all earn?'

But she makes an awkward little face, and shakes her
head. She really doesn't want to. Isn't it funny what different
people are shy about? 'Terry gets the same as me,' I tell her,
whether she wants to know or not. 'I don't know how he
eats in all those restaurants . . . She doesn't seem to pay
herself anything at all, but then I suppose she doesn't need
to . . . What about you? You're not down. They are paying
you, aren't they?'

'I don't know. We haven't really talked about it.'

She's blushing!

'You must have it out with them,' I say. 'They'll simply
make use of you if they get half a chance.'

But she's gazing at one dog-end of paper after another.
She can't believe her eyes. 'I don't really understand how
the Campaign operates,' she says. 'I suppose this accountant
of hers manages to somehow . . . I don't know . . .'

What's this? Some sort of expenses book ... And in a moment I'm laughing all over again. 'Oh, I see how he does it!' I say, but then stop myself. She won't want to hear anything about Terry ... Though I think she's too absorbed in the wonders of Jacqui's bookkeeping to notice.

And she's thinking. Illiterate and innumerate, she's thinking – and she's worked here ever since the Campaign started, doing the newsletter and the books. Why? she's wondering. What could possibly be the explanation ...?

She pushes all the papers back to me, and catches my eye. She's going to ask me if it's true! 'Jacqui and Terry ...' she's going to begin, not knowing quite how to put it. And I don't know quite how I'm going to reply! I honestly have no idea what words will come out of my mouth!

But she says nothing. She doesn't ask me if it's true. And I know why not – because she's afraid I might tell her.

Her face is changing. Her nose is sharper. She's quite plain – I can't imagine what could possibly have attracted Terry. She just happened to be there, I suppose. She was a possibility that had to be tried. Isn't that what usually attracts men?

Poor love.

'Never mind,' I say. 'I'll make us some coffee.'

'Never mind ...' I shouldn't have said that, because now she knows I know what she's feeling. Or is that what I intended? And as I make the coffee I start wondering if I always meant her to come back and find me here. Is this why I stayed behind to check the newsletter tonight – because I knew Terry wouldn't be here on a Friday – because I guessed she'd trail back all forlorn, with nowhere else to go? Up to my old tricks again, was I, making everything nice and neat on top of the desk, kicking the legs away underneath?

But I never meant her to look as beaky-nosed and wretched as this! I didn't! I really didn't!

'Why don't we leave all this nonsense?' I say suddenly, switching the kettle off. 'It's too depressing! Why don't we go out and see a film?'

I don't know where this idea comes from. Where do any ideas come from? Out of some locked and muddled drawer at the back of one's mind, like the accounts. But it's plainly my responsibility to cheer her up a bit. And anyway it suddenly seems a very attractive prospect. She could come back to my place afterwards – we could have a glass of wine together, and a proper talk about things. How would she get home afterwards? – She wouldn't have to! Chrissie's fellow's wife has gone off to Paris with her mother for the weekend, so Chrissie's with him, and Hilary could have Chrissie's room!

We can sort all that out when we come to it, though.

'Oh, that's very kind,' she says. 'But I can't, I'm afraid. I've got to . . .'

Got to what? She can't think. I just wait and say nothing. I've already put the mugs back on the side table.

'All right,' she says. She gives a little bleak smile. I know what she's thinking: anything's better than nothing. But I laugh – I'm really feeling quite cheerful.

'After all,' I say, 'she told me to borrow you.'

I put all the accounts and the old gloves and the painting of My Mummy back into Jacqui's drawer. It was all in such confusion before that I can't imagine she's going to notice much difference.

'Isn't it funny,' I say to Hilary. 'She keeps all this mess inside her desk – but you should have seen her when she came in one morning and found someone had messed things up on top of it!'

I close the drawer and set to work with the coat-hanger to relock it. It's only then that I realize what I've just said. Oh, no! The things that slip out if you don't keep your mouth properly locked! Hilary's glanced away – I don't know whether she's made the connection or not.

The drawer's as bad as my mouth – I can't get it locked up again. Never mind – as long as I hide the remains of the coat-hanger she'll think she left it unlocked herself. Hilary watches without comment as I put the accusingly deformed wire in the waste-paper basket under some newspapers.

Then on second thoughts I take it out again.

'Better be on the safe side . . .' I say. I take it into the copying-room and put it in Kevin's waste-paper basket instead.

I give Hilary a grin. 'Aren't we awful?' I say. And off we go.

17

Monday – and it's one of *those* Mondays!

Jasna's right – I've got to get off this switch, I've got to start doing audio. It's driving me mad, this thing, buzzing away at me every two minutes . . . Hold on – here we go again . . .

'Hello, OPEN . . .' And I've got to be all nice and friendly as usual, just in case it's not what I think . . . But it *is* – I knew it was going to be – it's the millionth time this morning. It's just going scream scream scream at me, because it thinks I'm a fax machine, which I'm not, though I'm starting to wish I was.

And here's me thinking we'd be back to normal again after all the fun and games last week. But oh, no – on top of which there's a terrible atmosphere in the office. It's Jacqui again – she's having one of her days.

I don't know what happened – she came in all smiles. 'The doorway downstairs, my sweet!' she goes. Oh, no, I thought – I've forgotten about it again! Here's trouble! But on the contrary. 'A lovely start to the week to come in and find it absolutely and totally clear for once,' she says. 'I assume that was you and not them?' I thought, Shall I say? Then I thought, If you don't say anything you can't say anything wrong, and I just gave her a nice smile instead. 'Thank you, Shireen!' she goes. So that was a bit of luck.

But after that everything was all wrong. First it was something about a smell. 'It smells *different* in here,' she kept saying. 'Can't you smell it?' So we're all sniffing away. 'What's it like, Jacqui?' we go. 'I don't know,' she says. 'Different.' And she's all put out.

Then something else happened. What was it? Oh, I know – the paper plates. She found these paper plates under her desk. First thing I realize she's tapping on the glass, holding out these disgusting things with all bits of dried-up spaghetti on them.

'Shireen, my love, is this you?' she cries. 'It's no good taking the rubbish out of the doorway and hiding it under my desk! That's an absolutely cretinous thing to do!'

'Oh, no, Jacqui, how awful! It wasn't me, honestly! I expect it was the boys, wasn't it?'

So off she goes, waving the spaghetti about in everyone's faces, and it wasn't the boys, oh, no, of course it wasn't, not them, it wasn't anyone. And now there's some other trouble, I don't know what it is – I don't think it's the plates this time – but she's raging away in there. I slip my headset off for a moment. 'I know it's not *you*, my love,' she's saying to Hilary, 'but *no one* in this office will ever take any *responsibility* for anything, it absolutely *enrages* me.' And Hilary's giving her a really funny look. Well, naturally – she's never seen her like this before. I remember what a surprise *I* got the first time. They were as thick as thieves last week, those two – but then so were Jacqui and Liz once, so were Jacqui and Terry. She falls out with everyone, that woman, you can see her doing it, it's a shame. I put my headset back, because my buzzer's buzzing and my light's flashing away at me ... 'Hello, OPEN ...'

Scream scream scream . . . But, oh, dear, that look on Hilary's face! Oh, and here's Liz, putting her head out of the library to see what's going on, and she's smiling, but it's that funny sort of smile she's got, and all it does is get Jacqui more worked up still. Now Terry's come out of his office, perhaps he'll calm her down . . . But no – five seconds, and he's got a look on his face as well, I don't know what sort of look it's supposed to be. A funny look. They're all in a really funny state.

Oh, now it's my turn again! Get the glass slid back before she starts banging on it . . .

'Shireen, my sweet, there was a wire coat-hanger behind the door on Friday. Where is it?'

'A wire coat-hanger?' It that all it's about?

'Yes, someone's taken it. I need it, you see. To unblock the lavatory.'

'Oh, no!'

'I won't describe the state the room is in.'

'Oh, poor Jacqui, what a morning! But no, I haven't seen the coat-hanger. Have you asked the boys?'

And off she goes again. It doesn't *have* to be like this just because it's Monday morning! We had a lovely Monday last week! Everyone being all cheerful and friendly because Hilary had arrived, and we wanted her to see how nice it was here. Or they were for a start. Yes, until Roy came in. Then it all changed, and people got a bit funny. There always has to be somebody who spoils it. If it's not Jacqui it's someone else. Why are human beings like that? Why's there always got to be someone who's left out of things, who's spoiling everything for all the others?

Buzz buzz . . . 'Hello, OPEN . . .' Scream scream scream . . . Why does it have to scream? Why can't they make it talk? It could just say in a nice friendly voice, 'Hello, are

239

you a fax machine?' Then I could say, 'No, sorry, I'm not, I'm just a human being, so it's no good going on and on.'

On top of which it's the weather. Maybe that's what's making everyone so funny. It's freezing out this morning, and not much warmer inside. The first real touch of winter – they were saying on the radio this morning. I'm sitting here with a woolly on and my scarf round my neck, but I've still got a draught on my knees. None of the windows fit in this place! I don't know what another four months of this is going to be like . . .

Slam! Back goes the glass! Jacqui, crosser than ever. I wonder she didn't break it.

'Oh, well done!' I say, try and cheer her up. 'Where was it?'

Because she's found her coat-hanger and she's unbent it, and she's holding it up in the air like that man they had on telly the other night who could divine things – gold, vitamins, anything hidden in anything, and all with nothing but an old coat-hanger, it was incredible.

'Kevin had taken it,' she says. 'Listen, Shireen, my precious. Is it you who blocked the lavatory?'

'Not me, Jacqui, I haven't been in there.'

'Look, my love, I don't want to hold a court of inquiry, I don't want to blame anyone. I just want to find out what happened so we can stop it happening again.'

'Well, it wasn't me, Jacqui. It was probably just Kevin, you know what he's like.'

'Yes, but I've found what the trouble was, you see, my darling, and whatever Kevin gets up to in there I don't think he'd put a sanitary towel down the loo. Let alone two sanitary towels together.'

'Oh, Jacqui, no!'

It's terrible. I can feel my face burning, but I can't manage to say anything else, because I don't like talking about that sort of thing. So she just stands there looking at me, and she thinks I'm the one. It's so unfair! I don't want to talk about it, because that's not the way I was brought up, to talk about things like that. I could simply open up my handbag, for that matter, and show her it *couldn't* be me, because I've got completely different sort of things, but I'm not going to, because I don't see why I should, I wasn't brought up like that. I'd rather leave, I honestly would, because if it's not friendly here, what's the point?

So she just stands there, and I just sit here, and it's awful, we're going to be stuck like this forever.

'I think this is probably my fault.'

Jacqui looks round – I look round – it's Hilary. She's walking over from her desk, and her face has gone a funny kind of blotchy red colour. But Jacqui just smiles and kind of closes her eyes in irritation. She doesn't want her precious Hilary involved.

'I know it's nothing to do with you, my sweetheart,' she says. 'And you don't have to worry about Shireen. I'm not going to be angry with her. I just want to *know* so I can make sure it never happens again.'

'Those two girls downstairs in the doorway,' says Hilary. 'I said they could sleep in here last night.'

Oh, no! The funny smell – the paper plates – oh, *no*! Jacqui can't even speak, she's so surprised. She can't believe it. She's just staring at Hilary, and Hilary's just staring at her. Oh, and they were so thick together!

'I'm sorry,' says Hilary. 'I should have mentioned it before . . .'

'I'm sorry,' says Jacqui as well, but sorry's the last thing she is. 'I don't understand. Those two girls . . .?'

'They slept in here,' says Hilary. 'On the floor. There was a frost last night.'

'What are you saying, my love? You're not saying that you . . . *invited them in?*'

'I told them to be out before anyone arrived this morning.'

'My honey . . .' says Jacqui. She's smiling, but she's got her eyes closed as well, so you can see all that shiny blue eye-shadow she puts on them, I don't know why. 'My dear sweet girl . . .'

'I'm sorry,' says Hilary. 'I should have made sure they'd left the place tidy.'

Jacqui's still smiling. She's really, really cross!

'I know you've been working in this office for all of a *week*, my darling . . .' she says.

Oh, so bitter! And to Hilary, too!

'I'm sorry,' says Hilary, 'but there was no one here to consult, so I had to make a decision . . .'

'Yes, but I don't imagine you'd have invited people in off the street in your *last* place of employment!'

'But if you've got an organization that believes in openness . . .'

'No, my darling! No! No! No!'

'But we can't really keep our doors locked . . .'

'No! Listen to what I'm telling you! *No!*'

'But when there are people outside who may die . . .'

'*No!* Quite simply – *no!*'

Jacqui's eyes are closed again, and her head's sort of trembling. We've had rows here, yes, but we've never had one like this! It would have to be her precious Hilary who's put her foot in it. I suppose Jacqui's like this at home with that poor daughter of hers. And Hilary's all red in the face, too – she won't back down! The more Jacqui says No the more she tries to explain, and the more Hilary tries to explain the more Jacqui won't listen. 'No!' she says, working herself up more and more. 'I'm sorry! No! No! No!' Terry and Liz have both come running out of their rooms, and everyone's trying to talk at once. The boys are messing around in the copying-room – I don't know *what* they're doing, they're killing each other – and no one's even noticed except me – and now my buzzer's going . . . 'Hello, OPEN . . .' Scream scream scream . . .

'OK, end of argument,' Terry's saying when I take my headset off again. 'It's all over and done with and we don't need to go on about it because it's not going to happen again.'

It's not over and done with at all, though, because now Jacqui's off on some new track altogether.

'Last night?' she's saying. 'What do you mean, you let them in *last night*? Last night was Sunday!'

Yes! Right! I knew there was something funny about it! So did Liz, by the look of her – she doesn't know where to put herself.

'Never mind about that . . .' says Terry.

No, but what was she doing here? We all want to know!

'I came in,' says Hilary. 'I had some work to do.'

'Work? What work?'

'Just some work of my own.'

But all this does is set Jacqui off all over again!

'This is your thing about all your old friends, is it?' she says. 'Yes, I do know about it, my precious, because it was lying on your desk and I had a look. I *assume* it wasn't supposed to be anything private or secret, and if we're going to start going in for this kind of personal revelation thing then I think we need to have a little talk about the principles involved.'

'Fair enough,' says Terry. 'We got to get it thrashed out sooner or later. Why not now? It's going to take all morning, though, so let's get ourselves sat down before we start.'

Hilary sits down at her desk at once, good as gold. No chance of getting Jacqui into a chair, though, now she's in this state . . . Oh, I beg your pardon! She is – she's sitting down! I think we're getting back to earth.

'*And* you, Liz,' says Terry. 'You'll drive us all barmy twittering about like that.'

And even Liz sits down. Genius that man is!

'Right,' he says, pulling up a chair for himself. 'Let's have a proper discussion. Should Hilary grass her old mates or shouldn't she? I call on Hilary to speak first, tell us what *she* thinks she's up to. Go on, then, Hilary.'

But Hilary's got that terribly funny look on her face she had before.

'I wasn't here with *him*,' she says to Jacqui. 'As it happens. If that's what you're worrying about.'

What's all this?

'With Terry?' says Jacqui. 'I know you weren't. What do you mean?'

'I just thought that might be what was worrying you. But as it happens I was on my own. Terry wasn't here at all last night.'

'I know,' says Jacqui. But she's gone a bit quiet.

'Never mind all that,' says Terry. 'Just tell us about this report of yours, Hilary. Are you naming names . . .?'

But Jacqui's forgotten all about the report.

'Of course he wasn't here,' she says. 'Why should anyone think he was here?'

No, because he was at home with her in Sunningdale, we all know that. But thinking about whether he was here or not seems to have put all sorts of ideas into her head. She's got to her feet, and there's something funny about her face. It's not just her eyelids – her whole face is sort of blue and shiny.

'I'm going out for a walk,' she says quietly. 'I don't feel very well.'

And before anyone can move, the door's closing behind her and the handle's jingling.

'I'm sorry,' says Hilary to Terry, but he won't look at her.

'I'd better take her her coat,' he says, and now he's gone all quiet as well. 'She'll catch her death out there this morning.'

He gets her fur coat off the hook.

'Wait,' says Hilary. But already the door's closing behind him, and the handle's jingling, and now Hilary's dragging it open again, and it's jingling behind her as well. I don't know why they don't get that handle fixed, it's going to be right off one of these days.

I look at Liz. Is she going to go running after them as well? She just stands there, grinning at me, she doesn't know *what* she's going to do. Then, yes, *she's* off! Only when she opens the door, there's Terry and Hilary still standing outside, and Terry's saying, '. . . but I been ringing your number all weekend – I rang you seven times . . .' I can't hear any more because by then Liz has got the door shut on them again, and the handle's jingling, and she's giving me another grin.

Oh, dear. It's boring here, says my knowall sister, nothing ever happens.

And now what? Liz has gone over to Jacqui's desk, and she's rummaging around in Jacqui's handbag. She looks up and sees me watching her.

'Oh, sorry,' she says, taking her hands away quickly. 'I was just looking for her keys. I think she may have left her drawer unlocked . . .'

I give her a nice smile. I don't want to know what she's doing! I don't want to know anything about anything!

Buzz buzz . . . 'Hello, OPEN . . . Oh, hello, Mr Donaldson – I thought you were the fax . . .! Oh, no, your voice is quite different . . . No, I promise faithfully, I'll get them to call you the moment they come in . . . No, they're all out – there's only Liz . . . No, sorry – *she's* going out as well . . . Beg pardon . . .? All alone here – what, me? Yes, isn't it awful – but no, thank you, Mr Donaldson, I don't need anyone to keep me company – I'm perfectly happy being on my own . . .'

'What – them?' I go. 'That what you worrying about, Kevvy? They all gone out, you dumbo! No one going to see nothing – int no one there to see!'

Kills me, old Kev does. Got this picture out of his bag, so I know he wants to give me a flash of it. Only now he got the bag on top of it and his daft face buried in the bag and he's giggling away like a little girl.

'Come on, Kevvy, don't be an arsehole!'

What's he got under there? Hiding it away like that.

'What – not doing it with animals? Not dogs and that?'

Shaking his head, giggling away. He loves it, the dirty monkey!

'What – Jacqui? You scared of Jacqui? Look! There's no one out there, right? There's only Shireen!'

Daft bugger lifts his head off his bag and looks. So I grab hold of the mag. He lets go of the bag to hang on to the mag, and what do I do? Let go of the mag and whip the bag! Mag – bag – I don't mind. If we can't look at one, OK, we'll see what he got in the other.

So I'm halfway to the switch before he knows what's happened. I'm going to show Shireen! That'll get him going!

'Hey, Shireen! Kevin's got this picture of you in his bag with no clothes on!'

'No! No!' he goes, and I'm pissing myself, because I've jumped up on Jacqui's desk, and I'm waving the bag in the air, and he's flapping around my knees like an old newspaper.

'What?' I go. 'That one on the motorbike! You said it looked like Shireen!'

'I never . . .!' He's going mad! He's a crazy man! Look at him – whirling his daft arms around like a couple of old bog rolls! Half an hour ago Jacqui was giving him all kinds of grief because he'd stopped the toilet up and I don't know what else! He was dead pissed off! Now look at him! I can always cheer him up.

'She'll love it, Kev! She'll know you fancy her!'

'I don't . . . I don't . . .'

'You *don't* fancy her? Shireen, Kev don't fancy you no more!'

Because here she is – she come out of her little cubbyhole, and she's trying to stop Kev knocking all the things off Jacqui's desk – you never seen him in such a skedaddle!

'Look, will you two stop messing around!' she shouts – cause she's in a real skedaddle herself! I got them both going! I never seen nothing like it! It's really wicked!

'Get out of here, the pair of you!' she goes. 'I've had nothing but messing around ever since I came in this morning! I'm sick of it . . .! And that's her bag!'

Cause the silly bollocks has knocked Jacqui's handbag off the desk. There's money and lipsticks and I don't know what rolling everywhere.

'Oh, now you done it, Kevvy!' I go.

So him and Shireen dive after Jacqui's doodads – while I tip the stuff out of his haversack over their heads – and now there's bums and bazoombas tumbling around on top of everything else like pins in a bowling-alley.

Yes, and there's the mag he wouldn't let me see in the first place — he's only dropped it on the desk while he goes chasing after all the other stuff! We got there in the end, folks! Only trouble is I'm laughing so much I scarcely got the strength to bend down and pick it up.

'Oh, so this is why you was hiding it away, Kev!' I go. Cause it's dead wicked. She's across the desk, with this massive pair of bing-bongs dangling over a typewriter. And I know which desk old Kevvy's got in mind — I'm standing on it, right?

'No wonder you gone off Shireen!' I go. 'You got Hilary on the brain now, haven't you, you bad boy! So this is what you was up to with all them chocolates and that! One moment it's Here's a box of chocolates for you, Hilary. Next thing we know it's Down over the desk, darling!'

I'm going to die laughing, and old Kev's going to die of a climbing accident — he's only trying to climb up my leg, that's all! He's going after the mag like a monkey after a coconut!

Only he's not. All of a sudden he's just standing there looking the other way. Everything's gone dead quiet.

Right. Hilary and Liz. There they are. They're back.

Not saying nothing. Just looking. Hilary is. Just not looking, Liz.

Same as me, except I'm up here on the desk. No mag in my hands, no grin on my face, no thoughts in my head. Nothing.

'I can't . . .' I say. 'I can't . . .'

I can't explain. I can't get the words out.

'I don't . . . I don't . . .'

I don't see why I should have to feel like this. I don't understand why I should have to crawl humiliatingly among their legs, trying to collect up these . . . these entirely private and personal things of mine. I don't see why I should be scarcely able to breathe for the injustice of it, and scarcely able to see for these helpless tears of shame in my eyes.

I'm so angry at myself for feeling like this and for not being able to explain. I'm so angry at *them*, too, for coming in and seeing my things. They shouldn't have looked at them! There are a great many things in my life that people shouldn't look at, because it will upset them if they do, and it will upset me to know that they're upset. Why should *I* be the one to be humiliated if they choose to look?

Their legs are all around me, like the bars of a cage. Why should I have to see Shireen's feet kicking my things away out of sight under the desk? Liz's feet turning this way and that way, trying not to look? Hilary's feet planted there rigid and unblinking? Why should I have to gasp for my breath, and struggle with my tears, and knock my head against the bottom of the desk, and hear all these voices above my head pretending not to notice?

'Get off the desk, will you please, Kent.' This is Hilary's voice, and in a moment yet another pair of feet descends and joins the barricade around me.

'Just half a chance, that's all they need, and they're in here making trouble!' says Shireen's voice.

'Are these Jacqui's?' This is Liz, and now she's down here with me, not looking at me, pushing my things aside and collecting up compacts and pieces of broken mirror. 'Where are her keys? There should be some keys.'

'I told them!' says Shireen. 'I begged them!'

It's so unfair! I kneel up, holding my things. All I need now is my haversack. Then I shall simply get up, fetch my coat from the copying-room, and leave without another word to anyone. I refuse to go on working under these conditions.

'Thank you, Kevin,' says Hilary, as I look round for the haversack. And I discover that all the things I have collected up are simply being lifted out of my hands and taken away from me.

'These are yours, are they?' she says in a horrible quiet voice.

I look at her feet. They don't move. And nor will I!

'I won't . . .' I say.

I won't explain!

'I don't . . .'

I don't intend to apologize!

I keep my eyes fixed on her feet. Her feet go on pointing at me.

'I won't . . .' I say. 'I don't . . .'

'Just a moment, Kevin,' says Hilary. 'I'm talking to Kent.'

To Kent? I don't understand. I look up at her . . . She's holding my things out and she's gazing straight over the top of my head. At Kent.

'I said, these are your magazines, are they, Kent?'

What? I look at Kent. He's shrugging his shoulders. 'No,' he's saying.

'They're *not* yours?'

'No.'

No. Of course not. But there may be some confusion about this answer, because it's what Kent always says. It should perhaps be made clear to Hilary that on this occasion no means no.

'I think . . .' I say. I think, I am going to explain, that I should in the circumstances perhaps rescind my original decision to remain silent.

'So how did they come to be in your possession?' says Hilary.

Kent shrugs again. 'Don't know,' he says.

'I think . . .' I explain.

'You don't know? How do you mean, you don't know?'

'Just found them.'

'I think . . .'

'Just found them where?'

'Don't know.'

'In the office?'

'Don't know.'

'So whose are they, Kent? Shireen's, perhaps?'

'Don't know.'

'Mine? Liz's? Kevin's?'

Kent shrugs.

I think it says something for Kent that he is refusing so adamantly to implicate me. But I think I must now absolve him from the task and admit my share of the responsibility. I get to my feet and pull at Hilary's arm. 'I think . . .' I repeat very definitely.

'What is it, Kevin?' she says, turning to me. 'Oh, sorry, you want your things.'

She extracts two of the items and hands them to me. One is *The Sopwith Camel at War*, the other is *Notable Triplanes*.

'I take it these are yours,' she says. 'Now, Kent, I know Terry's out. I know I've only been working here for a week. But there are things wrong in this office that have got to be put right, so let's make a start with this. Let's all agree – no more harassment and no more bullying. Yes? So take this stuff away, Kent, and look at it in private, if that's the best you can manage, but don't ever bring anything like it into the office again.'

She throws it all down on the desk in front of Kent, and wipes her hands with a tissue.

No one says anything. No one moves. There's the same kind of awkward feeling as there is when I go on for too long trying to explain something.

'I'm sorry,' says Hilary. 'Now I know we've all got a lot of work to do . . .'

I glance at Liz. I'm almost certain she's looked inside my bag sometimes when I've been out of the room.

'I think . . .' I say.

'What?' says Hilary, rather impatiently, as if it's somehow become my fault once again that everyone is so discomposed.

'Oh,' I say. 'No. Nothing.'

I pick up my haversack and my aircraft studies, and return to the copying-room. I think, from the little smile Liz gave me, that she wants her spying to remain a secret between us. And there are occasions, I know, when I must learn to curb my persistence. This seems pre-eminently one of them – more especially now that the agitation of the door handle has alerted me, if no one else, to the appearance of Terry and Jacqui on the threshold, and the imminence of further scenes. The magazines, after all, are still lying there on the desk where Hilary threw them down. And there's Jacqui's handbag, on the floor behind the waste-paper basket. So is one of the magazines still, open at a particularly unfortunate page . . .

18

Easy enough marching out. Difficulty is marching back in again.

Up and down Embankment Gardens we been, Jacqui half a pace ahead, with a face like a snowman and her fur up round her ears, me half a pace behind, very sympathetic, no coat, balls dropping off. Nothing much I could do except be nice and reassuring, make her see the funny side of it.

'Which one is it you're worrying about?' I been asking her. 'Tina or Donna or Hilary? Or is it all three of them?'

No answer. Just a few gawkers turning round to see if it was me, which it was, which it always was when they turn round to see. Reach the end of the Gardens and come back up them again. Have another try.

'Anything you want to know, love – all you got to do is ask me and I'll tell you. That's the system we've always worked on.'

'I *don't* want to know!' she says, keeping her voice down in a rather noticeable sort of way that makes four or five more people turn round to see what's going on. 'All right? I simply *don't want to know*! Because *that's* the system we've always worked on. I'm just angry with myself for being made such a fool of. And when I see her sitting across the desk from me and virtually *telling* me . . .'

'Telling you what, love?'

'Nothing. I don't want to think about it! I just *don't want to think about it.*'

Two more people turning round. Oh, old Terry's having a few problems with the ladies, they're thinking. Very comic.

Wasn't me that got through to her finally. It was the same as what brought Tina and Donna inside in the first place – the cold. Back we come, over our nice clean doorway – and no little jokes from me on the subject, though I got one or two on the tip of my tongue – up past InterGalactic and Jaypro, her a couple of stairs ahead, me a couple of stairs behind, very respectful.

Now here we are, we're back, with the old door handle jingling behind us. Here we go. If we can just get through the next ten minutes we'll be all right. If we can just survive the coming back and the sitting down again . . . if I can just find a word or two to say as we come face to face with Hilary . . . if they can find a word or two more apiece . . .

What's going on, though? No one on the switch. The little light's flashing its heart out – no one's answering.

'Come on, Shireen!' I say, because there she is, standing by the desk. So's Hilary and Liz, so's Kent, and old Kevin's sloping hurriedly off back to the copying-room at the sight of me. OK – I'll have a go at them – this'll get us back in business. 'What's all this – the Christmas party?' I say while Jacqui's hanging up her coat. Only it's not the Christmas party, I can see that soon as I've said it, because no one's saying nothing – they're standing there in silence, and it's the kind of silence people stand around in when they've just discovered Grandma left it all to the cats' home.

'What?' I say. 'What's going on?'

'Nothing,' says Liz.

'Nothing,' says Hilary, and she takes a great armful of glossy magazines off the desk. Glossy magazines? I don't get it. Everyone standing round silently reading fashion mags together? Shouldn't have thought that kind of thing was much up Hilary's street. And as for Kent . . .

And as for Kent – she's giving them to him! They're Kent's magazines! He's wrapping his arms around them very carefully – you'd think he was being given the baby to hold for the first time. Even old Kevin's amazed at this. He's peering through the window of the copying-room with his mouth open. He's never seen anything like it.

'What . . .?' I say to Kent, but I don't even have to finish.

'Nothing,' says Kent.

'Nothing. Hear that, Jacqui? Nothing.'

Jacqui shrugs. She's not playing. Goes over to the table with the coffee things, pours some hot water out of the kettle into a mug, and puts her hands round it. Count her out. Never mind – *I* still want to find out a bit more about all this nothing that's been going on, I don't know why. Funny feeling in the room, that's all.

'Come back, Kent,' I say, because he's just bunking off back to the copying-room with his mags. 'There's something up, I know that. OK, Shireen, you tell us. And don't *you* say "nothing", or I'll knock your block off.'

She don't. She just looks down at the desk. There's something funny about her, too . . . I know what it is – she's not smiling.

'I don't want to work here any more,' she says.

Oh. Well, that's the way it goes. You're just in the middle of one crisis, when some other crisis altogether comes up out of nowhere and clobbers you. You're just bending down

255

to soothe this savage dog that wants to bite your ankle – and some horse leans over the wall and bites your bum.

But Shireen? I don't get it. She loves it here!

'Shireen . . .' I say, and suddenly it all comes tumbling out.

'I don't want to work in this kind of office!' she says. 'I don't want to get all upset! I don't want there to be everyone arguing, and everyone not speaking to everyone! I just want to know what I'm supposed to do, and get on and do it. You say, "We're talking about secret things, you mustn't listen." So all right – I don't listen. You say, "We're all going to be in trouble." All right – so we're all going to be in trouble! I don't mind! You tell me – I'll do it! I don't want people quarrelling, that's all! I want to come in and do my job and be nice and friendly to everyone, and keep everyone happy.'

And she goes across to get her coat.

'Now, listen, Shireen, my darling,' I say. 'I don't know what's been going on in here . . .'

'*I* don't know what's been going on!' cries Shireen. 'It used to be nice here, it used to be friendly. They said at the agency, "You'll like it, it's a very friendly office. It's not advertising or anything, it's only politics, but it's very friendly."'

I go and put my arm round her, very friendly, just like they told her. But she won't have it.

'I know people don't always agree,' she says. 'I know they've got sad things in their life. *I* don't always agree. *I've* got sad things in *my* life. But I don't go round telling everyone and spoiling things for them. If people can't get on I don't think they ought to argue and make trouble for everyone. I think they just ought to put on their coat and go.'

And, yes, she puts her coat on. Only I sit myself down nice and calm in Jacqui's chair and I raise my hand and take command of the situation.

'Hold on, Shireen. Not so fast. Let's get to the bottom of this. I want to know what happened.'

She just stands where she is and looks at the floor. All right – try Liz. 'What was it, Liz?'

But all I get from Liz is shrugs and grins and won't-look-at-mes.

'Hil?' I been a schoolteacher, remember.

'Just some rather silly horseplay,' she says.

'Oh,' I say, 'oh.' I got there. It's Kent. Right.

I can't imagine what devilry he's been committing with a pile of old magazines and I'm not going to ask, because if I don't ask him nothing he can't say 'nothing' back. I just look at him and wait. He shifts off his right foot on to his left. Off his left on to his right. I think all those mags he's holding are starting to weigh a bit heavy. I go on waiting. Done a bit of waiting when I was a schoolteacher.

Yes, and now his eyebrows are going up, which they do on those rare occasions when he's thinking. I suppose they're connected with his brain. I do believe he's going to say something.

'Don't want to work in that room no more,' he says.

Another little surprise.

'Oh,' I say, very calm, very reasonable. 'So why's that, then, Kent?'

'Don't want to work with *him* no more.'

'You don't want to work with Kevin? Why don't you want to work with Kevin?'

'Just don't.'

'Just don't. All right, Kent. So what you want me to say? Can't take Kevin out of there, can I, because what else can he do? Can't take you out, neither, because what else can you do?'

He shrugs, and mumbles something under his breath.

'What?'

'Go on the switch,' he says.

Go on the switch? Kent? He's got some cheek, I'll say that for him. Though I can't tell from the look on his face whether he's serious or whether he's just trying it on. Either way there's only one answer, and it's very short and simple.

'No,' I tell him.

He shuffles about, and mumbles to himself again.

'What?'

'It's flashing,' he says.

'Yes, and it's going to go on flashing, I'm afraid, Kent.'

'Where's my bag?' cries Jacqui suddenly.

'So why can't I go on it, then?' says Kent.

'Hold on, Kent,' I say. Why can't he go on the switch? I don't know what the answer to that is if he can't see it for himself. Where's Jacqui's bag? That one I can do, because it's down here on the floor behind the waste-paper basket. So let's give Jacqui her bag first. Right, that's one problem solved. Now, Kent . . .

Just a moment. I've picked up something else that was down there on the floor next to the bag. One of Kent's magazines. Only now I look at it . . .

Yes. I see. That's what it's all about. That's what Kent's hugging to himself.

I'll tell you something: I don't like that kind of muck. If I was in the Home Office I'd have it all seized and burnt. So, what, I'm suppressing things now, am I? In this case, yes. Not very consistent of me? OK, so it's not consistent. There's a limit to everyone's consistency. Everyone's? *Everyone's.*

'Kent,' I say, 'first of all drop all that garbage you're nursing in the bin. Right. Now. Listen, Kent . . .'

Don't get no further, though, because Jacqui's off again.

'Someone's been going through my bag!' she cries. 'All the things are mixed up and broken!'

'Your bag got knocked off the table,' says Hilary to Jacqui. 'We had to put everything back as best we could.'

'As soon as my back is turned!' cries Jacqui. 'I can't bear people touching my things!'

She's working herself up. She's not going to have a scene about Hilary so she's going to have a scene about the bag instead. But what I'm thinking about is the picture in this magazine I'm holding. Fellow with a girl down across a desk. Not referring to anyone we know, is it? I put it away in the drawer a bit sharpish before Jacqui sees it. She's got enough to be worrying about for one morning.

'Get away from my desk!' says Jacqui. She's turned on me now. 'Get away! Go on! Out! I want to get at my things!'

OK, OK . . . But before I'm halfway out of her chair she's already pushed in front of me and yanked at the drawer.

'Oh, *no*!' she cries – and she's yanked so hard that the whole drawer has come out and scattered stuff everywhere. 'It was *locked*! I left it *locked*! I keep it *locked*! Which of you did this? Which of you broke into my drawer?'

Oh, yes, her locked drawer. Bills and accounts, so far as I can see, and a painting by old Poops when she was little. Also the girl over the typewriter.

'Don't touch it!' she screams at me when I try to get it back, and pushes me out of the way. 'This was Kevin, wasn't it. The coat-hanger! He picked the lock!'

Kevin? What's all this about Kevin? But she's staring at

him in there on the other side of the glass, and she's got pure hatred written all over her face. She's going to go in there and kill him. And he's staring back, with something written all over his face, too, only I don't know what it is. It might be guilt. It might just be terror.

'It wasn't Kevin. It was me.'

What? Who's this? It's Hilary. Oh, no. She's looking straight at Jacqui, and she's got those red blotches of hers all over her face. She means it, I know that, but it isn't true, she's lying, she's trying to save Kevin's skin. I think. I hope.

'I did it on Friday evening,' she says. 'I wanted to see what you'd got in there. It was very stupid and very wrong of me. I shouldn't have done it. I'm sorry.'

Jacqui's staring at Hilary now, but I can't look at her face to see the expression on it. I can't look at Hilary, neither. Perhaps she isn't lying. Perhaps she done it. I don't know what goes on inside Hilary. All I can see is the two pictures side by side down there on the floor – the one that Poops did of her Mum when she was little, and the one of the girl bent over the typewriter. They shouldn't be together like that.

A second goes by. Another second. We all wait. What's Jacqui going to say to Hilary?

Nothing. She don't get the chance. Liz says it first.

'It was me, actually,' she says, and gives one of those little laughs of hers. 'And I put the coat-hanger in Kevin's waste-paper basket afterwards.'

'Well,' says Hilary, 'we did it together.'

Oh, I see. Together. She's not lying.

No, I *don't* see. Jacqui does, though. She kind of gives up. Sits down in her chair, puts her hand to her face, opens her eyes very wide. Both of them together, then, she's thinking. Both of them hate me.

She takes her hand away from her face. She's just seen the pictures. She bends very slowly down and picks them both up, Poops's painting and Kent's magazine, side by side.

Just stares at them. Can't take them in.

'It wasn't them that put that mag in the drawer,' I say. 'That was me.'

Comic, really, the way it's all worked out, the way it's all tied itself into one vast great knot. *I* can see it's comic, anyway. Jacqui can't, though. All she can see is the three of us ganged up together, going through her things, putting filth in them, laughing behind her back. The only thing to do is to keep nice and calm, and explain very slowly and very carefully, and who knows, maybe we'll get this rusty old aeroplane back on the ground again.

Only before I can open my mouth to get started – jingle jingle. The door's opening. We all turn to look. The outside world, that we'd all forgotten about, is coming into the room and stopping in amazement at the sight of us there, like the fellow in the fairy-story finding the palace where everyone was stopped dead in their tracks and covered in cobwebs.

No one speaks, for some reason. No one moves. They all just stare at me in silence as I put the typescript I'm carrying down on the desk in the midst of them. I feel as if I've walked into a tableau of the Cabinet at Madame Tussaud's – the only creature of flesh and blood in a roomful of wax figures locked in waxen debate.

'The Government Agencies report,' I say. 'At long last.'

'OK, Roy,' says Terry. 'Thanks.'

Very quiet and preoccupied. No jokes, no earthy wisdom. What's going on? Almost the entire staff seems to be assembled. I suppose a waxworks Cabinet meeting is almost exactly what it is – some admirably democratic discussion about the future of the Campaign, with everyone invited to put his views. Or everyone except me. No one's answering the telephone – they've fetched poor Shireen in from the switch to take part, though she can't so much as get anyone's name straight. They've even brought in one of the two lads from the copying-room. Well, I salute them. I'm a great believer in participatory democracy. Which is why I've been forced to take the step I have.

'Plus a personal letter,' I say, laying my letter of resignation down on top of the report.

Terry nods. I think from the expression on his face he can guess what it is. He must have seen it coming. He can't expect to organize disorderly demonstrations, then fail to consult me on an issue such as Hilary's employment, and still expect me to remain part of the organization. He knows what I think about his behaviour on a personal level; not that *that's* anything to do with my decision. He seems very phlegmatic about it. Well, perhaps they don't need me quite so much now they've secured the services of their new professional consultant. Who, I see, has come out in those curious red blotches I remember so well, and which I imagine now betoken embarrassment at the sight of me.

At least she's registered my presence. The rest of them have scarcely noticed me. What a cosy little world it is. It seems infinitely remote already, like the view down the wrong end of a telescope, or something in one's childhood. I can't quite remember now how I first became involved in it. I take a last look at Hilary, since I imagine that's why I've brought the report in personally. And I feel . . . yes, nothing. Almost nothing. Merely surprise that I ever did.

Well, arrangements change. We all move on. And I've left them rather a good report to remember me by.

'So,' I say. 'I'd better leave you to your labours. Good-
bye.'

'Cheers,' says Terry. Horrible usage. Liz grins. *She* knows
what's going on. She's always known. I see that now. She's
the real driving-force behind this organization.

The door handle rattles behind me. In all the time I was
working for them they never managed to put even *that*
small wrong to rights.

Jingle jingle, goes Roy, and the freeze-frame comes to life
again. What was I saying? Oh, yes. 'Not them that put that
muck in there, Jacqui. Me.'

Because they're still in her hands, the two pictures, and
she's still staring at them.

'Now, listen, love,' I say to her, because I think we all got
a bit of quiet explaining to do if we're ever going to get out
of this one. Only before I can think what to say Kent's
started up again.

'Why not?' he says.

Why not what? I don't know what he's talking about.

'Why can't I go on the switch?'

Oh, the switch. Forgotten all about the switch. The
world's moved on since then.

'Hold on, Kent,' I tell him with amazing politeness consid-
ering what I feel about his taste in reading matter. 'Let's
just get this other business sorted out first.'

I concentrate the entire force of my personality on Jacqui
again.

'Listen,' I say, very quietly, very reasonably, entirely truth-
fully, and even maybe just about believably. 'I don't know
nothing about picking the lock on your drawer. May have
been them – wasn't me. All I know is that I found that thing
lying on the floor just now. How it got there I have no idea,

though I can guess, and me and Kent are going to have a little private chat about that later. And I put it out of the way, first place that come to hand, so you wouldn't see it. OK?'

She's still looking at it.

'Why didn't you want me to see it?' she asks, and she's talking just as quietly and reasonably as me. Funny question, though. Hadn't expected that.

'Why didn't I want you to see it?' I go. 'Well, it's obvious . . .'

'Is it?' she says. 'Yes, I suppose it is. I suppose it's absolutely obvious. I don't know why I didn't think of it before. I just wonder why you did it on *my* desk instead of yours. I wonder if you know yourself. I wonder if you've even thought about it. There's something very twisted hidden away there, my sweet.'

'Now come on, love,' I say. 'I don't know what you're talking about.'

And I take hold of her by the back of her neck the way I sometimes do, to gently shake the nonsense out of her. But she won't have it. She just pushes me off like Shireen done before, and starts to pick the things off the floor. Right, so now what? Another little trip to Embankment Gardens, by the look of it. Only before I can get up to fetch her coat, Hilary's pitched in.

'Well, we *do* know what she means,' she says quietly, 'and it's true.'

Oh, dear. I knew she was going to go and say it, sooner or later. I knew that's where the whole system was eventually going to come unstuck.

Jacqui just glances at her, then starts very carefully rolling up Poops's painting, and looking for a rubber band to put round it.

'Hilary . . .' I say, just as quiet as her, just as nice and reasonable, we're all doing very well on the politeness front. Only I don't know what to say next in my nice quiet reasonable voice.

'But we've got to have it out sooner or later,' she says.

Sooner or later – exactly. But why does that always have to mean sooner? Why don't it sometimes mean later?

'Because it is rather absurd, isn't it,' says Hilary, still very quietly, as if they was ordinary sensible words she was laying out on the desk in front of us, and not little packets of dynamite. 'Here we are fighting against secret judgments and secret decisions – and all the time we're making secret judgments and decisions ourselves. We've got all kinds of secret understandings that no one ever mentions. You and Jacqui, for instance.'

Now she's looking at the floor. All the red blotches in her face have joined up until she's just one great big red blotch. Jacqui's all blue – Hilary's all red.

'OK, Hil. But I don't know whether this is all that much interest to Kent and Shireen and Liz . . .'

'Well, yes, I think it is,' says Hilary.

'I don't mind,' says Shireen. She's standing there with her coat on, waiting to go. Liz gives one of her laughs. Kent gazes at the little light flashing on the switch.

'I imagine they all know,' says Hilary. 'Or they all know something. But I think we should be told clearly what the arrangement is, so that we all know where we stand. It was very painful for me to be left to guess at it, and it's very difficult for me to accept.'

'Right. OK. Now . . .'

'But I'll try, I'll try. Only I think you ought to tell people clearly what the arrangement is between you and me, too. So that we all know where we stand on that. Particularly *her*! Because it must be even more difficult for her to accept than it is for me.'

I look at Jacqui. She's putting all the bits and pieces out of her drawer into her handbag.

'I know it's not easy to talk about this,' says Hilary, and I can see it isn't, because she's still looking at the floor, and she still puts me in mind of a pair of Victoria plums. 'It's not easy for any of us. But it's what you said, that first evening. You said we were making a city where all the houses had walls of golden glass. Transparent gold. Inside the houses people were living all kinds of different lives, with all kinds of different arrangements among themselves. Some very *comic* arrangements – that's what you said. But nothing hidden. Everything visible.'

A red face and a blue face – that's what's visible to me. Red face is looking at the floor, not meeting anyone's eye. Blue face is putting on her fur coat.

'This is the Book of Revelation?' says blue face. 'Yes, I've heard all the Revelation bit, all the heaven bit. So why don't you do it in front of us all? On the desk. Now. Why not? It's not quite high enough for comfort, I know that from my own experience, though I have to admit that was some years ago. You could perch yourself up on the files again, the way you did before. Or how about using the accounts? They're all yours now.'

And she throws all the paperwork that she had in her drawer down in front of Hilary.

She's going for good, then.

'You want to know how you got a job here?' she says to Hilary. 'Because I told Terry to give you one. You want to know why? Because I thought you were a kind of daughter. You want to know what he's going to be thinking when he's got you sitting up on the accounts? The same.'

Hilary looks at me. Just for a moment. Then she looks back at the floor. So do I.

'I don't know what Kent's making of all this,' I say. Can't think of anything else.

'Well, let's ask him,' says Jacqui. 'Everything open and above-board. Everything on display. What are your feelings about all this, Kent, my sweet?'

He shrugs. 'Want to go on the switch,' he says.

I don't know why, but I finally flip. Got through the whole minefield, step by step, inch by inch, and now for no reason at all I go up in smoke.

'No!' I yell at him, so loud and sudden he actually sways back on his heels. 'I told you! No!'

Right. I think I got through to him. Only now I started I can't stop.

'You want to know why not?' I say. 'OK, Kent, I'll tell you why not. Because you haven't got the brains. Because you haven't got the style. So you'll just have to go back in the copying-room with Kevin. And don't tell me you don't want to work with Kevin. Tell *him* – tell Kevin. Kevin . . .!'

And I'm out of my chair, I'm out of the room, I'm dragging Kevin in from next door, knocking envelopes out of his hands, banging him into tables and chairs. I got boiling molten metal running in my veins, and I don't care who knows it. Nothing hidden? Nothing hidden, then!

'In here, Kevin! Kent don't want to work with you no more, Kevin. Go on, Kent – why don't you want to work with him no more? Tell him!'

But Kent just gawps. His head's empty. He's out. He's away. So I'm going to bring him back and nail him down to the floor.

'I don't see how this is going to help,' says Hilary. Oh, don't she? So that's *her* nerve gone!

'Tell him!' I say to Kent.

'Don't take it out on Kevin!' says Jacqui. And there goes hers!

'Tell him!' I say, and I'm not taking it out on Kevin, I'm taking it out on Kent, making him say. I'm taking it out on all of them, making them listen.

Kent shrugs – and that's one shrug too many.

'OK, Kevin,' I say, 'I'll tell you why Kent don't want to work with you. He don't want to work with you because he don't like you. He don't like you because you can't talk properly and you can't walk properly and you can't do your proper share of the work. And he don't like being lumped together with you because that means we think he's just as useless as what you are. And he's right – that *is* what we think. OK, Kevin? OK, Kent?'

I let go of Kevin. I been holding him by the arm all this while – I never knew. And not a sound out of him from start to finish.

'OK, Jacqui? OK, Hilary?'

Hilary sits down in her chair. Jacqui buttons her coat.

'At least you'll get the newsletter properly spelled,' she says to Hilary. 'You have to keep writing to all the branch secretaries. They'll never send you anything otherwise.'

People take what you say, though, they twist it round, and then they throw it in your face. So now I've twisted it round again and thrown it right back where it come from.

'OK, Liz? OK, Shireen?'

Liz laughs. Shireen looks at her. That's it, folks – the show's over.

'I couldn't spell,' says Jacqui. 'But I did manage to make the books balance. Five years, and never a moment's trouble with the books.'

'Right,' I say. 'Anyone who's going – go. Anyone who's staying – back to work.'

Five years it took to put all this little lot together. One morning was all it needed to blow it apart.

19

'Hello, OPEN,' I say, for the fifteenth time. 'No, Terry's not here at the moment. Can I help . . .? Well, Jacqui doesn't work here any more, but perhaps I could . . .? No, I'm not Shireen – I'm Hilary . . . *Hilary* . . . Fairly new, yes . . . Shireen? Oh, she left, too . . . Sorry . . .? Oh, a field-day, yes – quite a field-day . . . All right, I'll tell him.'

And I scribble down the message in great haste, because I can see Kevin in the copying-room, struggling to lift a fresh case of stationery down from the top rack, and about to fall backwards off the chair he's standing on and crack his head against the machine if he goes on trying to do it by himself.

'Are you all right?' says Liz anxiously, when I get back from helping Kevin. She's sitting opposite me at Jacqui's desk, trying to fit the drawer back into its slot.

I don't know whether I'm all right or not. I feel as if the world around me were remote and unreal, audible only through the ringing in my ears after some great explosion. In any case I haven't really had time to think whether I'm all right or not. Between us Liz and I have got Jacqui's accounts sorted out from the rest of the confusion on the desk. Everything else has been put with Kent's magazines –

out on the street in a black bin-liner alongside the rest of the garbage. The bills and receipts and the exercise books full of muddled figures are spread out on the desk in front of me. I've obviously got to make some sense of them if I'm going to take control of our finances.

'I couldn't look,' says Liz. 'I mean when Terry finally went for them both. It was like being in a thunderstorm. I just wanted to put my head under the covers.'

The drawer still won't go back, I don't know why not, and as I watch Liz struggling with it what I'm thinking is that there must be other hiding-places in the office which we still haven't found. In one of them are two plain brown envelopes. I've kept quiet about them up till now, but I mustn't keep quiet any longer. They must be brought out, like everything else. Brought out into the open, openly discussed, made openly available.

'And you!' says Liz, laughing. 'You were so angry! You went a lovely deep red, like the wallpaper in that Indian restaurant we went to!'

But then she takes a look at the expression I've got on my face now. She stops laughing and puts the drawer down.

'Look, don't start feeling guilty!' she says. 'You were right to say all that! And it's a good thing she's gone – you know it is! She was useless. She just put everyone's back up ... What – Shireen and Kent? They'd have gone anyway, Hil, sooner or later. And they'll find other jobs perfectly easily. Well, Shireen will.'

But now the switchboard's buzzing again.

'Hello, OPEN ...' The only response is the scream and warble of a fax machine, as unanswerable and unignorable as the cry of a baby. I think this is the seventh time it's rung, and as soon as I switch it off the buzzer goes again. This time it's a voice, a man's voice. 'You're a naughty girl,' it says, in tones as blatant as the pictures in Kent's magazines, before I can collect myself and switch it off. 'You promised me faithfully! I'm going to come round there and put you over my knee and give you a good sound spanking . . .'

'Just some man making obscene suggestions,' I tell Liz, very shaken, as I sit down in front of the accounts again.

'Oh, no!' she says, biting her lip in sympathy. 'Pigs, aren't they, such pigs.'

Not senior Civil Servants, in this case. Men, I assume she means, though she is too tactful to be specific. But I'm still thinking about what this particular man said – 'promised me faithfully'. Perhaps it was simply a wrong number . . . Or not even a wrong number. Perhaps the sweet and smiling Shireen was living in some private world inside that glass booth as grotesque and pathetic as Kent's inside the copying-room.

'Listen,' says Liz, 'I expect now you'll have things to do next weekend . . .'

Will I? I suppose that's being decided somewhere not far away even as we speak. Somewhere between here and Waterloo station. He ran out after her again, just as he did before. Well, naturally. Something had to be said, something had to be arranged between them.

'I mean,' says Liz, looking everywhere but at me, 'I assume . . . well . . . you know . . .'

Yes, *I* assume . . . What do I assume? Well, that this time he'll at any rate tell me what the arrangement is. Won't he?

'But if you *do* ever want someone to talk to . . .' says Liz. 'Or somewhere to stay . . .'

And she's grinning away to herself again, intent upon the problems with the drawer. A curious thought has just come into my head. The first time I walked down Whitchurch

Street, looking for Terry ... It was Liz I thought I was coming to see. Or I think that's what I thought. For a moment I catch a glimpse of some quite new and different pattern concealed in the muddle of events.

I've no time to think about it, though, because I'm also beginning to see some quite new and different pattern emerging from the muddle of figures in front of me. I think I have uncovered the organization's deepest mystery. I think I have found the secret of its birth and life.

'These accounts,' I say. 'I suppose she was balancing them with her own money, was she?'

Liz shrugs. 'I don't know,' she says. 'I've never thought about it.'

I look at her. Three years she's been with the Campaign. And never wondered where the money came from. All the things in life we never wonder about!

'It'll be all right,' says Liz. 'Don't worry. I'll help with the books. We'll do them together! We'll manage somehow!'

'Will we?' I say. Because actually I don't think we will without Jacqui's subsidy. It's just come to me as we sit here. I think we're finished.

'We've still got us,' says Liz. 'We've still got you and me!'

'And Kevin,' I say. Because I can feel him on the other side of the glass behind me. He's up on the chair again, I know, he's struggling with something else that's too heavy for him to lift on a shelf that's too high for him to reach. Not a word did he say after Terry told him he couldn't talk properly or do his proper share of the work. He just picked up his haversack and went back to the copying-room. He'll be with us now until the ship goes down.

'And Terry!' says Liz, grinning again and not looking at me.

Oh, yes. And Terry.

'I told her it was me, you know,' she says.

She says this in the specially offhand tone she uses for specially significant things. The significance is lost on me, though – I don't know what she's talking about.

'Told her what was you?'

'Who messed everything up on top of her desk that day.'

I can feel the blood rising to my face again. So she knew it all the time, knew it from the very first, knew it even when we sat here on Friday night. Knew it and never said.

She should have said then! Or not said now.

But which I can't think, because the door handle's jingling, and there's Terry, breathing hard from the climb. He comes slowly into the room and then stands there, saying nothing. I glance up at him. The collar of his jacket is still turned up against the cold, and his face is grey and gaunt. He's slowly rubbing his hands together, not looking at me. I look back at the figures on the desk. Liz has already scuttered discreetly away into the library to leave the two of us alone together. We're still not looking at each other, though, we're still saying nothing.

I can hear the slow rubbing of his hands, then a sudden spasm of shivering. So what was decided, out there in the raw November cold?

He comes across to the desk. Without lifting my eyes from the figures I know that he is picking up the letter that Roy brought with his report. He's turning it over unopened in his hands, and still not looking at me. The switch buzzes and I go to answer it, still not looking at him. What's happening? Why can't we look at each other?

'Hello, OPEN . . .'

'We were cut off in the middle of things, my darling,' says the same voice as before. 'Call-us interruptus . . .'

I switch it off and go back to my desk.

'Don't worry,' says Terry. 'We'll ring the agency and get a temp in.'

I don't think we will, though, because so far as I can see there's no money to pay a temp with. Doesn't he know that? Didn't he realize what Jacqui was doing?

I must tell him, then. Obviously. But I can't, because it would mean referring to her figures, talking about her, mentioning her name. And that, just at this precise moment, seems for some reason impossible to do.

'I sent you two batches of photocopies,' I say instead, still not looking at him. 'One was the file on the Hassam case, the other was the Special Branch report on the Campaign.'

'Yes,' says Terry, still not looking at me. 'We're going to have to have a little talk about that, Hil.'

Why can't we look at each other? What's gone wrong? And why have I brought up the question of the photocopies? It's obviously a disastrously wrong moment. But now I've started I can't stop.

'I'd just like to know what we're going to do with them,' I say, but he's opened Roy's letter and he's busy reading it. 'I'd just like to be sure that we are going to make some use of the material.'

He throws the letter across for me to read.

'Conscience,' he says. 'Same reason as you.'

I pass the letter back to him. I'm not interested in Roy's thought processes.

'Where are they now?' I ask. 'The photocopies?'

'Somewhere safe, don't worry.'

'What, you mean – not here?'

He doesn't answer. He just goes across to the library and puts his head round the door. 'OK?' he says to Liz. 'Exciting start to the week, anyway. Never mind. Stick at it. Don't worry. We'll all settle down again.'

He comes out and closes the library door. Yes – this is why he went and talked to her. It was simply a way of getting the door closed.

'So where, then?' I ask. But I already know the answer. They're with *her*. He's taken them out to Sunningdale.

I put my life into his hands, and he passed it on to her for safe keeping.

He sits down in Jacqui's chair. He's not looking at me – he's looking down at Roy's letter, folding it up again, for some reason, and putting it back in its envelope. I'm looking at him, though. He's old. He was huge and frightening in that horrible moment when he stood grasping Kevin and holding him up in front of Kent – he filled the room with his anger. Now, sitting here fiddling with the letter and the envelope, and all the anger gone out of him, he's shrunk. He's a little shrivelled old man whose job has been done. And when I think of him like that some disturbing memory that I can't quite identify hangs in the air between us, making him smaller and more shrivelled still, as if he needed to be helped back to bed.

I suppose I love him. Do I? How strange – I've never thought of the question before. I'm like Liz with the money. It was just *there*, unidentified and unremarked, as natural as daylight.

So do I? I suppose I must, since I've thrown in my lot with him.

He looks up. 'I won't do it, Hil,' he says. 'I won't publish them. You can cut your own throat, and I can't stop you. But if you've put the knife in my hands I'm not going to do it for you. I can't, Hil, and that's that. The old fellow with his son in the Bible – yes. Me – no.'

The blood's coming back to my face again. But this time it's anger.

'I know what she said,' I tell him, 'but you're *not* my father, and I don't think it's your decision.'

'Now come on, Hil,' he says. 'We got to be sensible about this . . .'

But Kevin's in the room, his hands held out in front of him covered in some kind of black stuff.

'The copier . . .' says Kevin. 'The copier . . .'

'Oh, Kevin,' says Terry. 'Sorry you lost your chum.'

'I shall endure that . . .' says Kevin.

'Also sorry about the aggro I was giving you earlier. Won't happen again. OK?'

'I shall endure that . . .' says Kevin.

'OK,' says Terry. 'Lets say no more about it. Buzz off, then, Kevin, there's a good lad. We got things to talk about.'

'. . . with reasonable equanimity,' says Kevin.

He goes back towards the copying-room.

'No, wait a moment, Kevin,' I say. 'We *have* got things to talk about, and I think we probably all ought to talk about them together.'

'What's this, Hil?' says Terry, but I'm already opening the library door and calling Liz in.

'Anyway, I'm quite pleased . . .' says Kevin.

'Sit down,' I say to him. 'Here are some tissues. Wipe your hands . . . Sit down, Liz . . . There's something that needs to be decided that affects all of us here. In fact there are a lot of things that need to be decided . . .'

I stop, because the switch is buzzing. Terry glances round at it, then looks at Kevin.

'*You* don't want to go on the switch, do you, Kevin?' he asks, but it's not a serious question.

'No . . . no . . .' says Kevin. 'And I'm quite pleased . . .'

'That's right,' says Terry. 'Because you're going to be too

277

busy sitting in here helping Liz and Hilary decide about everything.'

I get up to deal with the switch myself.

'Sit down, love,' says Terry, waving me back. 'I'll get it.'

He picks up Jacqui's drawer, holds it against the slot with one hand, and hits it very hard with the flat of the other. It slides effortlessly back into place, and he walks across to the switch.

'Because if we're going to run this place as a committee,' he says as he picks up the headset, 'I'd just as soon sit here all day with this thing over my ears . . . Hello, OPEN . . .'

'Oh, dear,' says Liz, and gives one of her little laughs.

'And I'm quite pleased,' says Kevin, 'if sometimes other people . . .'

'Oh, hello, Mr Donaldson . . .' says Terry. 'Been hanging up on you? Have we? Staff problems, I'm afraid, Mr Donaldson . . .'

'. . . have to say difficult things,' says Kevin.

'Let's get started,' I say, because I'm not going to let Terry bully me out of it. 'I think perhaps the first thing we need to decide is how we *do* decide things . . .'

We done Environment. We done the MOD. Done them five times. Not bad going for a handful of ignorant monkeys in a garret who didn't know nothing about nothing and never knew where the next pound was coming from.

OK, we never done *you*, you bugger. The Home Office. There it is still. Great ugly devil peering out over the trees like some nosy copper that's grown a hundred foot tall. We *nearly* done you – we *could* have done you. Could have kicked you right in the balls, so bad you'd never have stood up straight again.

Nearly. Could have.

Makes me sick to see it there, all nice and peaceful again. Lights coming on in the windows against the murk of the day, all snug and shut up in itself. Week before last they had Mr Hassam stuck in their gullet like a fishbone. Now they choked him down, they digested him, they forgotten all about him. Mr Hassam? Who's Mr Hassam? That was over a week ago! We've had Chorleywood since then. Now even that's gone. There's a scandal this week about the contractors on one of the new motorways – that's back to Transport. There's a great cover-up going on over an accident on an oil-rig – that's the Department of Energy. The Home Office can slip off into the shadows again.

Well, we'll get after Transport. We'll chase up Energy. We'll do our best. Fact remains, though – we could have given the Home Office a beating, and we didn't.

This is the first time I thought about Mr Hassam myself this week, I may as well admit. Everything goes, everything buds and flowers and dies. Even down here where I am, six foot two above ground level.

But we could have had them. A little more moderation, that's all we needed. A little less of everything else. The information alone – yes, I'd have raised hell with it. The informant as well – I couldn't do it.

And now what's she doing? Only reorganizing the Campaign! Only shoving the old man out in the cold! Be putting me in a home, next thing I know. You got to laugh. Cheeky kid!

What's worse than people not doing what you say? I'll tell you – them doing it.

Moderation, that's what old Hilary's got to learn.

Have to hand it to her, though. She's got the go, she's got the brains, she's got the guts. They might find a few surprises waiting for them yet up there in the Big Nick, if my little Hilary has her way.

Might get a few more, for that matter, if some anonymous informant rings in from a Sunningdale call-box and tells them where their former employee is now and what she's trying to do. Can't hear a phone giving a sneaky little tinkle up there now, can I . . .?

No, she wouldn't do that. Not old Jacqui. Five years, though, and ending up like that, too frozen to speak, on the steps in front of Waterloo station! I'll give her a ring, see if she's all right. Have to go down there some time, anyway, pick up my stuff. I'll miss old Poops. I liked her. Took me a long time to get it straight, which was Poops and which was Pippy, but I got there in the end. Used to make her breakfast now and then, three o'clock in the afternoon, her mother raging away, me kidding her about all her smart chums. 'Terry,' she'd say, 'you're an absolute Sidney, but you do make the scrummiest fried bread.'

Got my coat on this time, but it's still too cold to hang around Whitehall, counting off what we done and what we never done. So now I'm heading back to the office. *If* I've still got an office to head back to. Don't fancy our chances too much, tell you the truth, now Jacqui's gone. Money, that's going to be the catch. I never asked her where it come from. Never talked about it, never thought about it. Kept myself pure, let her do the worrying. But wherever it come from I don't suppose it'll be coming no more.

I'll be all right. No worries there. Go up the Swiz tonight, go down the Pic, see what's stirring. Something'll turn up. Always does. Always has. I'm still me. Still six feet two inches from top to bottom, two feet six inches from shoulder to shoulder. Still got the face I always had. Trooper on his horse in front of Horse Guards – *he* knows who I am – I can see him giving me a crafty little grin behind his chinstrap. Copper who's guarding the trooper – him, too. Real dirty look he's giving me.

Any luck I'll be getting that summons. Should be fun. Something to keep me occupied, anyway, something to keep the old pot boiling. Then what? Do a few of the chat shows. Get a good agent and I could earn enough to keep the Campaign on its feet for a bit. Anyway, I'll write my memoirs. Always said I would, soon as I got someone to take the pressure off me in the office, and now I have.

I'm out of it with Hilary, though, I know that. She don't want me around no more. Saw her looking at me this morning. No use messing around where a woman's concerned. All it takes is one look and you know whether she wants you or whether she don't. Am I bitter? Oh, come on. Lot of worse things than this have happened to me, and when have I ever been bitter? Sad, yes. But it wouldn't have lasted in any case. Nothing lasts.

Anyway, it's all down to me in the end. Either I should have been better than I was, or else I should have been worse. Excess of moderation, that's where I went wrong.

Two girls coming towards me now as I cross Northumberland Avenue. Nudging each other – look, it's him! 'You tell 'em, Terry!' says one of them as they go past.

'I'll tell 'em, love.'

I will, too. Yes, don't worry about me. I'll just happen to run into the right person, like I did before. I'll dodge into the espresso in Villiers Street for a moment, say, get out of the cold. 'Anyone sitting here?' I'll say. 'No, please – all yours,' says this woman, moving her Italian snakeskin handbag off the seat next to her – one look at that bag and you can see a grand or two either way don't mean much to her – I don't know what she's doing in a sandwich bar in Villiers Street.

'I just lost two lady-friends in one morning,' I tell her. 'Not to mention one copying clerk, one switchboard girl, my legal adviser, and all visible means of support.'